as wide as the sky

as wide as the sky

Jessica Pack

KENSINGTON BOOKS
www.kensingtonbooks.com

KENSINGTON BOOKS are published by

Kensington Publishing Corp.
119 West 40th Street
New York, NY 10018

All Kensington titles, imprints, and distributed lines are available at special quantity discounts for bulk purchases for sales promotion, premiums, fund-raising, educational, or institutional use.

Special book excerpts or customized printings can also be created to fit specific needs. For details, write or phone the office of the Kensington Sales Manager: Kensington Publishing Corp., 119 West 40th Street, New York, NY 10018. Attn. Sales Department. Phone: 1-800-221-2647.

Kensington and the K logo Reg. U.S. Pat. & TM Off.

eISBN-13: 978-1-4967-1818-1
eISBN-10: 1-4967-1818-6
First Kensington Electronic Edition: August 2018

ISBN-13: 978-1-4967-1816-7
ISBN-10: 1-4967-1816-X
First Kensington Trade Paperback Printing: August 2018

10 9 8 7 6 5 4 3 2 1

Printed in the United States of America

To Jennifer Moore:

Thank you for planting the seed for this story
and being part of the lovely view from my window.

Acknowledgments

The idea behind this story began when my good friend, and fellow author, Jennifer Moore, suggested the idea of a short story that involved something lost and something found. When I finished the short story, I knew it was not enough. It took two more years for that idea to become this book, and the finished product was different from anything I had written before. That it found a home at Kensington was beyond anything I'd dared let myself imagine.

Thank you to the many people who helped brainstorm this story over the years: Ronda, Becky, Jody, Jennifer, Nancy, Cory, and Emily—each of you at some point saw this story more clearly than I did. Thank you to my agent, Lane Heymont, for championing this story and finding it such a wonderful home. Thank you, in advance, to my readers who will take a chance on this book. I hope it touches you.

I am so blessed to not only do what I love, but share it with the world. I could not do that without the love of my family and thank my Father in Heaven for everything listed above and so much more.

1

Amanda

Two hours, forty-three minutes

Amanda's eyes fluttered open when the alarm went off at five a.m. She lay perfectly still in the solitary darkness. Waiting. An advertisement for a new pizza place in town filled the silence while she willed her tense muscles to release. It was over. There was nothing left to brace herself for, but she needed to hear the words said before she got out of bed. She needed the confirmation that her son was dead before she could make sense of the life ahead of her. Life that had reset today, counting the minutes and seconds of her existence as though entirely new.

Knowing she'd slept while her child died filled her with guilt. There hadn't been live coverage, so it wasn't as if she could have known the moment it happened even if exhaustion hadn't overtaken her. Or could she? If she'd stayed awake, would a part of her have reacted, broken, died right along with him as though the poison were sliding through her veins? Would a mother feel the difference in the world the moment her child left it? Maybe she would have felt nothing and been shattered by that. Was it a mercy that she'd slept? Or a sin?

A used car dealership's commercial came on. She waited. Did Melissa, her only living child now, already know? Ohio was in a different time zone, so it was six o'clock in the morning there, but probably too early for Melissa to have heard the news.

What would she feel when she heard confirmation? Could mother and daughter talk about Robbie now that he was gone?

Not gone. *Dead.*

"Dead," she said out loud after the car commercial turned to a traffic report. The word bounced around the empty room and echoed back to her like a boomerang, striking her hard in the chest. "Dead," she said again, this time her voice catching in her throat as she pulled the covers to her chin and closed her eyes against the peeling agony of knowledge.

Dead.

Still no tears. Perhaps because of all the tears she'd cried for all the years she'd cried them until the numbness had set in. Mourning her son had been an incremental process that had stealthily overtaken her identity and broken her into jagged bits. But today was a different kind of mourning. Today she mourned the most basic elements of life: lungs breathing and heart beating and brain thinking. The opposite of the moment of Robbie's birth, when he'd taken his first breath and the room had cheered in triumph of new life. He'd had the cord wrapped around his neck and the last few minutes of the delivery had been frightening, yet they had ended in celebration that had dissolved the fear. Today, her son was *dead,* and a different group of people would celebrate. The significance of his death marked a change, a turn, an irreversible pivot for her life—she would *never* see Robbie again or hear him say, "Hi, Mom, how ya doin'?" Anything that he could have said or done to remove the iron weight she'd carried in her chest for four years—and she'd thought of *so* many things he could have said or done that might have brought some measure of peace—could no longer be said or done. *Ever.* His sentence could not be commuted. His execution date could not be stayed. He could not in any way make all the wrong even a little bit more right. Robbie was dead. Her son. Her baby boy. *Never* was such a long time. Infinitely long, and it had begun.

Amanda had thought she understood what those parents and husbands and wives and children of his victims had felt the day Robbie killed the people they loved, but she now knew she'd been wrong. Perhaps she had understood to the full extent of her ability, or maybe she understood fully from a place of supposition and sympathy and horror, but *now* that ability was different. Expanded. Focused. Hollow. Cold. Now it was *her* son dead. *Her* child gone forever. How could she ever have thought she understood what that loss felt like before now? What a terrible assumption she'd made. One of so many terrible assumptions. And yet he had deserved his punishment, whereas his victims had not. Did that change her grief? Could she still not know what those other parents felt like?

"My beautiful boy," she said to the empty room. Rather than spin around the corners and come back to her, these words dribbled past her lips as though the very air would not hold such a description of the mass shooter Robert Mallorie. That's how everyone would forever know him. That was his legacy and, through him, hers too. Robert Mallorie's mother. *His* mother. That monster's mom.

The icy tendrils of winter gloom had seeped into the house like a cat burglar in the night—surely that was the only reason she was so cold—and she pulled the blankets tighter beneath her chin as she continued to stare at the ceiling and wait for the inevitable. A car drove by on the street. An ordinary morning of an ordinary January day for the driver. The streetlight on the corner shining through the blinds made lines of light on the ceiling. Stripes. Bars?

After the traffic report and a reminder of the University of Sioux Falls basketball game that night, the commentator moved on to the day's headlines. Amanda's fingers gripped the blanket.

"Police are still trying to get both protesters and supporters to leave the South Dakota Penitentiary in Sioux Falls following the execution of Robert Mallorie, which took place at two o'clock this morning. It was the third execution in South Dakota in five years amid the continued controversy over the so-called fast-track process that put Mallorie to death only four years after his crime, despite numerous pleas from advocacy groups against capital punishment, his own mother, Amanda Mallorie, and his attorneys, who feel he was incompetent at the time he waived his appeals. Barbara Hansen, the mother of Carlee Hansen, one of Mallorie's victims, was allowed to witness the execution." The commentator's voice was replaced with that of a middle-aged woman Amanda knew from the news stories. Amanda had looked Mrs. Hansen up on Facebook once. She was two years older than Amanda, and she had turned forty-five years old two weeks after her daughter had been killed by Amanda's son. A journalist had written a story featuring a photograph of Mrs. Hansen holding a "Happy Birthday" balloon while she stood in front of the still-fresh grave of her daughter. No headstone yet, just the plastic markers they stick into the ground while they wait for the official monument. The dormant grass had been a sickly yellow-brown in between patches of hard, graying snow.

The air of Amanda's bedroom held the words of Mrs. Hansen coming through the radio: "I believe that my daughter can finally rest in peace now that Robert Mallorie is in hell, right where he belongs."

Amanda flinched, though the reaction surprised her—she wasn't used to feeling things deeply enough to react. The therapist Amanda had seen for a few months after the shooting had recommended she write letters to the victims' families as an exercise to begin healing after what Robbie had done. To describe the task as difficult was like describing Mount Rushmore as a paperweight. Barbara Hansen had been the only parent who wrote Amanda back—a scathing letter full of such anger and vitriol that Amanda had torn it in half with shaking hands when she finished reading it. She'd immediately felt guilty, as though she were passing judgment on this woman whom Amanda had no right to judge. But the letter had shaken her. It was proof that reaching out was risky. Amanda kept seeing the therapist for a few more months, but then she met her allowable mental health benefits on her insurance and couldn't afford to pay for the $200 per session on her own. Once she hadn't attended for a couple of months she wondered if it had done her any good in the first place. "How do you feel about what your son did, Mrs. Mallorie?"

"Sick. Devastated. Confused. Abandoned. Stupid. Lost. Lonely. Culpable. Horrified."

"And how does *that* make you feel?"

Amanda had expected to try therapy again. Maybe with a female therapist this time. But she never did. Distrust of people led to isolation that led to depression she rightly deserved. Or maybe the depression had caused the isolation and distrust; she couldn't be sure. Either way, once enough people close to her had turned on Robbie, the idea of sitting across from a stranger and laying out her most precious thoughts and feelings felt like walking naked down the street.

The radio commentator continued in the same tone he'd delivered the traffic report a few minutes earlier. "Mallorie was convicted of the Cotton Mall shooting that left nine people dead and twelve injured just before Christmas four years ago. After his automatic direct appeal failed to overturn his conviction, Mallorie waived additional appeals. Prison officials confirmed Mallorie's death by lethal injection at 2:17 this morning. His last meal consisted of root beer, onion rings, and macaroni and cheese with sliced hot dogs."

Amanda's throat tightened around a gasp, and she lifted her hands to her face while the commentator's voice moved on to the day's weather. The faces of Robbie's victims came into her mind as they so often did—they haunted her—but she made them leave, pushed and begged them to leave. Just for today. *Let me mourn just Robbie today.*

When the faces of the longer dead left her alone, she poured her sorrow into the empty spaces. *My boy,* she thought as grieving bubbled up in her chest like lava. She pictured her Robbie in a white sterile room eating his mac and cheese with sliced hot dogs off a plastic tray. Alone. Savoring every bite of the meal he'd loved as a child, knowing with each bite that he wouldn't be alive long enough to digest it. Amanda had made mac and cheese with hot dogs for him and Melissa when they were little. Had he thought about Amanda as he ate? Had he remembered the day she taught him how to make macaroni and cheese all by himself? Amanda had given herself a mental pat on the back for being a good mother that day. Good mothers taught their sons to cook. Boys who learned to cook grew up to be good citizens and helpful husbands. They mowed their lawns on Saturdays and stopped at stop signs. They didn't kill people in cold blood at Christmastime. They didn't drain society of millions of tax dollars necessary to keep them alive until the government killed them. They didn't ignore the pleadings of their mothers to not give up their appeals so that they could live a little longer. Because surely if Robbie had lived a little longer she would make sense of what had happened, wouldn't she? Someday. Somehow.

I should have been at the execution, Amanda thought, clenching her eyes shut. *You should have let me be there.* She could feel the tears building, but she wasn't ready to feel *that* much. Maybe if she'd seen him take his last breath she'd . . . what? Feel better? Believe he was gone?

But she *did* believe he was gone. The world *was* different today because Robbie was not in it. The world would continue to be different every day of the rest of her life. Had he wished, in those last minutes, that he had loving eyes upon him as his life slipped away? She would have mouthed "I love you" over and over and over again until his eyes closed. She would have been with him to the very end if he'd let her.

Amanda opened her eyes and let out a breath. The fleeting anger left with it. It *was* over and done. For the last four years, she'd given up one piece and then another of her emotion, identity, and place in the world. She'd let the numbness settle. Not that she didn't ache for everything that had happened. She ached all the time. But it was a bit frightening that just this morning she had *felt* different. She had *felt* something other than the familiar aching. *I should have been there,* she thought again, testing how she felt about such a statement. She didn't feel angry this time, but she felt . . . clarity. What right did Robbie have to deny her the chance to see this through? Why was his choice more important than what she wanted? There was no answer for that, of course. There never would be.

Over the years of his incarceration, Robbie had not called her very often—the outside world crashing against his inside world was chaotic for him. Sometimes he wouldn't even allow her to visit. Usually those moods coincided with adjustments to his medications, which affected his paranoia and delusions. The prison psychiatrist had always been adjusting his medications, trying to find the best combination at the cheapest price for the taxpayer's interests. Amanda had tried to keep Robbie on her health insurance in the beginning or pay for his meds herself, but there was a policy against that. She was no longer his mother; the prison was. In some states, because he had a death sentence he was already considered legally dead. Because Robbie's mental health was unstable, she had never known from one week to the next whether her name would be on his approved visitor list or not.

Ten days ago, the warden had officially filed the date of Robbie's execution. Amanda had last seen her son Monday afternoon—three days ago—at a special meeting arranged by his attorneys where he was free of his chains and ironically stable with his medications. All her other visits over the years had been non-contact, but this time she held both his hands the whole time they talked, nearly an hour. He'd hugged her. Twice. Despite the overgrown beard and prison tattoos across his forehead and down his neck, he had seemed more like Robbie than he had in years. The son he'd been before the shooting, before everything went so horribly wrong.

When Amanda's hour was up on Monday, she hugged her son for the last time—holding and smelling him and taking note of the exact place on his shoulder where her cheek rested. Robbie had begun to cry as the embrace continued. Frightening emotion built in her own chest, but she hadn't been able to free it then.

"I'm glad it's almost over," he'd said as he pulled back but left his hands on her shoulders as he looked at her. Over the years, Amanda had deciphered that clear eyes meant Robbie's head was clear, too—a double-edged sword. When Robbie had been stable, he was crushed by what he'd done and wracked with anguish. When his brain chemistry had been volatile, however, he was angry at how he was being treated, defiant with the guards, and hard to talk to; hard to even look at with the intense postures and glaring eyes. As prison took its toll, he was less Robbie and more Robert Mallorie.

"I'm not putting your name on my witness list for the execution, Mom," he'd said as he blinked those clear blue eyes.

Everything inside her had gone still. "But—"

"I don't want you haunted by yet one more thing I've done to you."

Amanda hadn't argued. Later she had felt like a coward for not trying to change his mind. She had considered calling his attorneys and insisting, but her hand had never gone to her phone. Maybe she hadn't really wanted to be there. The thought brought those tears back up behind her eyes again. Her sinuses tingled. She suppressed them again. *Not yet.*

An article in yesterday's *Leader* said sixty-two people had petitioned the penitentiary to be one of the prosecution's witnesses to Robbie's death. Sixty-two people believed that watching him die would improve their lives somehow. Only a fraction of the requests had been approved, but those few had made up the audience to Robbie's death—devoid of anyone who loved him. "I can't have you there, Mom," Robbie had explained on Monday, his hands still holding her an arm's length away.

Amanda closed her eyes in the darkened bedroom and let the memory of that final meeting wash over her. He'd been so lucid, so . . . Robbie. He'd been allowed to walk her to the door of the private visitation room, where two guards had stood on both sides of him the whole time. They stopped at the threshold. She looked into those clear blue eyes and said, "I love you, Robbie. So very much."

Tears filled his eyes again, and the tattoos and beard melted away until he was for that moment the young man he'd once been. Just Robbie. Just her son. "I love you, too, Mom."

When Amanda had returned home from that final prison visit, the emotions had been churning like the paddles on a river boat. She would never see her son again. He would die without her and she would go on living, such as her life was.

Without Robbie nearby she had no reason to stay in South Dakota, and so she had returned from that last visit and immersed herself in packing up seventeen years of life she'd lived in this house. For the most part, the work had kept her from thinking about the fact that even though he would live another three days behind steel and concrete walls, she would never see her son again.

Those three days were over now. The thing she'd lived for—to be Robbie's mother—was gone. Dead. Finished. The blockade she'd kept against feeling and being and having room for anything but him was no longer necessary. And she knew she could not "live" if she continued to hide behind that defense. She took a deep breath, then let it out while some of the numbness she'd held close seeped through the mattress to the floor and into the frozen ground beneath the house. It was done. Robbie was gone. Pounding sorrow in her head and chalky regret thick in her chest.

Peace?

Not yet.

Had his death brought peace to those people he'd damaged so much—those who had loved the innocent shoppers who died at his hand? Would knowing that the monster Robert Mallorie no longer breathed help them to heal? Could Mrs. Hansen find peace now?

With all her might Amanda hoped that each of those people devastated by what Robbie had done woke up this morning with less hurt in their hearts, a lighter burden on their shoulders. It was harder to hope that she might feel the same. They *deserved* peace; did she?

Amanda pushed back the covers and swung her legs over the side of the bed as she sat up. The air of a new life moved in and out of her lungs with each breath. She brushed her hair to the side and looked at the digital clock. It was 5:32 in the morning of the first day.

2

Darryl

Three hours, two minutes

Darryl gripped the coffee cup tighter and lifted it to his mouth with shaking hands. He kept his eyes glued on the TV above the counter of the greasy spoon he'd happened to be in front of when he realized he couldn't go to the office like this was a normal day. And he couldn't go home after the fight with Clara. "This is not the life I want to live anymore, Darryl," she'd said last night when he'd told her he wouldn't be able to make it to Riley's play—it was the last night of the three-night play and Riley was just a sunflower. Darryl could make a thousand dollars and impress the partners, or sit in a school gym and wish he were making a thousand dollars and impressing the partners. Clara had been furious. "Maybe you can pencil in some time to find an apartment, then."

He'd left, letting the door shake the walls of their new house in Shindler, one of the upscale housing areas of Sioux Falls. The house reflected how far he'd come in his career and had all the features *Clara* had wanted: six bedrooms, six baths, a huge family room, fully automated lights and alarm system, wraparound deck, formal dining room, central vac, double ovens, gas and electric cooktops. The whole house was essentially run by an app on their phones. The schools were good and the address was better. Everything about it confirmed that he'd made good on all the goals he'd set for his life. Except in regard to his marriage; specifically, his wife, who seemed to have forgotten that this was the lifestyle she'd dreamed of too. Now she wanted him home and involved with the kids, but she sure didn't mind spending the money he earned by *not* being home. She didn't mind the monthly trips to the hairdresser, infinite lunch dates, and new shoes anytime she was in the mood. Clara was spoiled, that's what she was, and ungrateful and judgmental and cold. He couldn't remember the last time he'd reached for her in the dark when she hadn't shaken off his touch.

Listing his wife's deficiencies could only distract him for so long, however. The TV drew his attention back and the shaking in his hands reminded him.

I watched a man die today.

Darryl set the cup on the saucer, clattering the dishes against each other. The waitress looked in his direction and came toward him with the coffeepot.

"A little early to have *that* much coffee in you, isn't it?" The waitress had a nose ring and spiked black hair. He wondered what her father did for a living as she topped off his cup. He smiled politely, but his eyes stayed on the TV. There was no sound, just footage of the protesters waving signs and giving silent interviews outside the prison. They looked so angry. Did they come out for these protests because they truly believed that capital punishment was wrong, or because they were naturally angry people looking for a reason to vent their rage? Did Darryl believe capital punishment was wrong? Did he feel differently now that he'd watched it happen?

He fixed his eyes on the countertop and was transported back to the witness section of the Death Room, where he'd been escorted at 1:30 this morning. By the time they opened the curtain that had covered the glass partition, Robert Mallorie was already strapped onto the gurney, with an IV in his left arm and another tube disappearing into the waistband of his prison-issued jumpsuit—it would be for the main IV in his femoral artery. The tube in his arm was just backup. Mallorie was ready to die, welcomed it even.

Darryl had been running through his daily to-do list until

that curtain opened. The rest of Mallorie's defense team had been unable to make it. In an instant Darryl had gone from feeling heroic for representing the firm, to wondering why he hadn't been able to find an excuse to skip this too. Darryl was the newest member of the team working for Robert Mallorie, who was going to be dead before Darryl stood up from his chair—he wouldn't lodge a complaint about not having his attorneys present. The other witnesses in the room were associated with the victims and had whispered to one another as they'd looked through the glass. Darryl was the only person there on Mallorie's behalf, but he'd only come to show the firm how dedicated he was to their clients. He was partner material—could there be any doubt?

Mallorie had been calm, maybe even relieved as he stared at the ceiling. Thick leather wrist and ankle straps held down his hands and feet; another strap crossed his upper arms and chest, and a final strap stretched across his thin hips. Darryl had been told that Mallorie had lost nearly forty pounds since coming to prison, but because Darryl had only known him the last year he looked the same to him—thin but muscular, with a bushy beard that made him look like the guys on that Alaskan wilderness show. He shaved his head, which kept his facial tattoos easy to see. Darryl had never asked what the green-blue markings meant. He hadn't wanted to know but realized that no one would ever know now.

The prison official asked Mallorie if he had any last words, and he stared at the ceiling as he said the words he'd rehearsed with another member of the firm. "I offer my sincerest apologies to the victims and their families." He'd wanted a longer final statement, but whatever Mallorie said would be picked apart in the press, so after considering a dozen different paragraphs that included regret and apology and maybe a little self-indulgent hope for forgiveness, they'd decided on something short and simple. The agreed-to statement sounded cold and dismissive now, though. Maybe a man's last words shouldn't be scripted and Mallorie should have said what he wanted to say.

Darryl had looked around the Death Room to see if any of the witnesses were affected by the words. Amid the shaking heads and narrowed eyes, he hadn't been able to gauge any positive reaction.

Darryl looked from the diner's TV to the leather satchel at his feet. On the way out of the prison Darryl had been handed the bag of Mallorie's personal effects—a book and some photos and . . . a letter to Mallorie's mom. Darryl had still been trying not to show how the execution had affected him as he took the plastic bag and put it in his briefcase. He'd have to return the items to Amanda. Would he go in person? The idea made him feel woozy, as though it were whiskey instead of coffee he was drinking this early in the day. How could he look at her after what he'd just witnessed? *It isn't your fault her son died today*, he told himself. *You did everything you could to help him.* But did Darryl help him? Even a little? Had he thought of Mallorie as a man or just a task to check off his list?

Mallorie's crimes had earned him an automatic death penalty sentence in South Dakota—a man couldn't gun down a kid and a security guard and holiday shoppers and not get the death penalty—but his attorneys had still fought for fair treatment in prison and his rights to psychiatric care. There was nothing for Darryl to regret about the work he'd done on this case he'd joined only fifteen months ago. But the man had been killed right in front of Darryl, and Darryl was not okay. His hands were shaking. His thoughts were scattering. He couldn't talk himself out of the fear and dread he felt. He wanted to curl up with his knees to his chest like a little kid.

Darryl had slid into the driver's seat of his imported sports car in the prison's parking lot and wanted Clara's arms around him in the worst way. He had wanted to be back in the dumpy apartment they'd rented when he was finishing law school, when the best part of his day was going home to his wife and talking about the future. How was it that he was now in *that* future and . . . miserable and scared?

Back in that dumpy apartment they hadn't talked about how

his work would one day include fourteen-hour days, six days a week, and golfing with clients on Sunday afternoons. They hadn't talked about Clara taking the kids to school and lessons and school and lessons all day every day—Darryl didn't even know what lessons the kids had. Karate for Joseph, he thought. Did Rose still dance? They hadn't imagined that one day he would suggest Clara start shopping at higher-end stores and maybe get a boob job so she looked more like the other attorneys' wives. Never fathomed that when he presented her with a trip to Europe, she would tell him she would rather he just come home for dinner a few nights a week. He'd blown up at her. She'd blown right back at him and slept in the guest room. That was three weeks ago and he'd been waiting for her to apologize ever since. She hadn't apologized and then, last night, when he'd told her he wouldn't be able to make it to Riley's play, she'd said that she was considering divorce. Last night, the words had pissed him off. Today, they terrified him. He couldn't see such a radically altered future. *She loves me*, he said to himself and he knew, just as surely as he knew Robert Mallorie was dead, that it was true. Clara still loved him. But she had told him to leave anyway. That's how hurt she was by his absence from their life.

Darryl put his elbows on the counter and pushed his fingers through his hair, pulling at the roots. *I watched a man die today. I watched the state kill him.* A man he had tried to help, a man who could have been different save for a few key choices in his life. Mallorie had died alone; he hadn't let his mother come even though she was the only person in the world who wanted to be there for him. He had died hated, and even though Darryl wasn't a mass shooter and for all intents and purposes was respected and admired, he felt as alone as Mallorie had been on that gurney. If Darryl died today, would Clara be relieved? Even a little bit?

"This isn't the life I want to live," Clara had said last night. He'd left the house and gone back to the office to prep for an upcoming hearing for a man he was trying to get off on manslaughter instead of the second-degree murder charge he probably deserved for running over his neighbor after a property line dispute. Darryl had a case of Red Bull in the trunk of his car, and this wouldn't be the first time he'd gone a day or two without sleep. There was so much work to be done if he wanted to make partner one day. Didn't Clara want him to be successful? Then he pictured the three partners of his firm—Perkins was currently separated from his third wife. Stone seemed to be making his second marriage work even though his wife chose to live in Chicago with their kids. Grimke hadn't bothered to marry. He'd brought a twenty-something redhead to last year's Christmas party, and no one dared tell him that at sixty-four years old he looked pathetic showing her off.

Was that the life Darryl wanted to live?

The memory of watching Mallorie's eyes flutter closed, tears disappearing into his shaggy beard as his arms tensed and re-laxed and tensed and relaxed, came to Darryl's mind again. He didn't know his own children the way he should. He wasn't nur-turing his wife. He was on track to attain every worldly goal a man could want. But did he want it alone? Did he want it at the expense of the other things that were important to him? At the expense of actual people? In an instant, he knew what he really wanted, and what he—for reasons he could not fully define—was hiding from.

He took a gulp of his coffee, forgetting that the waitress had topped it off and so it was hot again. He coughed into a napkin as it burned all the way down; then he lifted his eyes back to the screen of the TV, where a middle-aged woman he recognized as the mother of one of the victims spoke into the camera, her face hard but her eyes sad. Darryl thought of the plastic bag with Mallorie's effects in his satchel and the letter with *Mom* written across the front of the envelope. What had Mallorie written in-side? What had he wanted her to know that he hadn't told her during their visit on Monday?

What would Darryl's last words be—that he regretted hurt-ing the people who loved him, or that he was disappointed he hadn't made partner sooner?

Darryl didn't have to make partner. He didn't even have to

work in litigation and justify his defending the guilty. He told people that working as a criminal defense attorney was balance for the system, that everyone deserved a solid defense to keep the wheels of justice turning fairly. He still believed those things and fought for them, but he'd gotten a guy off on rape charges three months ago and the guy had been arrested last week for doing it again. Darryl got murderers five years instead of fifteen. Was that the mark he wanted to leave on the world? If he and Clara were willing to change their lifestyle, he could get a different job. Maybe they should go back to Tennessee and live near family again. Part of him screamed at the injustice of that—he'd left that life because he wanted something more. More wasn't working out so good, though.

You can choose different. He nodded in answer to the voice in his head to show he understood. Mallorie had made choices that took away his freedom. He'd lived the last years of his life as a hostage to his terrible mistakes, but Darryl's choices were not like that. Nowhere near what Mallorie's had been, but he could still choose different. A different choice could change everything. Even if it was hard.

He pulled his phone from his pocket and typed out a text message to the wife who wanted to leave him. It was early, but she was up at 5:30 every day. He used to compliment the way she could get so much done in the hours most people spent in bed. She'd smiled at the compliment and shrugged her shoulders. When had he last said something like that? When had he last complimented her at all?

Darryl: What time do the kids go to school?

That he didn't already know when his kids went to school further impressed upon him the changes that needed to be made. He'd never been very close to his own dad, but he'd had breakfast with him every morning before they all went off to their respective schools—Dad had taught history and coached football at the high school. Very Beaver Cleaver, that. And not impossible for Darryl to re-create if he changed his focus.

Clara: I drop Joseph off at 7:40 and the girls at 8
Darryl: Can I meet you at the house after you drop off the girls?

Before he sent the text, he looked at the time on his phone. It wasn't even six, which meant he had time to do better than that. He deleted what he'd written and tried again.

Darryl: If I drop off Joseph and you drop off the girls, can we meet back at the house and talk?

It was several seconds before Clara responded. Darryl was holding his breath. He had a nine o'clock associates meeting and back-to-back appointments from ten until five that he'd planned to prep for before anyone else came into the office. He was supposed to go out for drinks with Perkins tonight and talk strategy on another upcoming case. What if he told Perkins over drinks that he wanted out instead? Darryl got dizzy thinking about it, so he stopped. Clara. Joseph. Rose. Riley. His own sanity. Those had to be at the top of his list. What was it his mother used to say? "No worldly accomplishment will make up for failure in the home." He wished he could talk to her—they'd always been close and if she were still alive he could call her up and say, "Mom, I could use some advice." The thought gave him pause—he'd taken this job a few months after his mom died. Hadn't he felt almost desperate to get away from Tennessee after that? The job had seemed like an answer to the frustrations of not moving ahead as quickly as he'd have liked at his firm back there, but maybe it was the opposite. Maybe he'd taken this job because he wanted to be overwhelmed and distant from people he loved because his mom had died and it had broken his heart more than he'd expected. Could he talk to his dad? They'd never had that kind of relationship, but . . .

Clara: Talk about what, exactly?
Darryl: This isn't the life I want to live either. Please tell me it's not too late.

Another pause. More breath holding. Would she trust him? Was he trustworthy, or would he change his mind again and want the job and the house and the prestige after all?

Clara: It's not too late.

Darryl let out the breath and felt tears sting his eyes. In an instant, he knew that if his mom were here, this was what she'd have told him to do. She'd have told him to quit the firm if he had to but be a good husband and father. *Nothing will make you happier*—he could hear her words in his head. *Nothing.*

Darryl: I'm on my way.

3

Amanda

Three hours, seventeen minutes

Amanda shivered in the cold of the morning and reached over to turn on the lamp she hadn't packed yet. The light didn't fill the room, but instead created a bubble of yellow light that encompassed her, the nightstand, and the bed. Once she was moving around and had a cup of coffee in her, she wouldn't notice the cold as much. Melissa had already warned her that Ohio wouldn't be any warmer than South Dakota.

Amanda slid her feet into the fuzzy slippers Melissa had given her for Christmas. She wriggled her toes in the plush softness and felt her mind pulled toward a memory. She stopped the process as though pushing the pause button on the remote control. She took a breath. Was she ready to . . . remember? She slid one foot forward on the carpet as though she were about to step onto an iced-over lake. She put her hands on the edge of the mattress and let her mind roam her database of memory as though it were a dusty file drawer. She ticked through the files until she landed on the one that had tempted her, back when her son had been whole.

The mind-file creaked from lack of use, and she let her thoughts hover on the edges to gather courage. Then she took a mental step forward. And another. It wasn't ice after all, but warm water that beckoned her forward.

"I got one for Mom!" Robbie popped up from where he'd

been foraging beneath the Christmas tree, a red and gold papered box in his hands. Melissa, who had been digging through her stocking, looked up and then also jumped to her feet, crossing the room so that she was standing right next to Robbie as he handed the present to Amanda. It was Christmas morning, a long time ago.

"It's from both of us," Melissa said, her eyes as bright as Robbie's. Amanda accepted the gift and shared a look with Dwight— he must have taken them shopping. The tender warmth she'd felt at the realization of his unexpected thoughtfulness had been another gift of that day.

Amanda brushed her hand over the wrapping paper, which reflected juvenile skill.

"I wrapped it," ten-year-old Melissa said proudly.

Robbie nodded, his bright-blond bowl cut shifting with the motion. "Yeah, Melly wrapped it."

Present-day Amanda smiled to remember the nickname Robbie'd had for his sister when he was little. By the time Melissa turned twelve she had made him promise never to call her that stupid name again.

"Melly," Amanda said out loud; it felt like melting chocolate on her tongue. After a moment of savor, she returned to the memory, surprised how real it could feel after having been sealed up for so long.

"But it's from us both," Robbie added quickly. He bounced on the balls of his feet, which were naked beneath the hem of the Transformers pajama bottoms she'd given him the night before. Melissa's pajamas were Barbie themed that year, and Amanda had known even as she'd purchased them that it would be the last year Melissa would put up with such a thing.

Amanda oohed and aahed over the wrapping and then carefully popped the first seam.

"It's slippers!" Robbie suddenly yelled, making Amanda jump.

"Robbie!" Melissa's hands were instant fists at her sides as she turned on her brother in the same moment that Robbie put both of his hands over his mouth, his eyes as wide as Christmas bulbs. Dwight laughed, a deep, rich sound none of them heard very often. Amanda had reached out for her angry daughter and horrified son, the half-unwrapped present on her lap. She put one arm around the waist of each of her children and pulled them against her.

"I love you guys to the moon!" she said, giving each of them a smoochy kiss in turn. They had both tried to pull away, but she'd successfully taken their minds off of Robbie's outburst. They'd begged her to put the slippers on, so she had, keeping to herself that they were at least two sizes too big. She'd eventually put a sock into each toe, and she'd worn those slippers for years, until Melissa had given her another pair. Every Christmas now, Melissa gave Amanda slippers—including these ones that were lined with sheepskin—and yet it had been a long time since Amanda had let herself remember where the tradition had started.

The ringing phone shut off the memory like the closing of a music box. Amanda picked up the phone automatically, noting the unfamiliar number on the display. Did the movers need to verify some information? She'd been told they would call for confirmation.

"Hello?"

"Is this Amanda Mallorie?" asked the male voice on the phone.

"Yes."

In the time it took to confirm her identity she realized that 5:49 in the morning was too early for the movers to be calling. But not too early for the press. Never too early on a day when there was fresh blood in the water. How did they get this number? She'd had it changed six months ago after a producer of some criminal justice television show had called her every day for a week in hopes of her participation in a Mother's Day special made entirely of mothers of notorious killers.

The hounds.

The vultures.

The ordinary men and women trying to make a living.

"This is Mark Johanson from the *World-Herald*," the voice said on the other end of the line. "I'm looking for the more human side of your son's story and wondered if I could get a statement from you in regard to his execution despite your petitions to have his appeals reinstated."

Amanda had been hanging up on people like Mark Johanson for years. Hanging up and then getting a new number. She'd learned quickly after Robbie's arrest that the press was holding a completely different trial from the one in front of a judge and jury. Not that she blamed them, not really. She just couldn't be part of the campaign against the flesh of her flesh and the bone of her bone. There were enough people willing to take that role. Her part—as his mother—*had* to be different. Her silence had made her that much more enigmatic, however, and the continual bombardment, along with the turning of too many people she'd trusted, had driven her further and further into isolation. A year ago, at the conclusion of the automatic direct appeal mandated for every death row inmate, Robbie had waived his remaining appeals and asked to be executed as soon as possible. That request was the only thing that could have brought Amanda to the forefront of the firestorm, but she'd come running. She'd written letters to her public officials, she'd done an interview on the ABC affiliate news station here in Sioux Falls—though she'd been labeled cold and robotic. She'd met with the warden and hired an attorney. For two months, she'd fought what she thought was a good fight and put herself in the center of a target in order to save her boy's life. Until Robbie asked her not to. "This life is worse than death, Mom, the things that happen here . . ." He started to tell her. She made him stop, then went home and stared at the wall for hours. It had felt good to have a cause, and it had felt like she'd been doing the right thing by advocating for her son. But he didn't want her advocacy. He wanted to die.

Amanda had withdrawn her arguments and run back to the hidey-hole of her life, pulling the lid on tighter than she ever had before. She hadn't said a word publicly since.

Today, however, Robbie was gone and Amanda had no one to protect, though she never felt as though she'd truly protected him from anything. That one attempt had been like tying herself to the bumper of a runaway truck and thinking she could slow it down if she pulled hard enough. "You're calling me three hours after my son's death in search of the *human* side of this story?"

The reporter didn't skip a beat. "How do you feel, Mrs. Mallorie?"

She almost hung up. Almost. But instead she paused and then said the words that came to mind. "I feel like maybe we can all find some peace now. I hope so."

"By *we*, do you mean—"

She ended the call and put the phone in her lap. Was that really what she felt? Did she truly believe there was peace to be found? *Believe* might be too strong a word. Maybe *hope*. She had hope, didn't she?

In the next instant, her entire body ached in anticipation of how long the day would be. If one journalist had her number, they all had it. Whatever peace she hoped for would not begin today. The thought made her feel decades older than her forty-eight years, and she ran her hand through her sleep-tousled hair. She thought of all the television producers and newspaper writers who had contacted her over the years; all the friends and family members who had offered up their connection with Robbie in exchange for fifteen minutes of fame—offerings that were then twisted and posed to push whatever agenda had spurred the contact in the first place. Some writers wanted to sympathize with Robbie—son of an alcoholic father, child of divorce, victim of inadequate mental health services in our country. Another would frame him as a sociopath—charming, manipulative, and violent. Others simply called him evil. Soulless.

Amanda finished finger-combing her hair and began weaving it into a French braid that would keep it out of her face—she had it trimmed twice a year when she went to Cincinnati to visit Melissa. People didn't recognize her as easily in Ohio. The strawberry blond had faded to dusty rose, but she couldn't commit to regular maintenance, so she hadn't had it colored for years. She stood and shuffled into the kitchen, flipping on lights as she went and still shivering. For a moment, she wondered why she wasn't moving to Florida. Then she remembered Melissa and felt guilty. She had work to do there. Being Robbie's mother had interfered with her being Melissa's.

Amanda started the coffee before heading into the bathroom. At the sight of the tropical-fish-themed shower curtain she felt her mouth twitch into a smile; a desperate one, perhaps, but a smile all the same as another memory long ignored played out in her mind like a cherished home movie. She'd bought the curtain for a carnival at the kids' elementary school. Robbie had begged her to run the fishpond—his teacher had pushed the kids to involve their parents and the fishpond was Robbie's favorite game. Amanda had never been *that* mom, the PTA-room mother mom. But she agreed to do the fishpond and then panicked when she realized she had to put the entire booth together. Why hadn't she just agreed to sell tickets like she usually did?

Her angst had resulted in a fully enclosed frame built of PVC pipe, actual fishing rods the kids could cast and reel with clothespins instead of hooks, and *The Little Mermaid* soundtrack playing behind the tropical fish shower curtain she'd searched five stores for. Dwight had helped her build the frame—it was one of the last things they'd done when she'd felt like they were friends. She'd shown up at the carnival that night to find that her setup was more elaborate than the other games, which had utilized desks and chairs and tables from around the school for necessary props. Instead of cheap candy and plastic rings, she gave away notebooks, mechanical pencils, and small stuffed animals—nicer prizes than the other booths. The compliments she'd received had made her feel as though everyone thought she was trying to impress people when what she'd really wanted was to just be like the rest of them. Robbie, however, had loved it so much that he hadn't played any of the other carnival games and instead gleefully helped her clip the prizes and throw the line over and over and over again. On the way home, Robbie hadn't stopped talking about how much better her fishpond had been than *any* other fishpond he'd *ever* seen. Amanda tried not to think about how much money she'd spent on the stupid thing or what judgments had been flung her way for overdoing it.

The fishpond setup had been relegated to the basement, and residual anxiety had kept Amanda from volunteering to do anything but sell tickets at future events. During a de-junking phase following Robbie's conviction she'd found the remaining pieces, including the shower curtain, and decided that the upstairs bathroom could use a little color. Today she dared to specifically like the way the curtain reminded her of Robbie and a time when she'd made him proud. The smile faded. Maybe if she'd been a better PTA-type mom, none of this would have happened. Maybe if she'd volunteered regularly and made petitions to circulate about unfair practices in the district, her son would have avoided becoming a pseudo-commando killer. Either way, Robbie was dead.

She said it out loud. "Dead." The windows did not shatter. A lone wolf did not howl at the injustice. The clock downstairs kept ticking. *Tick. Tock. Tick.* Nothing had changed. Everything was different. Was she different? Could she be?

Her phone rang from where she'd left it in the kitchen and she let out a tired breath—it was still too early to be the movers.

4

Melissa

Melissa hadn't been able to sleep. She'd tried, telling herself that staying up would not change anything, but her thoughts had cycled and spun until she'd slid out of bed around midnight and come downstairs. She'd found the box easily enough, even though she hadn't looked through it for years. She'd taken the box to the family room, where she turned on the gas fireplace, lifted the lid, and let the memories overtake her. Photo after photo of her and Robbie. Her dad was in some of the earlier ones, usually toward the side of the frame. Sometimes looking at his kids, other times looking off at something else. Usually holding a beer. Melissa stared at the pictures of him but was still unable to decide how she felt about the man who had been distant when she was little and then gone when she was older. She didn't know him, never really had, and now, at the age of twenty-nine, with a child of her own and another on the way, she didn't want to know him.

She had sorted through everything in the box—a collection of keepsakes from childhood, high school, and college—until she had one perfect pile of everything relating to Robbie. It wasn't much. Prior to the horrible thing he'd done, she'd never considered a need to save bits of his life. After the horrible thing he'd done, she hadn't wanted to look at him. It was too hard to reconcile the brother she'd grown up with and the demon he'd become. Each time she thought too much about it, she'd feel this tearing sensation in her head, as though she were moving at warp speed and the ship was beginning to fall apart like on those old episodes of *Star Trek*. So, she tried not to think about him and she'd become pretty good at it. No one here in Cincinnati knew that her brother was on death row—well, there had been that one article, but that was years ago. She paused and looked at the green digital time on the DVD player. With a loud exhale, she realized he wasn't on death row anymore. He was dead. A lump rose in her throat and she put a hand to her mouth. Somehow she'd become so distracted with evidence of the past, she'd forgotten the present entirely. Maybe that was some kind of coping mechanism; maybe she'd been avoiding the realization. Hot tears filled her eyes and soon she was sobbing into the cushions of the couch, overwhelmed with so many emotions that she couldn't sort one from the other—guilt for having not been a better sister, confusion as to whom she was mourning, embarrassment for her connection to him, and excruciating sorrow to know that he was gone.

The baby within her moved, as though reminding her that he was still there, and she put her arms around her belly. Things had been different with Lucy—Melissa had been naïve and overjoyed to be pregnant and could go weeks without thinking of her brother who was sentenced to death a few states to the west. She had built a perfect little life for her and Paul and Lucy in Ohio. Melissa had loved being a mom—met other moms in the area, learned how to manage a home and a child, and basked in the purpose of her life. When Robbie did enter her thoughts, she pushed him away. There was no time. When her mom entered her thoughts, it was harder. She'd begged her mother to come with her and Paul when they decided they couldn't stay in South Dakota. Robbie was six months into the trial and Melissa was suffocating. Leaving was the right thing for them and, she was certain, the right thing for her mom. But Mom wouldn't leave. She said she needed to stay for the trial. And then there was the appeal. And then . . . it didn't matter why she stayed, only that she chose Robbie over Melissa. Over Lucy. Over everything and everyone.

When Robbie had dropped his appeals and asked to be executed, Melissa had breathed a sigh of relief. The memory caused her to clench her eyes and cry even harder now, still cradling her belly. What a horrible sister and person she was to have been glad that there was an end in sight. And then she'd found out they were pregnant again. She had expected the new baby to distract her from her first life the way her pregnancy with Lucy had. It hadn't distracted her this time. It terrified her.

Maybe because Lucy was growing up. Maybe because this child was a boy, like Robbie. Maybe because you can only run from the truth for so long. She'd had anxiety attacks. She struggled to sleep. Mom was coming to Ohio, and Melissa was terrified that the move wouldn't be enough to fix what was broken between them. The physical distance had served as a good reason to be disconnected all this time. What if they still couldn't connect? What if all the hope Melissa had of them being mother and daughter again came to nothing? The idea made her insides feel like sand.

A hand on her shoulder startled her and she snapped her head up to see Paul, his hair tousled with sleep and his eyes worried. He didn't say anything, but slid onto the couch, somehow moving her onto his lap in the process. He wrapped his arms around her and she turned into his shoulder and cried again.

"It's going to be okay," he said, stroking her hair with all the tenderness he had always had. He was her gift, her foundation, and her treasure. She shook her head, unable to speak, yet knowing he understood. They talked about everything—he knew every hurt and fear.

She cried for a long time, then finally lifted her face to look at him. "He's dead, isn't he?" Paul would have confirmed it on his phone as soon as he woke up, then come looking for her.

He nodded. "Official time of death was 2:17, Central time."

Melissa nodded and wiped at her eyes. "I need to call Mom; she said she'd be up early."

"She just texted." There was the barest hint of apology in his voice. Melissa waited for him to continue. "The press got her number. She's been getting calls all morning but didn't turn off her phone because the moving company hadn't called to confirm their arrival. But I guess they just did, so she's turning off her phone. She said she'll call when she's on the road."

She didn't want to talk to me, Melissa said to herself. She lifted a hand and smoothed her hair behind her ear as she slid off Paul's lap. "She didn't ask how I was doing." It wasn't a question.

"She's overwhelmed, that's all."

Melissa stared into the fireplace. "What if this is a mistake?" she whispered. "What if she comes all this way and still isn't . . . here."

Paul put his arm around her shoulders and she relaxed back into him. "It's going to be okay, Mel. Maybe not easy, maybe not right away, but it is going to be okay. Give her a chance."

"I've given her a hundred chances."

"Then giving one more won't be too hard."

5

Amanda

Five hours, fifty-two minutes

The first media van showed up at 8:05. Amanda had already hung up on five reporters by then. At 8:30 the movers finally called her to confirm her address. As soon as she hung up, she sent a text message to Melissa, explaining why she had to turn off her phone and promising a call later in the day. She shut off the phone. The silence was sharp and comforting. Amanda was good with silence.

A second van arrived at 8:40 and a third five minutes after that. At ten minutes after nine o'clock, the moving van backed into the driveway and Amanda opened the garage to allow the men easy access to the house. As the garage door lifted, anxiety peaked and rolled in her chest like those tiger cubs on TV that you know are perfectly capable of annihilating one another if they choose to. Amanda had to take deep breaths and repeat affirmations of strength and push-through-it. She never let anyone in. Not Mormon missionaries promising her peace. Not neighbors holding out wavering friendship. She hadn't had her carpets cleaned or bugs sprayed for four years. She'd fixed her own sink, recalibrated her own furnace, and reattached a section of rain gutter all by herself. Thanks to YouTube videos and DIY bloggers, she'd managed to avoid asking anyone for anything. She'd have never hired help for the move if she'd been capable of hauling couches and mattresses on her own. Letting the five men wearing matching orange T-shirts that said COAST TO COAST MOVING in through the garage door seemed to shatter a little bit more of the haven her home had been. But maybe letting them in would make it easier for her to leave.

The burly men of various colors looked out the living room window at the press vans and then back to her. How she wished she could keep hiding. Instead, she gathered her fortitude and pulled her shoulder blades together, forcing herself to stand a little straighter and hopefully look a little more confident and comfortable than she felt. "I'm Amanda Mallorie," she said. "My son was executed this morning. That's why they're here." She waved through the window and worried the gesture looked as though she didn't appreciate the intensity of what she'd said.

She watched their expressions shift; the supervisor seemed embarrassed for her, another blandly accepted the situation, two looked at each other with raised eyebrows as if to say, "Dude, did you hear that? This is that murderer's *house*." The fifth man's face darkened as he put his hands in his pockets and turned away, staring out the window. Amanda wished she could tell them it was fine if they left, but she kept her mouth shut and her shoulders squared even though the panic chipped away at her ability to stay in this room with these strangers.

"If I ignore them long enough, they'll leave," she lied. The supervisor seemed to ponder another moment and then nodded. Thank goodness. "Thanks for explaining that, Mrs., uh, Mallorie."

She'd used her maiden name on the reservation—not to be deceitful but because she always used her maiden name these days. She felt like a coward who had tricked these men into helping her. To apologize would make it worse, though, so she didn't apologize. She didn't say anything at all.

After another second, the supervisor turned to face his crew. "This is just like any other job. We'll start with the basement and move our way up with the hope that we'll finish loading the truck by noon." He turned back to Amanda. "Did you put a yellow sticker on anything you don't want us to put in the van?" She'd read the instructions that had been e-mailed to her several times.

"Yes," Amanda said. "I'm leaving the major appliances and some tools in the garage." She'd been sorting the house for months in preparation—taking apart what furniture she could manage herself and dropping things off at various Goodwill establishments throughout eastern South Dakota. The furniture that remained only emphasized the bare spaces that had once been so full of living. There *had* been happy memories here. She had to believe those memories would come with her and that the empty, burning feelings of these last few years would stay behind.

"I have a few boxes to finish packing upstairs," she said once the supervisor had ushered his workers to the basement. "I'll be finished by the time you reach that level."

The supervisor nodded and Amanda headed for the second floor. On her way up the stairs, she heard an angry, though hushed, conversation. She took the stairs two at a time in order not to overhear their discussion, but thought of the man who had turned away when she'd announced who she was. If she didn't hear what he said, she wouldn't have to repeat the shrinking words in her head. There were too many other words she could not unhear.

Monster.

Demon.

Terrorist.

I hope he rots in hell.

It took fifteen minutes to clear the nightstand and take the bedding off her mattress—the bed frame was already disassembled and stacked against the wall. She put the bedding into the last open box marked "Master Bedroom" and then taped it closed. The condo in Cincinnati had two bedrooms—one more than she needed.

She stacked the box on top of the others, then glanced around the room. After the divorce, she'd gotten a new bedroom set through a classified ad in the *Leader* . . . and cried herself to sleep the first night she'd slept on the unfamiliar bed. The marriage had not been great, but there had been security in being part of a pair. How would she manage a house, career, and two kids by herself? Should she have fought harder to make the marriage work?

Melissa had heard her crying and slipped into the bed beside her. Robbie had come in a few minutes after that, and they had all three fallen asleep in Amanda's new double bed. She'd been the first to wake up the next morning and had looked from Melissa to Robbie. She wasn't alone. She was part of them and they were part of her and they would be all right together. The huge chest of drawers from that bedroom set had been picked up with some other big pieces by the Salvation Army last week since it wouldn't make it up the stairs of her new place. No longer a set, just pieces.

On her way out of the room, Amanda ran her hand along the curved headboard, feeling the barest hint of excitement at the thought of arranging her new room in a new place in a new city. Excitement, she remembered fleetingly, was nice. It would be a couple of weeks before she'd see her furniture again—the discount moving company shared a semi-trailer among three or four people moving to and from the same places—but she liked that she was looking forward to the delivery. Surely, by the time her furniture arrived she would be ready to start this new life of hers, right?

She pulled the bedroom door shut too hard and jumped at the sound, which reverberated strangely through her chest. It had sounded like a shot and drove away the soft feelings she'd found comfort in. She opened the door again to convince herself everything was fine on the other side of the door. She was still shaken by the slam, however. Too shaken. She didn't do well with sharp noises. She'd been at a grocery store one day when a balloon in the floral section had popped. She'd had to leave without completing her shopping. She couldn't watch anything on TV that had gunshots. That therapist she'd seen a million years ago said her reaction was a form of PTSD, but that didn't make sense. Amanda hadn't been at the mall the day Robbie walked in with an assault rifle.

Amanda went into the extra bedroom, which she'd used as a kind of study. She'd given away everything except her filing cabinet, office chair, and a few boxes—one of which she hadn't sealed because she kept adding more and more things to it as she worked through the rest of the house. She took a moment to organize all the items she'd haphazardly thrown in these last few days, but her hands were still shaky and she couldn't focus her thoughts.

The Westroads Mall shooting, committed by a young man named Robert Hawkins, had shaken the state of Nebraska—the state just south—in 2007. Robbie had been sixteen years old. Omaha was only a few hours away and mass public shootings, which were now almost common, had been rare back then. The Westroads tragedy had ignited gun law debates and sparked finger-pointing campaigns against everything from public security to mental illness to video games. Robert Hawkins had a history of mental illness and making violent threats; the shooting had been motivated by his own wish to die in a way that made him famous. He shot himself after eight innocent people lay dead or dying on the second floor of the Von Maur department store.

Like everyone else, Amanda had watched the aftermath of the event play out in the newspapers and on TV. She'd been shocked that something so horrific could happen so close to home—people didn't shoot up malls in the Midwest. The only thing she specifically remembered about Robbie's reaction to the shooting was his pointing out that he and Hawkins shared the same first name.

Six years later, Robbie walked into the Cotton Mall in Sioux Falls on the anniversary of the Westroads shooting and repeated Robert Hawkins's fateful and fatal actions, shooting from the upper concourse of the mall into the common area below. A mall security guard tried to intervene and Robbie shot the man in the head. An off-duty police officer knocked Robbie to the ground moments later and other holiday shoppers helped hold him until the police came—Robbie never had the chance to seal his grotesque act with his own blood as he'd intended.

Amanda, Melissa, and Paul—Melissa's husband of only six months at the time—had been caught in the middle of the firestorm that followed. Amanda had resigned from her twelve-year teaching position at Jefferson High—one of the victims, Garett Draden, had been a student there. No one resisted her resignation. The numbness sank a little deeper. Paul and Melissa transferred to the University of Cincinnati five months after the shooting, inviting Amanda to come with them to Ohio.

"This is too much, Mom," Melissa had said after announcing their plans. "No one can expect you to stay here after all that's happened, not even Robbie."

Amanda chose to stay, just until after the trial, she'd said. But after the first trial came sentencing and then the next trial; then Robbie dropped his appeals. There was no point at which Robbie hadn't needed her.

Melissa had gone on with her life. Amanda visited her twice a year, and each time Melissa resurrected the idea of Amanda moving to Ohio. Two years ago, when Melissa became a mother, Amanda was not there. She met Lucy four months later when she went to Cincinnati for her usual week-long visit in July. She saw Lucy again six months later when she went to Ohio for Christmas. During her trips, she got haircuts, went off-the-rack shopping, hugged Melissa, smiled politely, deep-cleaned anything that needed it at Melissa's house, and took her granddaughter to the park as though she were a normal person. Then she scurried back to South Dakota and pushed away the rising guilt of having abandoned her daughter for the sake of her son.

"It's time," Melissa had said four months ago when they got the news that Robbie's execution date would be in January. "This isn't doing you or Robbie any good, Mom. Just come to Ohio."

"I can't," Amanda had said into the phone. "And I hope you never know what it feels like to be the only person in someone's life."

Melissa had been angry and ended the phone call. She and Robbie had exchanged letters during his incarceration, but his medication and state of mind influenced the content of those letters. After a particularly difficult letter Paul had called Amanda and told her that they would not be accepting any more of his letters; would she please explain that to Robbie? After that, Amanda and Melissa didn't talk about Robbie very much. Amanda understood that Melissa needed distance from her brother, but he had become Amanda's life. He needed her.

Robert Hawkins—the Westroads Killer—had threatened his stepmom with an ax when he was fourteen and had spent years in and out of psychiatric institutions and state care. He'd been diagnosed with depression before the age of six. Amanda, like everyone else, assumed Hawkins was damaged from the start; that there had always been something "wrong" with him and he had turned homicidal on that fateful day in 2007.

That impression of Hawkins, and other mass shooters of the last decade, easily played into people's desire to think that some-one they loved could never be so evil. Yet someone Amanda loved as much as anyone in the whole world had done some-thing horrific. Something beyond imagination. Everyone needed to believe that there *had always been* something deep and dark and twisted about Robbie, but there hadn't been. Yes, his father had had an alcohol problem that resulted in Amanda being the sole breadwinner for many years. Yes, his parents had divorced when Robbie was twelve, and the relationship with his father had become fractured. Robbie had dealt with those things the way millions of other kids dealt with them and continued to be successful and "normal." Yes, he was eventually diagnosed with a serious mental illness. Yes, he could have lived a normal life if he'd taken his medications. No, Amanda had never imagined his not taking his meds would lead to *this*. Never in a million years had she considered the possible outcome to be anything like it had been. To everyone else, Robert Mallorie was all Rob-bie had ever been. Only Amanda believed that his kindness, goodness, humanity, and innocence had ever existed. Only Amanda knew there was more to Robbie than what he became.

Men's voices downstairs brought her back to the present, and she blinked at the box she'd finished organizing in the extra bedroom. She taped up the box and crossed off "finish packing study" from her mental to-do list. The movers were calling to one another from the main level—had they finished the basement already? She walked quickly into the hallway, not shutting the door this time, and felt her mind pulling out of the heavy thoughts. Thank goodness. Unlike memories of her children when they were little—which she'd let in only today—thoughts of the shooting and all that happened before and after always surrounded her. Over and over she wondered what one thing she could have done differently that would have changed the outcome. After four years, she had looked at every piece of her mothering from every angle and found no solid answer, but a thousand possibilities. She had been too strict about homework, but too lenient with curfews. She hadn't made her children do enough chores, then grumbled about doing everything herself. She had served too many processed foods but didn't make enough cookies. She was home too much, but then again she worked, so maybe she was home too little. She'd yelled. She'd spanked. Sometimes she wished she could leave her children and move to Hawaii all by herself.

Amanda looked down the hall at the last door—with the two-toned black and silver stickers that read DANGER ZONE. Robbie's bedroom.

The letters weren't straight—Robbie had been nine when he'd put them up. He'd thought himself so clever, convinced that if the rest of the family believed he had something dangerous behind that door, they would never be tempted to come in. He had explained that the ruse would keep Melissa from "messing with my stuff." Melissa had rolled her eyes. At the grand age of eleven, she had no interest in his Transformers or Legos and claimed that everything in his room smelled bad. She was right about the smell part. Amanda had tried for years to get his room not to smell like socks. When had it finally stopped? When he was fifteen and started liking girls?

It had seemed so overwhelming back then to be a mom when the kids bickered relentlessly and nothing was ever clean, and yet it had actually been so simple. Feed them. Love them. Make sure they did their homework and showered regularly. Robbie had asked for some stickers to make a sign on his door and she'd given him the ones left over from putting the name "Mallorie" on the mailbox. Simple. Easy. Cute. Good mothers let their sons take ownership of their bedrooms as a matter of pride and responsibility.

Part of the D in "DANGER" had been ripped off—an attempt to hide that nine-year-old silliness from his sixteen-year-old-self years later. Removing the sticker after seven years had taken the varnish with it and Amanda had insisted he leave the rest of the letters up until she could figure out how to get the stickers off without further damage. They'd argued about it for three days—Robbie hating the immature warning on his door that was so "not cool."

"It's my house," Amanda had finally said in a stop-arguing tone of voice. Dwight had been gone four years by that time, so the house really was hers. "I'm not letting you ruin that door."

Once Robbie had realized that no counterargument could trump her position, he had put an Aquabats poster over the stickers. The band was ridiculous—a bunch of grown men dressed as pseudosuperheroes singing ska music—but it preserved the door, which was what she'd wanted. She wasn't sure when that poster had come down, but at some point Robbie had decided that an uneven warning about a danger zone was better than the Aquabats.

Amanda ran her fingers over the letters, imagining his little-boy fingers putting them in place. He'd have had his tongue poking slightly from the left side of his mouth, like it always did when he concentrated. He'd have been focused and determined—she had loved the way he could be so intent upon a task.

The walls of Robbie's old room were empty save for some nail holes. All the furniture had already been donated, but she'd thrown personal items into boxes as she'd disassembled the room. History. Memories. Bits and pieces of life from better days. Four boxes containing the sum of her son's life were lined against the wall, the tops gaping open like the mouths of baby birds. Rather than waiting to be fed, however, they were waiting for her to sift through the personal objects of her son's life and determine what was reasonable to keep. She considered taking the boxes to Cincinnati and going through them when she didn't feel so raw, but she wanted to arrive in her new condo without so much baggage—literally and figuratively. Crossing the South Dakota border without the burden of this task heavy upon her shoulders would be a big step on this new journey toward living. Wouldn't it?

Amanda had already decided to allow herself only one box of mementos, which meant that each item in the four boxes would need to be weighed against every other item. She had decided to keep photographs, but certificates, trophies, and things without sentimental value would be discarded.

Was it a chore to go through Robbie's things, she wondered, or was it an indulgence?

Robbie would laugh to hear her thoughts—or would he? She hadn't heard his laughter for years. Prison and declining mental health had changed him. Had there been room within him these last years to find humor in anything at all? Should there have been after what he'd done?

She didn't know. Would never know. Robbie was gone. *Dead*. Yesterday she had two children, and today she had one. Did that make her half the mother she'd been?

Had it been today when that changed? Or had she lost her son years ago when the voices in his head became louder than hers? Or had the change been at some different juncture entirely, a choice she'd made along the way that turned him that fateful degree away from the man he was supposed to be. Too many shoot-'em-up video games? Not enough chores? Too much sugar? Not enough discipline? Was not properly punishing him for sideswiping a post at the drive-through responsible for his having become so callous about human life? Amanda let the familiar thoughts move through her as she settled herself on her knees in front of the first box and carefully poured the contents onto the sand-colored carpet. She emptied the second box too.

She'd use one now-empty box for garbage and the other one for things she wanted to keep. She pulled a marker out of her back pocket and wrote "Robbie" on the keeper box to make it official, then attached a yellow sticker so that the movers wouldn't accidentally load it into the van.

Within the hour, this would be all that was left of Robbie's life. She took a breath and got started.

6

Larinda

Four years, one month, five days

Larinda shifted into drive and pulled up behind the car in front of her. She turned the radio back up, but when the commentator started talking about the execution she changed the station. No sense dwelling on the negative. She'd gone to the prison like Barbara had wanted her to—though she had stayed outside—and it was over now.

A car ahead of her got their order and pulled away, allowing Larinda to pull up to the payment window. She shifted sideways as best she could and handed over her credit card. The cashier had to lean halfway out the window to take it. Larinda avoided eye contact, not wanting to see the judgment in the girl's face. When the cashier returned the card, Larinda put it in the change compartment of the middle console—it was her "fast food" card and she left it there so that it was easy to find.

Larinda's cell phone pinged and she picked it up with her right hand, glancing at the screen as she pulled forward a few more feet. She was the next car in the pickup line now and her mouth watered. Cheese, potatoes, and white flour were her love language.

The ping was indication of a new voice mail, and the fact that she didn't recognize the number meant it was probably another reporter. After the shooting, she'd done a few interviews, but that was almost a hundred and twenty pounds ago, and she hadn't ever been what one would call slender. Plus, she knew that dwelling on the greatest tragedy of her life was not in anyone's best interest. Whenever her mind seemed to get bogged down in the memories of losing Nora, she forced her thoughts somewhere else—once she was back home she would make that dipping sauce she liked out of salsa, sour cream, and lime juice for the hash browns. So good!

Larinda reached the pickup window and leaned over to take the bag and the drink holder that would keep her shake and Diet Coke from spilling on the drive home. She was breathing heavily once both items were on her passenger seat. She shifted into drive again and pulled forward, anticipating how she would navigate the few blocks to home, turn on the TV, and eat while she watched whatever mindless show might be on. She liked the fixer-upper shows and the ones about dogs. She *didn't* like the commercials that talked about weight-loss programs and health crises—there were always a lot of them when the new year started. It made her think of how her toes were getting tingly more often and the headaches that seemed to come on every afternoon. She didn't complain to Ken because he'd want her to go to the doctor, and the doctor would tell her she was sick and getting sicker. He would tell her to lose weight. Like that was the big solution to everything.

The new radio station began talking about the execution and she changed the station again. She hadn't avoided cameras completely at the prison this morning and Larinda was anxious about how she'd looked. A few weeks ago, she'd passed a former coworker when she'd stopped to pick up a couple of pizzas. The woman had made eye contact, smiled like she would to a stranger, and gone back to whatever she was doing on her phone. And Larinda had been relieved. She didn't have to answer the inevitable "How are you doing?" that everyone asked her all the time. She didn't have to push on that smile and say, "Things are good," while pretending the other person didn't notice all the weight she'd put on since they'd seen each other last.

Larinda had worn a turquoise blouse and black pants under the long black coat she hoped was more slimming than it felt—

the waistband of these pants were killing her. She would change into her pajama bottoms as soon as she got home. Before she ate? She made a face, not sure which was better—eating in comfort or eating as soon as she could.

The food smelled amazing and it took all her willpower to keep from ripping the bag open with her free hand and downing all the greasy goodness right now. But she'd promised herself last week that she wouldn't eat in the car anymore. It was one promise in a string of promises she'd made and broken over the years, but she was determined to keep this one. It was the first step to getting things under control. She just had to get through the stress of the execution, the increased coverage and renewed attention to the man who had killed her daughter. After things died down she'd feel less confused and she'd get some help putting her thoughts back in line. Maybe she'd take down some of Nora's pictures—over the years she'd framed every photo of Nora and put it on display in the house. Ken had called it a shrine, and even though she knew he had meant it in a bad way, she had kind of liked the word. It kept Nora alive somehow. Sometimes Larinda talked to her daughter when she was home by herself. "I think the girl completely manipulated that man," she'd say regarding the *Judge Judy* episode she was watching. "Poor guy."

When the garage opened, Larinda was surprised to see Ken's car was still on his side. He hadn't come to the prison with her because he had work. "I don't need to be there when the man dies to move past this, Lari. I've made my own peace." Larinda had said she had, too—it wasn't like she was a rage-monger like Barbara Hansen, or was drinking herself into oblivion like Valerie Simperton's mom. Larinda donated to the Boys & Girls Clubs, made care packages for new mothers at the hospital, and had faith in a plan bigger than this one. She knew where Nora was and it gave her peace.

Larinda parked her car next to Ken's and looked guiltily at the food on the passenger seat. Maybe she could convince Ken that she knew he'd be home and so she'd bought breakfast for both of them. And she'd gotten fast food instead of coming home and making something healthier because . . . it had been a long morning at the prison. He'd see right through that, but he wouldn't want to fight, so he'd let it go after giving her a reprimanding look. Maybe she could just eat it all right here in the car before she went inside. But what if he came out and found her shoveling fast food into her mouth? Plus, she wouldn't even enjoy it if she scarfed it down, and that would make her want to get more. She let out a breath and then lifted her chin—it was what it was.

She moved the seat all the way back, then opened the door and put out first one foot and then the other, awkwardly turning her bulk in the seat until she was facing sideways. She grabbed the side of the door with one hand and then pushed up on the dashboard with the other to get to her feet. First try—that was success. Maybe she was down a few pounds since making her no-eating-in-the-car promise. She closed the door and lumbered to the passenger side, where she picked up the drive-through bag and decided to leave the shake and the drink in the car. It was cold enough that they would be okay for an hour or so. Until Ken left. Hopefully he wouldn't notice them as he crossed the garage to his car. He wasn't staying home all day, was he? She couldn't remember the last time he'd done that.

With the bag in one hand, she used the other hand to help her climb the three steps that led to the kitchen door. She pushed the button to lower the garage door.

"Ken?" she called as she entered the kitchen, putting the bag on the counter next to a collage of Nora's dance team portraits. Larinda kissed her fingers and pressed them to the glass as was her habit, then looked longingly at the bag of comfort she had to leave on the counter for now. She hoped the burritos wouldn't be completely cold by the time she was able to eat them—the hash browns could be warmed up in the microwave easily enough, but eggs never reheated right. "You didn't go to work?"

She put her keys on the counter and made her way toward the doorway into the living room, where the computer desk was that Ken worked from when he worked from home. Fifty photographs of Nora filled that room—every bit of shelf and wall space filled with her beautiful smile. It was a happy place. "Ken?" She was taking off her coat when she reached the doorway, looked up, and froze.

"Hey, sweetie."

Larinda held her husband's eyes for a moment before scanning the other faces in the room—each of them dear to her. Each of them a betrayer. Her face instantly caught fire with embarrassment at the sure knowledge that they had gathered here to confront her. She started to turn in a vain attempt to pretend this wasn't happening, but Ken was beside her in a flash, one hand on her back, another on her arm, pulling her gently into the room. "Let go of me," she hissed through her teeth.

"No," Ken said, simple and bold. He led her to the couch, where their sons waited. They stood to hug her, but she remained stiff as a board. Had she ever felt so humiliated in her whole life? Her eyes met the only unfamiliar set in the room—a woman with red hair and sharp eyes. Over the woman's shoulder Larinda could see a collection of Nora's baby pictures. She'd been such a pretty baby. *Can you believe what they're doing to me, sweetie?*

"Have a seat, Larinda," the interventionist said.

Larinda wanted to argue as she looked from the face of her sister to her best friend to her mother, brother-in-law, daughter-in-law, and then Ken again. All the people who loved her best gathered in one room for the purpose of saving her from herself—she watched the shows, she knew the drill, but she'd never in a million years expected to be the . . . addict being confronted.

She sat, but closed her eyes, unable to look at these people. Ken started. Ken, who was supposed to love her unconditionally but wanted her to change. She waited for him to say that he only wanted what was best for her. That she was eating too much and he was afraid of losing her to health problems that would inevitably result from her lack of self-care. She knew all that—it was why she'd made the promise not to eat in her car anymore. She wasn't stupid. She knew she'd let things get out of control, but she didn't need to be shamed into doing better. She was already doing better this week than she had last week. Except she had enough fast food for four people in the kitchen.

"I can't keep doing this," he said, then sniffed and looked at the paper in his hand. "I *won't* keep doing this, Larinda. You're killing yourself slowly and I can't watch it anymore. I need my wife back, and our kids—the ones who are still with us—need their mom."

"I'm right here," she said, but she was crying too. Each of her boys took one hand. Derrick had come from California for this?

"No, you're not, Mom," Randy said. "You're stuck in what happened, and it's killing all of us. Nora's gone."

"I know that," she snapped, then took a breath and stared at a spot of carpet rather than make eye contact with anyone. Their oozing pity was too much. "And I've made my peace with it. She's in God's care and there's comfort in that."

Ken was shaking his head. "We all admire your faith, Larinda, but it's not enough. There's more that needs to be addressed. You're out of control and—"

"I'm dealing with it," she snapped. "I've formed some bad habits, but I'll get them under control."

"I don't think you can do that until you properly mourn Nora." Ken waved his hand around the living room. "There's no room for anyone else anymore, Lari. You're completely lost to us."

Larinda wanted those breakfast burritos more than ever and wished she dared make a run for them, sprint into the garage, and lock herself in the car until her stomach was full and her thoughts were mellowed. The irony that she couldn't sprint because of the many times she'd numbed herself out that way was stark.

"And we can't risk you not getting better, Mom." This was from Derrick. He gave her hand a squeeze and she was tempted to pull it back.

"They feel like they've lost you," the interventionist said. "An—"

"They want me back," Larinda cut in. She'd meant to speak first in order to put the woman in her place, but instead the words pierced her. *They want me back*. Her loved ones had come from all over the state, some from other states, to tell her that they wanted her back. She still wanted to defend herself, but she also wanted them all to leave so she could eat her food and watch TV and numb out. She didn't want to think about the piece of her heart she'd lost the day Nora died. She didn't want to think of the years Nora didn't have, the accomplishments she hadn't made, and the motherhood Larinda had lost. She didn't want to think about any of that.

"We're here because we love you," Larinda's mother said, speaking for the first time. "And we want you to be happy again."

Happy? She couldn't see that happiness was possible, and that's what scared her the most. That's what kept her eating and eating and eating some more. What if she tried to be happy and couldn't? It was better not to try than to try and fail. The arms of her sons encircled her. Someone else took her free hand.

The interventionist began talking about a facility in South Carolina. Larinda stared over the woman's shoulder at a picture of her daughter on the day of her junior high graduation. She wondered how many pictures of Nora she would be able to bring with her and what kind of food they served. Who was going to end up eating those burritos?

7

Amanda

Eight hours, forty minutes

Pokémon cards, progress reports, and sports memorabilia went into the garbage without much hesitation even though she ached a bit with each item—these were the type of things she'd expected to pull out and show Robbie's children one day. She would have told his son what a good runner Robbie had been, and a math whiz—always an A student. The never-to-exist grandchild would finger the old paper and smile proudly—his dad had been great. His dad had always had greatness in him. See what he achieved? See how he put his mind to things?

Amanda had naïvely expected branches upon branches of his family tree—*her* family tree—spreading out for generations behind him. Children for Robbie. Grandchildren for Amanda who would one day give her great-grandchildren. Robbie would grow into a man and become a husband and lose his hair and thicken around his waist and have to get glasses and learn how to grow tomatoes. That's what she'd always expected. Not believed. Not hoped for. *Expected*. It had been her God-given right as a mother to have these things.

These expectations *had* been fulfilled by Melissa, Amanda reminded herself as she threw away Robbie's high school graduation program. Amanda had only seen her granddaughter four times in two years, though.

Amanda thumbed through a folder containing the career testing Robbie had done in high school—accounting, business, design. He was naturally analytical but had good people skills. He would be a good manager and should pursue graduate school so as to maximize his potential. *Mass killer* was nowhere on the list of future occupations. She threw the folder out.

In the keeper box went items that had been important to him—like the purple rock shaped like an egg. Her memory banks were oiled up now and quickly connected the memory with this rock. Robbie had found it when they'd stayed at a KOA in the Black Hills. Robbie would have been six or seven at the time—she remembered that both kids had missed a day of school so they could take the trip to Mount Rushmore for Labor Day weekend. Dwight was supposed to go with them but at the last minute decided to get some work done around the house—they'd lived in an older house in Watertown at the time and there was always something to be fixed. That Amanda hadn't minded leaving her husband behind, was actually relieved, in fact, reflected the state of their relationship, though it would be six more years before they decided to legally acknowledge their distance. When Robbie had showed Amanda the purple rock, she'd put aside the novel she'd been reading and leaned forward with her elbows on her knees.

"I bet a big purple bird laid this egg." Robbie's bright blue eyes danced with excitement as the story behind his discovery grew in his mind. He'd cradled the egg in his hand as though it were the baby bird he was imagining. "And then the world froze and all the dinosaurs died. This egg was frozen for so long that when people were born they just thought it was a rock, so they didn't even try to eat it. One day the rock-bird will hatch and fly into the sky with *huuuuge* wings that will blow over trees when he moves them up and down 'cause it will make tornados." Tornados had fascinated Robbie when he was little—she'd forgotten that. They'd once taped two water bottles together at the openings with some doohickey Robbie had brought home from school. They had filled one of the bottles with water. When you tilted the water into one bottle and then turned it upside down, a whirlpool formed in the center as the water drained into the empty bottle. Robbie had loved watching that funnel over and over and over again. He said he wished they'd put a tiny plastic cow in the bottle before they taped it up so he could watch it spin. Not that they'd had a tiny cow . . .

Amanda now turned the rock over in her hand, uplifted by the memory she'd matched to it. She'd originally thought Robbie had left the rock at the campground. A few weeks after the trip, however, she'd found it in his drawer when she was putting away laundry. She'd left the rock-egg in the nest of socks Robbie had made for it. She hadn't seen it—or even thought about it— since. The rock went into her keeper box. It was a good memory; intact and happy without any possible indications of what may have been always lurking in the darker corners of her child's mind.

Yearbooks went alongside the rock in the keeper box after she skimmed through them. She liked being reminded that Robbie had run cross-country. He'd wanted to join the shooting club that went to a rifle range a few times a month, but Amanda had said no. She hadn't been raised with guns and didn't want him to be either. The irony of this was not lost upon her. It wasn't until his trial that she learned Robbie had become fascinated with guns in the years before the shooting—had been intrigued by them since childhood. He'd hidden his interest because he knew she wouldn't like it. Kind of like he'd hidden his drug use and dabbling into terrorist watch group websites; she wouldn't have liked that either. He'd tried to buy an automatic rifle of some sort the summer *before* but had been turned down because of his mental health history. So, he'd stolen an assault rifle from his roommate's father instead—ex-military with a broken lock on his gun safe who had showed off his collection when Robbie had been invited over for dinner with the other guys who shared the apartment. If she hadn't been so phobic about guns, would Robbie have developed a healthier relationship with firearms? Maybe if she'd taken him shooting or somehow shown him what damage guns were capable of he'd have . . . what? Known that his delusion was a delusion? Told her his plans so that she could get him the help she didn't know he'd needed?

Robbie's choices in high school activities had assured Amanda that he would continue to achieve and progress as he grew up. He'd been a good student; 3.5 GPA; he'd scored a 23 on his ACT test. He'd helped decorate for the Halloween dance even though he hadn't gotten up the courage to ask anyone. He'd liked that one girl . . . Kaitlyn, but she was a year older and "totally out of my league, Mom, like, far, far outta there." Amanda looked up Kaitlyn's picture in Robbie's sophomore yearbook and wondered what she was doing now. College graduate? Married? A mother? Did she have a son of her own she was teaching to go pee-pee in the toilet and imagining what kind of man he would grow up to become?

Surrounding the black-and-white photographs forever recording this time in the lives of Robbie and his classmates were notes from fellow students hastily written on the last day of school. Things like, *I will miss you so much, Robbie. Thanks for making Mrs. Larkin's class bearable,* and *Rob, let's get together for a Halo-fest this summer!*

None of those kids had ended up in prison for killing nine people and forever changing the lives of countless others. Justin Farnsworth—Robbie's best friend in junior high—had gone on to dental school and recently returned to work in his father's practice; there'd been an article about it in the *Tribune* last spring. Jannie Mendon, Robbie's date for the junior prom, had gone to NYU on a dance scholarship. A few months into Robbie's trial, Jannie and her parents had sold the prom photos to a tabloid. Nicole Carlisle—the girl Robbie had dated for six months during his senior year—was now Nicole Allen. She'd had two little kids with her when Amanda had seen her at the grocery store a few months ago. Amanda and Nicole's eyes had met when they both entered opposite ends of the cereal aisle, but Nicole had looked away quickly and then casually turned her cart around as though she didn't actually eat boxed cereal. After Robbie had broken up with her all those years ago, Nicole had come to the house and cried on Amanda's shoulder. "I just love him so much," Nicole had said with all the fervor and sincerity of a teenage girl desperately in love. "I know he's the one for me; I just *know* it."

How Amanda wished Robbie *had* been the one for Nicole . . . or Jannie . . . or even Kaitlyn. It wasn't hard to picture Robbie married to a sweet girl like one of them, kissing her and the kids goodbye before he went to work, having cookouts in the backyard on weekends while he complained about the office or the car in need of an oil change or the crabgrass he couldn't get out of his lawn. He could have been a great husband, couldn't he? He could have remained balanced on his meds, found behavioral controls for his anxiety like running or not eating gluten. He could have been whole and real and good. Was it better or worse for Amanda to fantasize about the possibilities? Was she missing some kind of peace by believing he'd had a chance? A chance he had discarded.

Amanda moved on from the yearbooks to another stack of papers—college brochures, a manual for his Xbox, his acceptance letter to the University of Sioux Falls. He'd wanted to go out of state, but he didn't get the hoped-for scholarships to any of those schools. Amanda had been secretly glad to have him closer to home. His freshman year at USF had been fun—parties and friends, a job at a burger joint; he'd even had a girlfriend for a few weeks, though Amanda had never met her because "we aren't serious, Mom. It's just a thing." He didn't do as well in his classes as he'd thought he would, and he wasn't sleeping well. Toward the end of his second semester he told her that he was having really vivid dreams that sometimes felt so real it took him a while to really wake up from them in the mornings. Amanda ascribed it to stress. College wasn't high school after all. Lots of kids struggled, and it was through adversity that we grow—Amanda's dad had always said that, and she found herself repeating it to her adult children on a regular basis. Robbie moved home for the summer after his freshman year and worked on the landscape crew where he'd been employed since he was fifteen—he was good with his hands and after four years of grunt work was now helping to put in sprinkler systems.

His sophomore year at USF was when everything fell apart.

He'd chosen a rigorous schedule and exhibited a new tension that surrounded him like a bubble. He was snappy with Amanda but would always apologize and admitted after a rough weekend that he wasn't sleeping well again. Sometimes when he came home for an evening or the weekend to do laundry, she'd catch him staring into a corner of the room as though looking really hard at something. When she asked about it, he shook his head, returned to what he was doing, and said he was just thinking.

It had been easy to chalk up his behavior to the continued stress of hard classes and then the stress of not doing very well that first semester. He'd come home for Christmas sulky and irritable—staying in his room most of the time and playing video games. When he'd been living at home she hadn't let him have a TV in his room, but he'd brought the TV and console from his dorm home with him at Christmas. Amanda didn't want an argument when their relationship had already become so strained. A stressed-out son coming home for visits and playing video games in his room was better than him not coming home at all.

Amanda had suggested that he talk to the therapist she'd seen after the divorce, but he'd shrugged off her suggestions. He was just tired, he said. College was hard. She suggested seeing a doctor; maybe he could take sleeping pills for a few weeks to get his circadian rhythms back to normal. He said he'd think about it. He didn't always return her texts; he said he'd come to Sunday dinner, but then forget. Amanda tried not to take things personally, telling herself that Melissa had gone through the same sort of transition in college. He was an adult and gaining independence—it was fine.

Two months into the second semester of his sophomore year, Robbie called the school's administration building to warn them about a bomb. He said he'd had a dream about it and if they didn't listen, hundreds of students would be killed. The administration had taken the call as a terroristic threat and had him arrested. When Amanda was called out of class so she could go down to the police station, she'd had a weird vortex-like moment of believing they were talking about some other kid with the same name. Another Robert Mallorie at USF. Or perhaps someone had used Robbie's name—that weird roommate who was obsessed with Call of Duty maybe. Her kid didn't make terroristic threats. Robbie was in college, working hard and learning life lessons.

She'd left the vice principal in charge of her class and arrived at the police station to find Robbie pacing back and forth in one of the interview rooms, his hands in his hair as he mumbled about a conspiracy no one knew about except him. Didn't they know how many people were going to die? Didn't they see that their detaining him was exactly what Al-Qaeda wanted? She had watched him from behind the glass with shock and fear and wondered, *Who is that guy?* It was Robbie, but it . . . wasn't.

What had happened?

What had she missed?

What did she need to do to fix it?

Robbie was admitted to the Avera Behavioral Health Unit instead of being taken to jail, and the charges were dropped, although he was put on probation with the university. Amanda hadn't seen him again until he'd been stabilized with medication—the longest three days of her life up to that point. Little did she know how truly long a day could become. When she was finally able to visit, Robbie was so upset by what he'd done. He remembered it all happening but said it felt like it had been someone else. Like a movie he'd watched. The school dropped the charges, but he was put on academic suspension and moved back home so that he could get his feet underneath him, find the right medication, and deal with his embarrassment and depression. He'd gone to a therapist and a psychiatrist, who confirmed Avera's initial diagnosis of schizophrenia.

Amanda knew what schizophrenia was, but the reality of its delusions—auditory and visual—and the paranoia they inspired was far different from anything she'd imagined. She'd never imagined that someone she loved—someone not only in her sphere of life, but her own child—could become one of *those* people who saw things that weren't there, heard things no one else did, and felt watched and monitored by everyone from the next-door neighbor to the CIA. In the year that followed that first hospitalization, she became an expert thanks to the library and Google. She clung to the understanding that with medication and awareness, Robbie could still live a normal life. As it turned out, Dwight had a cousin, and probably an uncle, with the same diagnosis. Did it make her terrible to be glad it was on his side of the family? Dwight wouldn't get into it with her; he just gave the history and then didn't return her calls when she asked for more information. She remembered telling Robbie once when he was particularly down about everything that "This isn't a death sentence, Robbie; it's just something we need to deal with." *Not a death sentence.* The memory made her shiver.

Robbie was diligent with his medications, which kept the delusions and his moods subdued but slowed him down in a lot of ways. Everything was harder than it had once been. He worked with the landscape crew again that summer, but Robbie wasn't "easy" with the work. He got frustrated and was clumsy. He made mistakes, which made him even more frustrated. He got angry one day and smashed a sprinkler timer on a customer's driveway while screaming obscenities. His boss called Amanda once they'd gotten Robbie to calm down to tell her that they would have to take the cost of it out of Robbie's check. "You know I love Robbie, Amanda, but maybe this is a little too much pressure for him right now. I think it would be better if he took off these last few weeks before school starts. We can look at things again next summer." Amanda had been humiliated on her son's behalf, but downplayed it to Robbie. She worked it out with his boss to pay for the timer herself so that Robbie would still get his paycheck. They agreed to tell him that work was slow and they didn't need him those last two weeks.

Robbie went back to school under probationary status that fall—determined to make up for the time he'd lost—but ended up with more failing grades than passing ones in the first semester. He had one more semester to get things right, but dropped out halfway through and moved to Omaha one weekend—one of the guys from the landscape crew had invited him to share an apartment. Amanda had been furious at such an irresponsible decision and refused to talk to him for three full weeks. Even when they made up—agreeing to disagree that this move was a good idea—he'd been defensive when she asked if he was taking his medication or experiencing any of his delusional manifestations. She learned later, during his trial, that he started drinking during that time and smoking various substances that were then not classified as illicit drugs—spice, black mamba, and other "herbal" blends that lots of kids were experimenting with. There were stories about these drugs causing psychosis in people *without* mental health issues.

Amanda had helped Robbie with his portion of the rent three different times because he wasn't working regularly—just picking up short-term jobs through a temp agency. She talked to him about being responsible, and he would tell her about the interviews he had lined up. "I just need one more month, Mom. Then it's all gonna fall into place." She talked to him about being an advocate for his health and he said he would. She sent him articles about people with schizophrenia who lived normal lives so long as they stayed under the care of a good psychiatrist. He finally told her in an e-mail that he didn't really have schizophrenia; whatever was going on with him was something else, and he was figuring things out. She'd called him as soon as she got the e-mail, but he didn't answer. She left him messages, reminding him to take his meds and offering to come to Omaha and help him find a new doctor. He finally texted her back in all caps:

IM TAKIGN MY MEDS. BACK OFF!!!

It had been such a frustrating and frightening time for Amanda. Robbie was so different from the boy he'd been in high school. She read articles on parenting adult children and then more articles about parenting adult children with mental illness. She read about schizophrenics who had learned how to live without their meds and she hoped that maybe Robbie *was* like them. She talked to her pastor, who told her that Robbie had to make his own way in the world and maybe this was a case of her not cutting the apron strings. Amanda had never thought of herself as smothering, but maybe she was. It was a strange kind of relief to take the blame. If it was her fault, she could fix it. She watched *A Beautiful Mind* and cried, but also found hope. Robbie wasn't bad; he was just sick. She prayed that he would find his way sooner rather than later.

Six months into this new phase of independence Amanda tried to convince herself was normal and nothing to freak out about, Robbie stole that assault rifle from his roommate's father's house. Three weeks later he drove past the Westroads Mall in Omaha on his way to Sioux Falls. He thought of the Cotton Mall as *his* mall and he believed it was the meeting place of a secret cell of Al-Qaeda. He had to get them before they could organize another attack like 9/11. His roommates later testified that he'd become obsessed with 9/11 and the first Westroads massacre—talking about the events incessantly and saying things like, "What if they're connected?" and "Robert Hawkins wasn't all that different from me, ya know." His roommates dealt with his odd moods by offering him another drink or smoke, which, they said, he never turned down. None of them were aware that he'd been previously diagnosed with schizophrenia or that he was supposed to take medication every day to keep his delusions in check. They thought his obsession was . . . funny. One of his roommates admitted to putting notes on Robbie's car a few times saying that Al-Qaeda was strengthening in his area. He later told Robbie that he'd made it up, but Robbie hadn't believed him. He was convinced there was a growing threat in Sioux Falls. It was a perfect cover—quiet Midwest town where nothing extreme ever happened—and even though he knew innocent people might die, someone had to take a stand, and God had somehow decided that Robbie was that someone.

Amanda had been filling his prescriptions every month and mailing them to him with little motivational quotes about determination and perseverance. The police found all the packages in his closet, unopened, after his arrest. Were all those notes now in an evidence locker somewhere?

In 2015—two years into Robbie's incarceration and appeals process—Nebraska repealed its death penalty; they would no longer execute capital offenders. North Dakota had repealed its capital punishment years earlier. In between those two states was South Dakota, with its single-drug lethal injection and fast-track executions upon the request of the sentenced inmate. It didn't matter that Robbie was mentally ill. He knew that what he was doing was against the law and had accepted that innocent people might be killed. He had planned his attack in detail, choosing a time he knew the mall would be busy—a Saturday afternoon two weeks before Christmas. If Robbie had committed his heinous crime a few hours north or a few hours south, he wouldn't have died today.

Not that she wished Robbie'd had the presence of mind to commit his horrible crime in a state that would not kill him, but because . . . nothing. There was no sense to make of her thoughts. In four years she hadn't come to grips with what had happened; why would she be able to now?

Amanda scanned the boxes full of things that represented the boy he was and the man he could have become and felt the anger rising for the second time today. He could have been a good man! He *should* have been a good man! All of *this*—she thought of the pain suffered by his victims, their families, the advocacy groups on every side of the debate, the judges, the courts, the people who had to read about what he did, Melissa, Paul, and their children, who would one day know what their uncle had done—all of this could have been prevented. *Robbie* could have made different choices and spared all of them. He could have spared her. But he hadn't. *Why?* It was the single most common word associated with every thought Amanda had had about her son for four years. *Why?*

The anger left her shaky, like caffeine after months of abstaining. She felt buzzed, and yet she relished the strange alertness of this unfamiliar emotion. When she'd felt anger in the past, she'd immediately felt equal guilt. Maybe even fear that if she allowed herself to get too angry, she might push herself away from Robbie and later regret it. But there was nothing to push away from now. He was gone. And she was pissed.

She went back to the boxes with renewed energy, throwing

away things she'd once expected she would cherish. The certificate he'd received for getting all As the second semester of his junior year of high school. The bridge he'd built out of toothpicks that took second place in the physics competition for holding the most weight before it broke. Maybe every item in these boxes had been garbage all along. Maybe he *had* been a monster from the start and she was as delusional as he had been. She pulled out one half of the plaster cast he'd had on his arm in sixth grade, and felt the anger pause. Robbie had been sledding with a friend and hit a tree. He'd gotten a concussion, a broken arm, and two broken ribs. The doctor had looked at the x-rays and shown Amanda where, but for a little more pressure, one of those broken ribs could have punctured his lung. At the time, she'd taken such comfort that he'd been spared; but for a bit more speed or her not being there to take him to the ER immediately, she could have lost her son that day. She stared at the dirty green cast scribbled with names and get well messages. What if he *had* died that day? She would have felt the heartbreaking loss every day from then to now, but she would have been spared the depths of pain these last few years had been steeped in. She choked on the realization of how much better the world at large would have been if he'd crushed his skull that day, or if that rib had gone through his lung and directly into his heart. She'd have never known what pain really was if he'd died in her arms that day. She'd have never wished her son had never been born.

She threw the cast away, shocked at her own thoughts. In desperation, she went back to the box, needing some sign that there had been a purpose in the years her son had lived between sixth grade and now. Was that what she was looking for in these boxes? Validation that Robbie's life wasn't wasted? Was all this emotion and confrontation a desperate search so she could be glad the cord had been safely removed from his neck on the day he was born? Was she frantically looking for proof that his life had meaning, to her if to no one else?

She found his school picture from ninth grade and felt some of the desperation settle into mere wavy lines instead of pitching points like those of a heart monitor. Robbie's hair was over-grown in the picture, he had two zits on his chin, and he was wearing his favorite blue *Star Wars* shirt. He was giving a rather saucy grin to the camera, as though it were she standing behind it, telling him to smile. Confusion entered where anger and frenzy had been moments earlier. Was it really *this* boy who went to that mall? Her son whom she'd loved as well as she could? He always ordered the chocolate chip pancakes when they went to IHOP. When their neighbor's dog was hit by a car, he'd cried himself to sleep. He'd been so very *good* once.

She picked up another photo—the team picture of the cross-country runners his senior year. He stood there with his tanned arms thrown over a teammate on either side and a genuine "show your teeth" smile. The photo was taken in the fall, with golds and reds of the turning trees serving as a backdrop. Who wouldn't look at this picture and not think every kid there was going to make the world a better place? She put the pictures in her keeper box and went back to the sorting, her storm of anger diffused for a moment. It was okay for her to miss him, wasn't it? Even after everything he'd done, could she still be a moral person and love her son? Could she be glad he'd been born and survived that sledding accident? And if she *could* be glad, if the powers that be approved that possibility, *would* she be glad? Would she *just* love the Robbie he'd been? Yet another question rose up to make her wince: Could she love her son and also be relieved he was dead?

Relieved.

Unburdened.

Free.

The thought pushed every bit of air from her lungs.

Every anti–death penalty group had tried to court Amanda over the years, wanting her voice to join theirs. They wanted her to say that the state's killing of her son was an act of depravity, that every life was precious and deserving of protection. Even his. She never returned the calls or answered the letters. Four different people had shown up on her doorstep to recruit her. She'd turned them away, threatening one particularly intense man that she would call the police if he didn't leave, even though she wondered if the police would come to defend her. Each time she shut the door on those faces, she would rest her forehead against the painted wood and ask herself what she thought of the death penalty. Was it fair? Was it cruel? She'd never made up her mind. Even when she'd protested against Robbie's being able to turn down his appeals, she didn't know if she believed the death penalty was wrong. Was she horrified that her son had been killed by the state that collected her taxes? Undeniably. Did he deserve it? A simple yes or no was an insufficient answer. Robbie's death seemed a form of mercy. An end place for the misery he'd invited into the world. For him. For the families of his victims. For her? *Was* she glad that Robbie was dead? The thought made her blood run cold and she focused, again, on the boxes.

She threw out the expulsion letter that had followed his dropping out from USF. His mental decline had been relatively rapid—less than two years between his first diagnosis and the shooting. She shuddered and turned back to the dwindling pile of what remained. Soon enough she'd cleared the floor space. She moved on her knees to the third box.

"Mrs. Mallorie?"

Amanda started and turned to look at the doorway where the moving company's supervisor stood. It was shocking to be reminded that there was a whole group of men downstairs, and she felt an odd vulnerability about not having been aware of that every moment since she'd let them in. "Oh, hi," she said, getting to her feet and standing in front of the boxes as though to hide the memories contained within them. Maybe she shouldn't have written Robbie's name on the box she was filling.

"My paperwork says you're taking the fridge, but there's a yellow sticker on it." He lifted the clipboard in his hand.

"I'm not taking the fridge—sorry for the confusion. It's too big for my new place." The kitchen in the Cincinnati condo was half the size of the one here. Everything in the condo was space-saving and efficient. Perfect for half a mother trying to figure out how to live her life again.

"Okay," he said, smiling politely and nodding as he turned out of the room.

"Is everything else okay?" Amanda asked. "Are we on track with the space and time I estimated?" She'd have to pay extra if she took more than the fourteen square yards she'd committed to in the truck or the four hours she'd estimated it would take to load. She couldn't afford more than the fourteen square yards and four hours.

"You might have overestimated the space, which would set you up for a refund except that one of the guys had to leave so it might take us a little longer. It should all even out, though."

"He had to leave?" Amanda questioned, thinking of the hushed argument that had been taking place when she'd escaped upstairs. Her rib cage pulled in a bit.

The supervisor pretended to adjust the band of his watch. "Yeah, he, uh, I mean he just . . . I guess he knew Claire Whiterock's family."

Claire Whiterock.

Claire had been fourteen years old and hung out with her friends every Saturday at the Cotton Mall, flirting with boys and buying perfume and cheap jewelry with her babysitting money. Claire was part Sioux, beautiful, smart, and the only daughter of her parents, though she had three younger brothers. She'd been hit in the neck by one of the bullets Robbie fired from the upper concourse of the mall and bled to death while her friends scattered in an attempt to save their own lives. The newspaper said that her dark hair had drawn his fire, since he claimed to have come to the mall to kill Islamic extremists. Three victims were light-haired. Four months after the shooting, one of Claire's friends who had been at the mall and watched from under the escalator as her friend died had hanged herself in her parents' closet. The newspaper had called Valerie Simperton the tenth victim of Robert Mallorie, and on several occasions Amanda would wake up from a nightmare in which she discovered the girl's body, only it was Melissa—not the Simpertons' daughter. All of the victims had invaded her dreams at one point or another, but Valerie Simperton was the one who came back over and over again. Perhaps because Valerie symbolized the burden left to the living, a burden that broke her months after the other bodies were cold in the ground.

The pain hadn't stopped once Robbie was behind bars. He had dropped a rock into a pond and the ripples of terror continued. Continued. Continued. One of those ripples had taken the last of Valerie's hope. One more innocent life ended. More parents shattered. More outrage. More heartbreak. It never stopped.

Perhaps Amanda also understood Valerie's desire to escape more than she wanted to admit. Perhaps she envied it. How many nights had Amanda lain in bed, staring at the ceiling and wishing she could disappear? Become nothing, feel nothing, want and need nothing. She couldn't count the occasions of those thoughts, yet she couldn't give in to the temptation. Sometimes Amanda felt like the shoreline of that pond Robbie had dropped the rock into, trying to absorb those ripples, hoping that maybe if she gathered them in no one else would be hurt. Only, by the time the ripples reached the shore, they'd already passed through all that water.

Not all of Robbie's victims died. Jaxon Blanchard was a paraplegic. Garth Harrington had been shot in the head and was now stuck in the mind of a ten-year-old. Christine Rocham had to learn how to walk again.

"Are you okay, Mrs. Mallorie?"

Amanda brought herself back to the present, realizing she'd been still and silent for several seconds while the moving company's supervisor watched her. He had a look on his face that asked for absolution for making her uncomfortable.

"I'm so sorry," she said, hating the inadequacies of language that made it impossible for her to truly express the depth of regret she felt for the pain still rippling through the lives of good people. "And I appreciate you and your crew very much—thank you for staying."

She watched as his face relaxed. "We'll get the work done as quickly as possible." He began to turn and then paused before turning back. "Do you know if the media will be in Cincinnati when we unload?"

Amanda hadn't considered that possibility. Surely the scrutiny was limited to South Dakota and would not follow her like a disembodied stain spreading to a new community it could darken. Surely two weeks from now the hounds and vultures would have found another carcass to pick apart, a new story to exploit so that they could pay for soccer practice and take-out pizza. "I sure hope not."

The supervisor nodded and left, his boots thumping down the wooden stairs to the main level. Alone again, Amanda turned back to the single box that would account for the life of her son.

She didn't blame the employee who'd left. She hoped he had a wife or mother or best friend he could go home and talk to. She hoped that confidante would put their hand on his arm and tell him how sorry they were for the resurrected pain. Amanda had had friends like that once. Soft places. They were all gone now, either by their choice or hers, but she could still remember what it was like to have people you trusted with your feelings. She hoped the employee took advantage of the gift and could work through this unexpected encounter with Robert Mallorie's mother. That monster's mother.

Amanda understood their hatred of *Robert Mallorie*. She hated him too. Sometimes she even imagined that Robert Mallorie had murdered her Robbie—swallowed him whole and then put on his face and his clothes as a disguise. Yet when Robert took his medications he was Robbie again, albeit an absentminded version who struggled to focus and sleep and never smiled. Then the frustrations would build and he'd go off his meds and feel like himself again. Since his delusions were reality for him, he would address *that* reality and try to fix the things happening there. That it wasn't anyone else's reality made sense to him because of his special power to hear the communications that regular people couldn't. He'd once tried to explain it to Amanda during a visit at the prison when he was lucid and therefore accepting visitors—she hadn't seen him for five weeks prior to this visit and asked him why he wouldn't just stay on his meds. "It's like all those books I read where someone has this superpower and doesn't know it, then discovers that they aren't ordinary after all. They're special, blessed. That's how I feel when I don't take these meds, Mom, and even though right now I know that's not true, it's so . . . tempting to feel that way. I want so bad to feel good again. Does that make any sense?"

Of course it did, and she told him so, but she was disturbed by the light in his eyes when he'd talked about those powerful feelings. She had wondered how long he would stay on his medications this time before the temptation would have him sticking his pills in the mattress again.

When she'd come for her visit two weeks later, he'd been agitated. She'd asked if he was taking his meds and he told her it was none of her business before ranting against his attorneys and how they had royally screwed him over in his trial. When she came again two weeks after that, her visit was refused.

8

Tony

Three years, ten months, twenty-two days

The light turned yellow and Tony punched the gas instead of the brake. The light turned red before he reached the intersection, but he kept going, flipping the bird to the car that honked at him. He swerved between two other cars, got honked at again, and let out a string of expletives no one could hear but him.

"Just give me a reason!" he said to no one and pounded his fist on the steering wheel. Leone said he wouldn't write him up for walking off the job—what a saint! He wasn't going to pay him either, or at least that's what he said. Tomorrow Tony would be in the office throwing a fit. They couldn't expect him to move that woman!

He took a corner too fast and almost hit a kid on a bike. He laid on the horn as he passed by—the kid's eyes were as wide as saucers. Tony slowed down. He forced himself to take a breath, but his heart kept racing. What if he'd hit that kid? He came to a full stop at the next stop sign and looked both ways before easing through the intersection. He managed to keep himself in check the rest of the way home, but just barely.

"Cherie!" he called as he threw open the door to their apartment a few minutes later. He slammed the door shut and then stormed toward the bedroom. She sat up in bed, blinking quickly as she pushed her frizzy black hair off her face.

"Wh-what's the matter?"

"The lady we were moving today was Robert Mallorie's *mother!*" He threw up his hands and turned back to the kitchen. Just as he'd expected, she got out of bed and followed him. She was still blinking as she leaned against the fridge, dressed in a tank top and pajama pants. She crossed her arms and rubbed the gooseflesh rising there.

"Robert Mallorie?" she repeated, still sounding half asleep.

"The dude who shot up the mall and killed Claire. The reason Valerie hanged herself. They finally killed him this morning, and so I guess his mama's flying the coop. You should see her house." He huffed. She lived in this nice suburban house and he was still kicking around apartments. That wasn't right.

"Oh," Cherie said, straightening up and swallowing. Finally, she understood. "Oh, wow, his mom?"

Tony grabbed a beer from the fridge, then scowled when he saw Cherie look at the clock on the microwave. It wasn't quite ten in the morning, but come on. Robert Mallorie's *mom*? If that didn't justify a beer, nothing did. He started composing the raging Facebook post he'd write about it—he'd get tons of comments. As he pulled back the tab he turned back to Cherie, waiting for her reaction.

Cherie worked nights at a nursing home; she'd gotten home right before he'd left that morning. She looked tired, but what good was having a girlfriend if she wasn't there for you? She shifted to lean her other shoulder on the wall. "So, you're not working today."

Her tone was cautious, but not sympathetic. He narrowed his eyes. "No, I'm not working. I'm not gonna pack up that woman's shit so she can go on with her life like nothin' ever happened. That whole thing ruined me, Cherie. Ruined me!"

"I know, baby, but we need this job." She pushed off the wall and walked toward him. "Let's go in the living room and talk about it." She put a hand on his arm, but he shook it off. What she really wanted was for him to put down the beer and he wasn't about to fall for it.

"I don't need to go into the living room to talk about it." His voice was getting louder as the adrenaline rose. He wanted a brawl—anything to release the pressure in his chest.

"Tony, stop," she said when he paused to take another swig of beer. Her voice was still calm and soft, which pissed him off even more. "The neighbors are gonna hear."

"I don't care if they hear!" Tony yelled, spreading his arms out. "I don't care if the whole world knows what that bastard did. You know how many lives he screwed up that day?"

"I know, baby. But—"

"But nothin'!" The cops had been called twice before when their arguments had gotten too heated. But they hadn't arrested Tony either time—Cherie was the one who left scratches on his face. In fact, he hoped the neighbors *did* hear him. He hoped they pounded on the door so he could get right up in their faces and tell them all the reasons why they could go to hell. He had gone to school with Claire and Valerie. He'd had math with Claire and his friend, Kayden, had made out with her once in the science hall. And then, just like that, Mallorie took out Claire and Valerie was all messed up and then, bam, she hanged herself. Killed herself at fifteen years old! That kind of stuff screwed with a guy's head, and there wasn't anyone who could argue with him about that, though he'd love for them to try. He had a whole list of ways life had screwed him over, but Claire and Valerie were the great-big-horrible thing no one could pat him on the head about. And it was all on Mallorie. Everything was on him. Tony was another one of the victims, and he deserved consideration for that. He deserved some sympathy, especially when he stood in the same room as that animal's mother! She was right there, looking all nervous and uncomfortable. Ha! He wished he'd told her a thing or two when he'd stood in her spick-and-span living room.

Cherie's hand was on his arm again. "Tony, you have got to calm down," she said. "I know that was so hard for you, but let's talk, not scream about it. We can't keep doing this." If not for the frustration in her tone, he might have listened. But she had no right—*no right*—to tell him how to feel about this. She didn't know Claire. She hadn't even lived in Sioux Falls when the shooting happened. She didn't know. Couldn't know.

"You'd better back off, woman," Tony said, glaring at her and clenching his jaw. "You ain't got any idea what I've been through."

"It was four years ago," she said, all sympathy suddenly gone. Her dark skin looked even darker, which happened when she was mad. Who was she to be mad at *him*? "And if you ask me, you're just using it as one more excuse to be a jerk. You barely knew her and—"

He slapped her before he'd even thought about doing it, and she stumbled back against the wall, then slid down it. "Oh please," he said, hiding his surprise at what he'd done, but not necessarily feeling bad about it. He took another swig of his beer. "Don't be so dramatic."

She looked up at him, the whites of her eyes stark against the black of her skin. "You said you'd never do that again."

"And you said you'd never act like this again!" he said, raising his arms and walking toward her. She cowered against the wall and he relished the feeling of power. "I've told you not to talk to me that way, Cherie, and it ain't my fault if you refuse to listen. Those girls died because of Mallorie, and they expected me to move her hoity-toity dining room set! Tomorrow I'm going into the office and I'm gonna kick up such a storm they won't—"

There was a knock at the door. Cherie looked at it with hopeful eyes. Tony threw his can of beer at her and stomped to the door. "Bring it on!" Tony yelled as he reached the door and pulled it open. A cop threw him to the ground before Tony could even register who was at the door. Tony went down swingin'.

9

Amanda

Nine hours, six minutes

Amanda knelt back in front of the box she'd been working through and moved faster than she had before, relying on the categorical decisions rather than pondering individual items—there was no time to be indulgent. She emptied the box quickly, most of the contents going in the trash. The final box was from Home Depot rather than one of the cartons she'd purchased from Walmart last month. It was older, more ragged and aged, and she'd left it for last on purpose. Unlike the boxes she'd been filling with odds and ends for months as she took apart the household, she'd found this box in the corner of Robbie's closet—he had filled it himself years ago. Amanda was in her robotic mode of packing and decluttering at the time she found the box and wouldn't allow herself the distraction of going through it then. Plus, it had frightened her—a time capsule that might create some kind of emotional explosion upon opening.

Now she couldn't imagine why she'd waited until she was under deadline and had strangers in her house. She'd added more tension to the moment, not less, and the panicky feelings she'd been trying to keep at bay increased. Maybe she'd waited because she knew that right now she'd be backed into a corner with her old life making up one angle and her new life making up the other. She had to empty this box in order to choose the future over the past. Or something metaphorical like that.

Amanda pulled back the cardboard flaps and easily discarded the old Nintendo Game Boy and a dead MP3 player—both of them too outdated to be of value to anyone. There was a cigarette lighter from a local restaurant they used to go to—Robbie said their chicken fried steak was *almost* as good as hers—and a bouquet of heart-shaped suckers she'd given him for Valentine's Day. She threw it all away. There was a golf towel in the box—she had no idea why Robbie had that—and a pair of soccer socks that had been his good-luck charm even though his community rec team had lost every game they played. They still smelled. She wrinkled her nose and tossed them in the trash box. There was a small teddy bear and a rubber snake he'd won at the Fun Plex. Hadn't he won the snake during the summer following his sophomore year? If she could figure that out she might be able to pinpoint when he'd packed this box. She'd been in the final throes of her master's degree that summer and it was his first year on that landscaping crew. She'd been so glad he had something to do so she could focus on her schoolwork. Robbie had spent time with new friends she didn't know and made plans without telling her beforehand. Toward the middle of the summer she decided to get him a cell phone. Good parents kept track of their kids. He'd agreed and then had done better at checking in with her. Problem solved. Good mother crown in place. Teenage boy properly managed.

That was the same summer Dwight had stayed in Sioux Falls for the week following Melissa's graduation. He'd taken Robbie fishing that first day. Part of her had hoped Robbie wouldn't have a good time; he'd come home all smiles. "Dad's been sober for six months," Robbie had said. He pulled a green coin from his pocket. "He gave me one of his ninety-day sobriety tokens and told me how sorry he was for all the bad stuff. He wants to give the other one to Melissa when they go to dinner tomorrow night."

Amanda had smiled and commented how great it was, but she burned eggs later that night to give her the excuse to scrub the burnt-on crud from the pan. Dwight had never apologized to *her* for all the "bad stuff," but now he could come back four years later and act like father of the year? If Dwight's sobriety resulted in his being more present in Robbie and Melissa's lives, she wasn't sure she could handle that. She and the kids had reestablished their family dynamics without him and she was anxious about having to make space now that *he* decided he was ready. Would he ask the kids to come to Pennsylvania for the summer? Would they go?

She needn't have stressed. Dwight stayed in Sioux Falls for the week, took the kids clothes shopping, which Amanda grudgingly appreciated, then went back to his wife and his job and his AA meetings. By the time Robbie graduated from high school two years later, Dwight said he wasn't able to get away—he'd just started a new job, he'd said. Amanda was pretty sure he was off the wagon and her wicked heart had been a little bit happy about it. "It's fine," Robbie had said, waving it off. "No big deal."

The month after Robbie graduated, Amanda got an official letter from the courts confirming that she would no longer receive child support payments—they'd already been decreased when Melissa had finished high school. Now Dwight had no financial obligation to his children whatsoever. And with those monthly checks went most of the contact. Melissa had confided her hurt a week before her wedding, when Dwight had e-mailed to say he couldn't make it, but he'd send a check—his *generous* two hundred dollars was almost enough to cover the cost of the cake. "How can he just dump us over and over and over again? How can he turn away so completely?" Amanda hadn't known what to say, but felt terrible for all the times she'd been glad she didn't have to make room for him. She'd held her daughter and let her cry. If Dwight hadn't been three states away that night, Amanda might have driven to his house and lit it on fire. And yet, she'd felt as though she'd done a pretty good job on her own. Until Robbie shot up a mall and killed nine people six months later. Maybe if she and Dwight had made things work, Robbie wouldn't have done what he did. Maybe if she'd insisted Dwight remain better connected to his children, things would have been different.

The green sobriety chip Dwight had given Robbie all those years ago hadn't been among Robbie's keepsakes—nothing in these boxes reflected Dwight at all.

Amanda sorted through game pieces and household items like fingernail clippers and paperclips—what was the organizational method behind these contents? It looked as though Robbie had just pushed everything off his dresser into the box, then put it in the closet. Maybe on a day she'd insisted he clean his room before he could hang out with friends. She wished she'd thought to ask him about the box during that last visit on Monday. A twist of her stomach accompanied the realization that she would never be able to ask him anything again.

At the bottom of the cardboard box was a small wooden one—six inches wide and maybe ten inches long. Mr. Rider, the shop teacher, had his students make their own gender-neutral treasure box—everyone else called them jewelry boxes—as a midterm project. Amanda had forgotten that Robbie had taken wood shop, and now she brushed her hand across the smoothly sanded top. It wasn't varnished, just stained, and didn't reflect any great skill. Still, the skinny blond kid from that cross-country picture had made it with his own hands, which were now limp and cold. Or maybe those hands had already been sent to the crematorium; she hadn't focused on the specifics of what would happen to Robbie's body after the poison had done its job of stopping his heart and lungs. She knew he'd be stripped naked, put in a large cardboard box, which would be put on a metal tray, and shoved into an oven. She closed her eyes against the images conjured in her mind and forced herself to take a breath. She would pick up the urn with Robbie's ashes at a funeral home in Cincinnati. She didn't know what she'd do with them after that. Would he be happy on her mantel?

She set the jewelry box aside and pulled out a small spiral notebook from the Home Depot box. The words *Robbie Mallorie's Leaf Journal* were written in sloppy handwriting across the front. Amanda smiled, another memory coming clearly to her mind.

"I found number thirty-three!" Robbie had said one day after school while Amanda corrected papers at the kitchen table. All the seventh graders collected leaves and used Scotch tape—clear, not frosted—to "laminate" the leaves onto individual pages of a composition notebook. Each page was labeled with the common name, scientific name, family, and genus of the tree from which the leaf came. The students got one point for each completed page, with ten pages being the minimum but no limit. Mrs. Web had told Robbie's class that the record was thirty-two different leaves. Robbie was determined to get thirty-three and spent hours wandering the neighborhoods around their home in search of leaves from trees not already in his book.

"This man saw me looking at trees and asked me what I was doing," Robbie had gone on to explain on that way-back afternoon. "I showed him my book and he took me to his backyard." Amanda had gripped her pen tight at the thought of a strange man inviting Robbie into his yard. "And he had a pygmy Japanese maple tree—it's little, not like a regular maple." He turned some pages to show her a regular maple tree; a red maple—Acer rubrum. The maple leaf was almost too big for the page. Robbie then flipped back to the last page in his book, where a smaller, delicate-looking maple leaf the color of orange sherbet was taped in. "The leaves start out pink and then turn red and orange and yellow in the fall—like this. Isn't that cool? Mrs. Web is going to love it!"

Amanda traced the lines of that last maple leaf with her finger, then set the notebook in the box of keepers and turned her focus to the wooden jewelry box again. She undid the cheap metal clasp and lifted the lid. Solidified bubbles of glue around the upper edge of the fake velvet lining spoke of Robbie's attention to detail. Inside were several ticket stubs from different movies he'd attended. Amanda wondered whom he'd gone to those movies with. Whoever it was had certainly gone on with their life, perhaps trying not to think about the blond-haired kid they'd been in dark theaters with. That blond-haired kid who rampaged through a shopping mall while screaming about the spies infiltrating his country.

In addition to the movie tickets there was a Pikachu-shaped pencil eraser, two sphere-shaped charcoal-colored magnets and . . . a ring.

Amanda cocked her head to the side as she regarded the ring a few moments before picking it up. Once it was in her hand she could see that it was a high school class ring. Amanda had offered to pay half of a class ring if Robbie had wanted one. He'd said rings were for girls. The stone in the center of this ring was blue, not black or gold, which were Jefferson's colors. Or purple—amethyst—Robbie's birthstone.

Amanda looked at the ring more closely and turned it as she read the name of the school printed in a circle around the stone. "Skyline High School," she read out loud, then turned the ring in search of additional identifying information. On the left side was the year 1989 above an image of a football upon which was imposed the number 76. On the other side of the ring was the name *Steve* and below it an image of a bear. Amanda held the ring away from her and lifted it so that the blue stone caught the light from the window—not sunlight, seeing as how it was overcast today—just daylight muted by clouds. A class ring that belonged to someone named Steve who'd graduated from Skyline High in 1989 and was number 76 on the football team. Amanda scanned her thoughts and memories, trying to find anyone she knew who might fit that description. A distant cousin? A friend of Melissa's? But the graduation date was 1989, which put "Steve" closer to Amanda's age than either of her children— she'd graduated in '87. She looked at the jewelry box again and tried to create a possible timeline for when this ring would have come into Robbie's possession. Robbie had made the wooden box in high school. She went back to the movie tickets—Robbie's sophomore year. A class ring was such a personal item with value limited to the person who ordered it. Why would Robbie have someone else's high school ring?

10

Steve

Ten years, five months, two days

Steve Mathis tapped the last item on the list with his pen. "The last of the converters will be here Monday to finish up the recalls, but I can send someone over the river if we need more before then."

Chuck nodded, his eyes not leaving the computer screen as he listened to Steve and updated the day's schedule at the same time. "We've four today and seven tomorrow so we should be all right until Monday." He paused long enough to make eye contact with Steve. "Anything else?"

"That's it," Steve said. He rolled the papers into a tube he then tapped on his knee before he stood, bringing him even with Chuck, who had pulled his desk up so that it was a standing desk this afternoon. This whole meeting—a mid-week service management meeting—was ridiculous. Steve basically repeated what he said in the production meeting Monday morning, let Chuck vent about the other departments, and called it good.

"Okay, thanks for the report. I wish the cashiers could get their crap together half as good as you guys do." This was Chuck's dismissal.

Steve nodded, exited the office, and hoped Chuck would soon realize what a waste of time this meeting was. Anytime someone got a new level of responsibility, they cocked around for a while: calling extra meetings, changing protocol, and introducing new "initiatives." Chuck had been promoted to Service Center Supervisor three weeks ago. Among the other employees there had been the typical eye rolling and grumbling, all behind the newly promoted's back, of course. Eventually the demands of the promotion would balance out the determination to be the guy who fixed the predecessor's problems, bringing Chuck back to the oil and parts that were the backbone of their job at Brigham Brothers', Florence's one and only Ford dealership.

It had only been two years ago that Steve had been promoted to manager of the parts department. He, too, had been determined to make his mark. He redesigned the way orders were placed, had a coffeepot plugged into the back of the parts room, and changed the staff meeting to Wednesdays instead of Fridays. Within a month, he was back to the old way of ordering and staff meetings were on Friday again. The coffeepot was the remaining tribute of the grand power of his promotion. Since he was paid on salary now instead of hourly and averaged close to fifty hours a week, he needed that coffeepot.

As Steve made his way away from Chuck and his weird desk, the TV in the waiting area caught his attention. He stopped even though the face that filled the screen above the ticker tape was unfamiliar . . . wasn't it? Prison tattoos covered the man's forehead and a reddish blond beard covered the lower half of his face. His head was shaved.

". . . executed by lethal injection this morning at the South Dakota Penitentiary, the latest fast-tracked execution performed in the state and the third execution in the last five years. Mallorie was pronounced dead at 2:17 this morning."

Steve consciously relaxed his eyebrows, which had pulled together, then reminded himself that he was at work and didn't have license to stop and watch TV. None of the waiting customers had noticed him watching, but as he scanned left, Tara at the cashier desk caught his eye and smiled. He smiled back, sheepishly, and looked quickly away before he started walking again. He tried to keep his back straight and his stomach pulled in, even though the action made him feel ridiculous. She was at least ten years younger than he, with an ex-husband in Louisville and two kids at home. Steve had worked with Tara for five years, but her general coworker politeness had turned into . . . flirting a few months ago. Embarrassment at categorizing her interactions as such made his head heat up. As though he were a man to flirt with.

Steve reached the scuffed door marked EMPLOYEES ONLY and pushed through to his kingdom: the parts department. He'd started working here a year after he'd come back to Florence and now he was the manager—not a bad trajectory for a man who'd been lousy at adulthood for the first fifteen years of being one. He slid the report he'd reviewed with Chuck into the slot marked WEEKLY ORDERS in the metal file shelves stuck to the wall above his desk, or, rather, his section of countertop.

Steve grabbed his "I'm a Grandpa" coffee mug off the desk and headed toward the coffeepot in the back. Max had forgiven Steve for not being the father Max deserved; having the generational title of "Grandpa" bestowed upon him had touched Steve deeply. And then Emma . . . that child had put his heart back into his chest the day he held her in his arms. He'd been a lousy father, but he had committed that day that he would do right by his grandchildren. That the role was so wholly enjoyable made the assumed sacrificial nature of his promise a moot point.

Steve watched Emma and her two-year-old brother every Friday night so their parents could have a date night. He made a mental note to bring over one of the big floor puzzles when he went over tomorrow night. Emma loved those, and Eli stood a chance of getting a piece or two in as well. On Saturday night, he'd go back to Max and Kassie's four-bedroom, two-bath house to celebrate Emma's birthday. He'd have to pick up something special for that—was she old enough to ride a bike? He couldn't remember when his boys had learned how—he probably hadn't been there.

At the back of the parts department, Steve filled his grandpa mug from his tributary coffeepot, added a little creamer, and headed back to the front. He only drank two cups of coffee a day and this was his second. He would savor it.

Kyle, the other parts worker this afternoon, grunted a greeting when Steve slid onto his stool at the front, where the counter looked out over the waiting room. Steve grunted back and took a sip of his coffee while he checked what e-mails had come in during his meeting with Chuck.

"You hear about that guy they executed? Mallorie?"

Steve's hand stopped on the keys and he swiveled on his stool to face Kyle, his attention caught by the topic that had already stopped him a few minutes earlier. Like Steve, Kyle sported a beard. Unlike Steve's, Kyle's was full brown—the beard of a young man—while Steve's was peppered with gray. The gray concentrated at his chin as though gravity were pulling it downward.

Seeing as how Kyle was twenty years younger than Steve, gray hairs were not yet on his agenda of things to worry about.

"Mallorie?" Steve said, his eyes drifting toward the waiting room even though he couldn't see the TV from here. "I just caught the tail end of it on the TV."

"He's the guy that shot up that mall right before Christmas a few years ago. I guess he turned down his appeals or something, so he was executed now instead of twenty years down the road."

"Huh," Steve said, still not sure why the name caught his attention. "What about it?"

Kyle was a news hound and always bringing up current events for them to discuss. At first, Steve had thought it was Kyle trying to show off. In time Steve realized that Kyle just found the stuff fascinating—especially legal and political topics. The kid was wasted in automotive parts, but then Steve knew Kyle's story a little too well. Smart kid, into sports, knocked up his girlfriend and did the right thing. Just like Steve. Except that Kyle didn't see settling down as *settling*.

"Well," Kyle continued, "by death penalty standards his execution was a success, with just the one drug. That's what's holding up Ol' Kentuk right now—the fails in Oklahoma and Ohio. There's, like, thirty guys on death row waiting for the courts to decide what they're gonna do." He shook his head. "Damn waste of taxpayer money."

Steve turned back to his computer since Kyle hadn't turned from his. For Kyle, this was ordinary Thursday morning conversation. Why wasn't it so casual for Steve? "What's wasting the most money, keeping them alive or taking the appeals to court?" Steve asked.

Kyle turned on his stool with a surprised expression and Steve smirked over his shoulder. "I read the papers sometimes." Only on Sunday, really, but there'd been something about Kentucky's death penalty cases last summer; the attorney and court costs of the multiple appeals.

"I'm impressed, Mr. Mathis," Kyle said, pleased as he turned back to his work. "And, quite frankly, both aspects are cutting into my paycheck and yours. You know about the one-drug system, then?"

"Only that there's some controversy about it." Or there had been six months go, which was honestly the last time Steve had even thought about the death penalty. *Mallorie,* he said in his mind. Did the name sound familiar? Maybe it had been mentioned as part of that article he'd read.

"It used to be that there were three drugs used," Kyle said, still typing on his computer. "But the three of 'em are expensive and one is only manufactured in Switzerland now, which won't sell it for death penalties. So, a bunch of prisons went down to two or even one, but that caused these dudes to, like, convulse and stuff—pretty miserable way to die, I guess. Kentuk, like a lot of other states, halted executions while they tried to find a better option. Other states have kept going, though. You for the death penalty, Mathis?"

Ah, here was the heart of the conversation. The only thing Kyle liked better than the news was a good debate. He and Steve had had some doozies about education, foreign policy, and the legalization of marijuana. The tattooed face from the TV came back to Steve. The eyes had been hard. The chin lifted in defiance. Steve didn't know anyone in South Dakota anymore.

"I'm not really sure how I feel about capital punishment. What do you think?"

Kyle took a breath and then launched into a dissertation on the pros and cons of the death penalty. Steve opened an e-mail from Ford Corporate about an upcoming parts management training. It would be in Atlanta in June. Steve was supposed to reply whether he would be attending. Kyle transitioned to the cost of the legal work that went into the appeals process. As he talked, the pit remained in Steve's stomach. Steve had lived in Sioux Falls once upon a time, but not for very long, and he didn't like to think back to that time. Was that what was bothering him, the reminder of the last stop on the deadbeat track he'd taken for six years?

Eventually Kyle was called into the service bay to confirm a parts order, bringing the topic to a close. Steve glanced at a picture of his three boys on his desk—Max, Jacob, and Garrett—taken a few years ago. They had been 17, 14, and 11 when Steve had come back into their lives and he marveled—*marveled*—that they'd made room for him. He needed to keep his focus, which meant not dwelling on things that unsettled him.

Steve confirmed that he would go to the Atlanta training and pushed the bearded, tattooed man out of his mind.

11

Amanda

Nine hours, thirty-four minutes

Amanda put the ring on her finger. It was huge, but of course it would be; it was a man's ring. She regarded it a moment longer before hearing one of the movers calling to another, reminding her that she wasn't done sorting the box—she should never have put this off until now. With quickened movements, she put the ring back in the wooden box, closed it, but then paused and opened the box again. There was something about this ring— something about the mystery of it—that felt . . . invigorating? Was that the right word? Interesting? Engaging?

How did it reflect on her that amid everything happening today—everything that *had* happened—a stupid class ring was demanding so much of her attention? It didn't have a memory of Robbie attached to it, which made it worthless by the sorting and keeping rules she'd set for herself. She stared at it again. Was there a Skyline High School in South Dakota? Maybe something across the border in Iowa? It wouldn't be hard to find out.

This was silly. She moved to put the ring in the box again, but her hand stilled and after another moment she put it in the front pocket of her jeans instead. Maybe she'd remember something. She leaned forward and began emptying out the last cardboard box faster than she had the others—should she keep the pocketknife with his name engraved on it? It had been a gift from her father when Robbie turned thirteen. Not for the first time she was glad her dad hadn't been alive when Robbie did what he did. Cancer had taken him a year earlier. It was the hardest thing Amanda had ever been through, losing her dad. She had believed it was the worst pain she would ever feel in her life. Little did she know.

She kept the knife.

What about the Toby Keith CD? Robbie had gone through a country music phase when he was fourteen and sang "How Do You Like Me Now?!" in the shower for weeks. She put it in the discard box.

Birthday card from Dwight's mother—garbage.

Collectible spoon from Pittsburgh—it had been Melissa's souvenir, not Robbie's. He'd likely taken it from her as a joke—or to eat his oatmeal with—and forgotten to return it. Amanda would give it back to her daughter.

A program for the school play his senior year—discard. He hadn't gotten the part he wanted and ended up in the ensemble. He'd made the best of it, but it hadn't been a great experience.

A pair of shoelaces—discard.

Tweezers—keep. She'd put them in her purse.

A thirty-eight-cent stamp—keep. Money was money.

Colored pencils—discard.

A charge cord for the DS—discard.

Dice—discard.

Old sunblock—discard.

A picture of Robbie and some kid she didn't remember taken in the hallway at school—keep.

At the very bottom of the box was another card—a Mother's Day card with swirling pink and purple printed roses and gold lettering that said, *For my mom on Mother's Day.*

Amanda had no memory of this card. She opened it and read the commercially printed words: *I love you more than words can say. Have a Happy Mother's Day.* Her eyes were already teary when she shifted her gaze to the handwritten words below the message: *Thanks for all the stuff you do for me and for being awesome. Robbie.*

Amanda sniffled, wiped at her eyes, and read it again—more slowly—while imagining Robbie sitting at the desk in his room and thinking of what he wanted to say to her. And then he hadn't given it to her. Maybe he'd misplaced it, maybe it was too sappy, maybe her theory about him cleaning off his dresser was right and that cleaning day had happened the day before Mother's Day. Amanda had no regrets about whatever had kept him from giving it to her back then; no way would it have been more powerful than it was right now. She held the card against her chest, wanting the juvenile words to burn into her heart, become a part of her, and drive away some of the ugly thoughts she'd had about her son today.

Someone cleared his throat behind her and she blinked her eyes open and pulled the card away from her chest. She'd wrinkled it and tried to smooth it out.

"Mrs. Mallorie?"

She wiped at her eyes, sniffled, and then turned toward the supervisor, knowing she couldn't hide her emotion. "Yes?"

"This is the only room we have left to clear out," the foreman said, then nodded toward the boxes surrounding her. "Are those boxes going?"

"They'll come with me," Amanda said, pulling the keeper box toward her and sliding the card inside. She picked up the discard items she'd scattered over the floor and threw them hastily into the other boxes. "Some of them are garbage, so I'll take care of them."

"Want my guys to throw them out for you?"

"No, the press will go through the trash once I leave." Amanda said this as though that were a normal concern for the average middle-aged woman moving out of state. For her, however, it *was* a normal consideration. She'd been shredding papers and taking any garbage of a remotely personal nature to Dumpsters ever since a reporter had found a letter Robbie had sent to her during a time when he'd refused his medication in jail. She kept his kind letters, but that one had been depressing and sad and full of self-hatred and thinly veiled suicidal thoughts. She'd torn it in half and thrown it away so as to never read it again, only to see it show up as a story in the *Leader* six weeks later and immediately get picked up by the Associated Press. The agenda behind making the letter public had been to ask why hardworking taxpayers should pay to keep death row inmates alive when they preferred death to prison. Robbie's letter validated the arguments.

"But thank you," Amanda said when she remembered that she wasn't alone with her thoughts right now. She seemed to have forgotten what it was like to carry on a conversation with another person.

"Well, then, after you make a final sweep of the house and yard to be sure we didn't miss anything, we can get your signature and close up the truck."

Amanda said she'd be right down. He went back to rejoin his crew, leaving her alone with the box of memories and three boxes of trash—a fitting metaphor of what Robbie had left behind. She sealed the one she'd keep with tape and folded the other ones closed. The task was done; she'd finished it. Did she feel better?

The moving truck pulled out of the driveway at 12:52. Amanda watched it disappear from where she stood by the living room window, then counted the media vehicles that remained outside. The KSFY van—Sioux Fall's ABC affiliate—was parked across the street. Two unmarked cars—one red and one black— were parked at the curb as well, and she could see a driver and passenger sitting within each of them. None of the vehicles was directly in front of her house, but she sensed their positioning was so as not to interfere with photographs rather than to respect her property. There was no realty sign in the front yard even though the house had been listed for over a month—she'd worried that the execution would draw unqualified buyers wanting to look at Robert Mallorie's house, so they had only listed it online and under her maiden name—her true identity could only be revealed to pre-approved buyers ready to make an official offer. So far, four different people had walked through, but no offers had been made. Maybe the prospective buyers had learned whose house it was some other way and decided that despite the larger-than-average backyard and newer fridge, it wasn't what they were looking for.

Amanda put the boxes and her suitcase into her car, which was parked in the now-closed garage, and then walked into the kitchen. Standing in the middle of the linoleum floor, she was suddenly stifled with memories. This was the kitchen where she had baked and talked and worked and laughed and cleaned for so many years. She did a slow 360-degree turn, taking in the details of where her children had grown up, feeling it deep and whole and beautiful. They'd been happy. Truly happy.

Melissa had taken her prom pictures on that staircase. Robbie had learned to Rollerblade in the driveway—and the kitchen, even though he was grounded from video games every time she caught him. She and Dwight had decided to get divorced on the front porch one Sunday night following two weeks of avoiding each other after yet another fight about who knew what. Dwight was the one to say he thought he should move out. Amanda had let the idea roll around on her tongue, then said, "Maybe that's where we're at." They had tried to conceal their relief from each other at having finally admitted how unhappy they were together. She'd been almost eager to go at life alone, no longer burdened by having to get Dwight's approval for every little thing. She hadn't loved him anymore and couldn't remember the last time she'd said it and meant it. But the divorce had hurt her kids, and she hadn't fully considered that when she told him to leave. She pushed that memory away. It had been revisited too many times already. There were far better things to remember right now.

Birthday parties. Barbecues in the backyard. Sleepovers in the basement and Sunday morning waffles before church. Melissa's bridal shower had been in the living room. After the party, Amanda and Melissa had taken some food to Robbie, who was a few weeks into his second year at the university—the probationary one. It had only been five months since Robbie's hospitalization, but his meds were working and he was determined to make up for the time he'd lost during his "illness"—

that's what they all called it back then, as though it were a cold or flu that his body would eventually recover from.

Amanda and Melissa had walked up the stairs to the third level of the complex and knocked on the door of the apartment Robbie shared with some guys he'd never met before the new semester—he didn't want to live with anyone who knew about his crash the year before. He'd pulled open the door with a huge grin and put out his arms so that they could both get a hug at the same time. He was six foot three, almost a full foot taller than Melissa, and wrapped his arms around them both, holding them tight for the space of two counts. His new medications had caused him to gain weight. He looked different. He smiled different, but he was Robbie and she loved him. "We brought you some leftover treats from the shower," Amanda said when he released them. Melissa held out the plate she'd somehow kept from being crushed by the bear hug.

"You take such good care of me," he'd said as they walked past him into the apartment, which was empty except for him. The rest of his roommates were out on a Friday night, but Robbie had pared down his social life, solely focused on his schoolwork.

They stayed for an hour watching funny YouTube videos and talking about Melissa's upcoming wedding. Amanda had been filled with wonderful mushy feelings about her children, who had somehow become her friends. Melissa went ahead to the car, leaving Amanda and Robbie to say their goodbyes at the door.

"I'm so proud of you, Robbie," Amanda had said, about to burst with the love she felt toward her children, who were growing up but not leaving her behind. Even Robbie's diagnosis hadn't troubled her that day; he was doing so well and Amanda had so much hope for him. She had friends, hobbies, a job she liked. She was healthy and capable, and so were her children. A man at church had hinted that the two of them try out a new Indian restaurant and Amanda was seriously considering it. She'd never wanted to date after Dwight left, there was no time or space, but maybe she was ready now.

Robbie had ducked his head and shrugged off her compliment, but then given her a big hug. "Thanks, Mom," he whispered into her shoulder. "Thanks for coming."

Amanda began walking through the house, pulling the memories from the walls and floors. Lego constructs that had sat in the living room for weeks. The time Robbie slid down the stairs on an old piece of carpet and nearly put his head through the wall. Fake spiderwebs on the bannister at Halloween. Mistletoe in the doorway of the dining room for Christmas. The first time they had Thanksgiving, just the three of them—that had been weird.

Amanda smoothed her hand across the handrail as she went up the stairs, then looked into each room. She remembered the time Melissa flooded the upstairs bathroom because she was talking to a friend on the phone and forgot that she'd been filling the tub. The red punch Robbie had spilled on the hall carpet. The time Melissa had tried to sneak out her window and fell, spraining her ankle. Amanda left Robbie's room for last and then stood in the doorway, picturing how the room had looked when he was little and waited in bed at night for her to tuck him in. She would cross the room, sit on the edge of his bed, and then pull the covers to his chin. She'd brush his blond hair off his forehead. "You're my favorite boy," she'd say.

"And you're my favorite mom," he'd say back.

She'd lean in and kiss him on the forehead. He'd give her a quick hug; then she'd leave the room, closing the door behind her and having no idea how limited those moments would be. It had seemed as if her children would be little forever. And then they weren't. How many of those hugs and kisses had Amanda hurried through, thinking about the assignments she had to correct or the dishes she wanted to get washed or the episode of *ER* she'd already missed five minutes of? How often was her head already on tomorrow instead of that moment? What would she give to have those wasted moments of her children's youth be the extent of her regrets?

She pulled the door closed for a final time, rested her hand against it a moment, then turned and walked down the hall. At the top of the stairs, however, she turned and looked back at the door. The missing D in "DANGER ZONE" looked different all of a sudden. Her smile fell and the sweet nostalgia faded. She stared hard at the words and imagined what someone else might make of them. Would the new owners see an unconscious warning to the world? Would a picture of Robbie's door end up on a newsstand tabloid? Her mind then flashed to a handful of personal touches he'd left on this house. Things that weren't only in her memory. Things that would stay behind.

Amanda swallowed and felt a moment of panic before her mind kicked into solution-mode. She could fix this.

She found the box cutter on the shelf of the garage with the other tools she'd marked with yellow stickers. She snapped apart the case, removing the straight razor inside, and turned her phone back on. The dinging alerts of voice mails accompanied her up the stairs as her phone came to life. *Thank goodness you realized before it was too late,* she told herself, ignoring the alerts. *It's not your home anymore, but no one can take the memories.*

She smiled nostalgically at the "DANGER ZONE" door one last time and then took a picture of it with her phone before using a razor blade to scrape the letters off the wood, all but destroying the door she'd fought Robbie about so many years ago. She imagined the new owners shaking their head at the damage. "We'll have to completely replace this door," the imaginary wife would say, her arms crossed in irritation. "We should reduce the offer to reflect that." How much did new bedroom doors cost?

Amanda turned to the next task, ignoring the emotion that beckoned her. She went down to the kitchen and opened the pantry door. Just a few months after they'd moved in, Robbie had scratched his name into the paint of the middle shelf. He was old enough to know better, but Amanda had seen it as his way of claiming this house as their own; a confirmation that they were putting down roots. He'd still lost TV privileges for a weekend, but she secretly thought it was kind of sweet. Innocent. Amanda took a picture of the scratched-in name, then used the razor blade to gouge it into oblivion, scraping and scratching until no one could tell what had once been there. The damage could be covered with some shelf liner, though the imaginary wife would shake her head at this too. Amanda turned to the doorway of the guest bath on the main floor, where a series of lines and pen and pencil markings had showed Robbie and Melissa's heights each year on their birthdays. After taking more pictures, Amanda got some toilet paper from the bathroom and her travel-size hair spray from her suitcase in the car, scrubbing until all the dates and ages and names were undecipherable. *I'm erasing him*, she thought, but not to destroy these scraps of evidence would be inviting people into the memories. Amanda didn't want that.

There was only one task left once the door frame was clean. She hesitated due to the fact that she couldn't perform this last erasing privately and wished she had remembered last night. Even this morning, before the news crews had arrived.

Amanda did a final check on the windows and doors to make sure they were locked—they were. Finally, she said "goodbye" out loud to the house, letting the words settle into the carpets and walls. She would never come back here again. There had been happiness in this house, but there had also been excruciating sorrow. She had peered out these blinds a hundred times to determine if the press was outside waiting for her. She'd scrubbed spray-painted swastikas and profanity off the front porch three different times. She'd hidden here, cried here, and felt the depth of all her misery until she was numb here. She turned her back on the rooms, returned to the garage, and said a prayer, hoping someone was listening, though she wasn't quite sure about that anymore. There was a time when God had seemed very real to her; today he was more of a desperate hope. Would that change now that the numbness was leaving?

The door from the house to the garage closed behind her with a swish and a silence. She was leasing the condo in Cincinnati for the first year, at which time she could buy it if this house had sold. A year seemed so far away, but then it also felt like a blink. The year after that would be another blink. And then another and another and another. Would she make friends? Did she still know how? Was it possible for her to live a life different from the one she'd been living these last four years? She couldn't imagine.

She'd left the rakes since the HOA would maintain her green space in Cincinnati, along with a miter saw Dwight kept saying he'd come for one day, and a smattering of other tools she didn't need anymore but that the new owners might find useful. One of those tools was a sledgehammer—thank goodness. What if she hadn't left it? What if she'd never owned it? The possibility of not being able to do what she *had* to do made her heart race. She had to pause and calm herself down again. *You did remember. You do have a sledgehammer.* With re-steadied determination, she reached out and wrapped her fingers around the handle.

When she and Dwight had bought this house, there had been a narrow walkway of pitted cement that led from the back patio to the small gardening shed barely big enough for a lawn mower. Had the path been a little more ragged or a little bit wider, it would have been quaint, but instead it looked like a weekend project undertaken by a previous owner who had never done concrete before. One summer—the one after her master's degree—Amanda decided she hated that stupid walkway. Melissa had created quite an impressive vegetable garden in the back corner of the yard, and Amanda had come to enjoy flower gardening. She had a lovely multicolored border of pansies and phlox surrounding the house, with snapdragons set behind for height. She had decided that the walkway threw off the overall aesthetics and should be replaced by a stone path instead. Her neighbor had put in a stone path a month before and she'd watched it come together. It didn't look hard to do and since Dwight had left, she'd become rather handy. So, she bought a sledgehammer and decided to tear out the walkway in a single afternoon. Surely it wouldn't take much longer than that. Robbie took over the demolition when she was barely halfway through. Her whole body ached from the impact of slamming the ten-pound hammer into the cement over and over again. Why hadn't she noticed that despite the poor quality of the concrete, it hadn't a single crack? Which should have told her it was thick. Really thick.

Robbie took out the last of it in half the time she'd spent on the first half. She went into the kitchen, washed her hands, and then watched him through the window. He had looked like such a man that day. Perhaps for the first time, to her eyes at least. He'd been wearing a Mario Bros. T-shirt, but it bulged at the shoulders as he swung and swung and swung. She'd been proud to be the mother of such a strong and helpful boy.

She'd made them sandwiches and lemonade. They'd eaten their late lunch on the patio. It had been a nice day, not too hot even though Robbie was sweating. As they ate and chatted she'd missed the little boy he had been even though she was proud of the young man he was becoming. She'd reminded him to wash his face so the sweat wouldn't cause him to break out.

Now she tightened her grip on the handle of the sledgehammer. Robbie wasn't here to help her this time, but it wasn't a whole walkway this time, just a few inches. She pushed the button to raise the garage door, took a deep breath, and headed toward that little spot of cement, underneath where she kept her garbage can when she wasn't worried that people would go through it. The can had been in the garage for weeks.

She tried to ignore the clicks of car doors opening and the whispered frenzy of "That's her," and "Quick, is the camera ready?"

She didn't look up as she walked to the corner of the driveway and leaned the hammer against the wall long enough to take a picture of the handprints frozen in the concrete. She'd never seen the handprints show up in a tabloid or newspaper, not that she followed the articles closely. The voices of the reporters were getting louder as they gathered at the edge of the street, but she refused to let her brain make sense of what was being said. She slid her phone back into her pocket and hoisted the sledgehammer over her shoulder. She let it rest a moment while she took a breath, then lifted the hammer higher and let its own weight carry the iron head into the center of Robbie's handprint. The concrete barely flaked, and for a moment she worried that she wouldn't be able to destroy this last bit of evidence the way she'd planned. But she reminded herself that she had taken out almost half of that walkway ten years ago. She lifted the hammer higher over her shoulder and swung it harder. This time it cracked right through Melissa's palm. The day these prints were made came back to her mind as she lifted the hammer for another blow.

The kids had been little, Dwight was still here, and they had used that year's tax return to replace the driveway, which had been falling apart since long before they moved in. It had been one of those projects they promised they would do the very next summer, then put off, and put off, and put off. But, finally, they got it done. After everything was poured and smoothed, Amanda had snuck the kids through the garage and had them press their right hands into the concrete. The cement was more set than she'd expected, and the prints weren't very deep, but it was enough. The kids had then written their names below their hands using a Popsicle stick. Then she'd added *2002*. When Dwight got home they showed him. He'd loved it, and told Amanda what a good idea it was. It *had* been a good idea. And a good day.

She lifted the hammer again and shattered the rest of Melissa's print. *Don't cry*, she told herself as the impact reverberated through her in ways that were only superficially related to the physical action. *Don't you dare cry over this in front of these vipers.* But she hadn't cried in months; why would she shed tears now? It was only handprints. Evidence of days gone by. She had the memory and the photo.

"What are you doing, Mrs. Mallorie?" a man called loudly to her from the street. She ignored him, lifted the hammer again, and swung. And swung. And swung. After what seemed like a dozen swings, the handprints were obliterated. Her chest ached. Her arms throbbed. There were half a dozen people standing at the end of her driveway now, calling out questions, pointing their cameras at her, and talking to one another about this "exciting development." She dragged the sledgehammer back into the garage without looking at them, leaned the black handle with the yellow sticker against the wall, and ignored the questions being yelled at her. The woman she'd imagined as one of the new owners of the house would shake her head at the broken concrete. "And we'll have to replace the entire slab because of this one corner. Reduce the offer by however much that's going to cost us."

Amanda slid into the driver's seat, pulled the door shut, and looked into her rearview mirror before backing out of the garage. Once the hood was clear of the door, she took the garage door opener from where it was clipped to her visor and got out of her car. The voices started again. She did not acknowledge them as she went into the garage and placed the opener on the steps so that the realtor would see it when he came tomorrow. He had the other opener already; she'd told him she'd leave this one here. She didn't look around. There was no need. It was over now.

She pressed the button to close the garage door, then walked quickly to the narrowing space between the bottom of the garage door and the driveway, and bent at the waist to fit beneath it. There was supposed to be a safety feature on the door, an invisible laser line that, when triggered, would raise the door to protect children and pets from getting trapped. Amanda had disabled the feature a couple of years ago—she'd worried that one night she'd come home, close the garage, and someone would throw something to trigger the mechanism at the last moment. She wouldn't notice, already in the house by then, and they would then have access to her life. She'd told herself it was a silly fear, that no one cared about her enough to put such effort into such a thing that was also illegal, but then someone spray-painted "Burn in Hell" on her driveway and she disabled the safety feature. She also installed motion lights at each corner of her house. There was a how-to video for everything on YouTube.

Amanda was back in the driver's seat before the rubber gasket of the garage door reached the concrete. She pulled the door shut again and put on her seat belt. The voices of the reporters were like birds on the telephone lines to her now. Slowly enough that the reporters could get out of the way, she backed out of the driveway. She didn't make eye contact with anyone—not the journalists vying for anything she might choose to say or the neighbors she'd once been friendly with who had come out to watch her go. The sense of community she'd once felt here had dwindled to almost no contact with anyone. The church tried to reach out to her, but she no longer invited anyone inside the house, and doorstep conversations didn't last long. Now and then a neighbor would come by to see how she was doing.

"I'm fine," she would say, then look at her watch as though she were late for something. "Thanks."

They would smile sadly, compassionately, judgmentally, and then go on with their lives. Many of them were sincere, she knew this, but she had lost perspective on whom she could trust and who was using her for gossip they could share. The platitudes of the first year had come to sound like the screeching of tires. "You poor dear." "I just can't believe it." "We all do the best we can." And then there were the betrayals. The secretary of the high school had given Robbie's transcripts and yearbook photos to a tabloid. A neighbor had sold pictures of twelve-year-old Robbie with their dog, Coon, who the neighbor claimed died under suspicious circumstances, insinuating that Robbie had had something to do with it. The truth was that Coon had been hit by a car and Robbie had been devastated. He'd always wanted a dog and Amanda had refused; she didn't like animals in the house. Amanda had burned with the desire to tell the truth about Coon when she learned of the article, but she already knew by then that the media didn't want the truth; they wanted a story.

Friends made comments to the press that were then taken out of context; schoolmates exaggerated experiences until it looked as though Robbie had been unstable all his life. The mother of one of Amanda's students—a woman Amanda had had continuing conflicts with the year before the shooting—claimed that Amanda should be psychologically evaluated, too, and have her teaching certificate revoked. Accusations were lobbed at Amanda for not recognizing Robbie's symptoms early enough for better intervention, for not getting him the help he needed once she knew, and for sending a ticking time bomb into the world. After enough of these accusations and betrayals, Amanda stopped letting anyone into her life. She resigned her teaching position over the phone after a month-long leave of absence that convinced her she couldn't go back. The principal's quick response regarding a plan B for her proved that he had hoped for this outcome. He had a friend who worked with an online high school based out of Utah. She could work from home and under her maiden name—having her master's degree would make her an asset to the company.

It had been four years since Amanda had started hiding behind her computer, and she didn't think anyone she worked with knew who she really was. She was just Ms. Stewartson, a good teacher who worked one-on-one with her students when they needed it and graded fairly. She had phone conferences with her supervisor three times a year. She didn't go to the in-person training held in Salt Lake City each August even though the company would cover her expenses. She'd never met face-to-face a single person employed by the company for which she worked. She used the picture of a puppy as her profile picture, as though she were bragging of her pet rather than distracting viewers from the fact that she didn't want to show her face. Isolation was her comfort zone. She was a rock. She was an island.

Once on the street, Amanda shifted the car into drive and headed down Mayfair Avenue, imagining that the press would now descend on her house like ants on a hill.

12

Jaxon

Four years, one month, five days

Jaxon pulled back slightly on the left wheel of his chair in order to turn sharply enough to make the doorway, rolled forward a few feet into the exam room, and then did a quick three-point turn until he faced the nurse standing two feet taller than he in the doorway. "Dr. Kubadia will be right with you."

"Thanks," Jaxon said.

She nodded and closed the door behind her. Jaxon backed up his chair so there would be more room for the doctor and unstrapped the fingerless glove from his right hand, then his left—the gloves made it easier to grip the hand rims of his wheelchair and kept his hands clean. He put both gloves in the narrow gap between his hip and the side of the chair, then flexed his fingers to get the blood flowing again. He couldn't wait for the day when he wouldn't need the gloves anymore.

Once circulation was restored, he took off the belt that kept his hips in the chair and pushed himself up using the arms of his chair and then back down—six sets of ten reps until his shoulders burned. It was one of a dozen exercises he did every day to keep his upper body strength. His legs, thin beneath the fabric of his jeans, barely moved with the effort—his feet were strapped in so that they wouldn't go askew. They didn't even seem like his legs anymore, but someone else's that had been sewn onto his body.

There was a tap at the door and a moment later Dr. Kubadia

came in. He smiled beneath his thick black mustache. Dr. Kubadia was a leading expert on spinal restoration.

Dr. Kubadia shook Jaxon's hand, then turned to the computer monitor, where he typed in some things. A few seconds later, the blank TV monitor mounted on the wall above the desk—four feet across—lit up with images Jaxon recognized as his x-rays and MRI scans. He looked back at the doctor expectantly.

"I am sorry I do not have better news for you, Mr. Blanchard," Dr. Kubadia said in his lilting English.

Jaxon closed his eyes and let his chin drop onto his chest. Dr. Kubadia continued to explain his extensive review of Jaxon's file, sent by the doctor Jaxon had seen in Dallas. He reiterated the severity of Jaxon's injury and said, as the other doctors had before him, that there was nothing further to be done. Jaxon tried to let the words sink in, but his body and mind and heart resisted.

The doctor stopped speaking and finally Jaxon looked up, hating the sympathetic smile on the man's face. "I would like to point out, however, what amazing strides you have made these last years. You have managed to improve far more than your initial doctors felt you could. Many paraplegics could find a great deal of inspiration in your story."

Jaxon shook his head. "I don't give a damn about inspiring anyone. I want to walk."

"That is impossible."

The doctor's answer was shocking. No one—not one of the six doctors Jaxon had consulted over the year and a half since his first doctor had said he was out of ideas—had ever said that word. "Nothing is impossible," Jaxon objected.

"Sadly, that is not true." Dr. Kubadia sat back in his chair, holding Jaxon's eyes. "I believe in optimism, but I do not believe in false hope, Mr. Blanchard. The facts are that you suffered an incomplete anterior severing of your spinal cord. The fusion of your L2 and L3 vertebrae was necessary to contain the injury and allow the physical therapy that has allowed you the usage you have now, but it limits our interventions. Additional surgeries will not increase your mobility."

"But the scar tissue could be interfering with—"

"You've had two surgeries to remove scar tissue; another one would do no good. You have maximized your potential. You have some feeling in your right leg, correct?"

"Some," Jaxon said. It was not a victory.

"That is an astounding thing for someone with your injury."

"It doesn't do me any good. It doesn't help me walk."

"But you can feel if you are developing any skin irritation, which means you can address that before it becomes a leg ulcer."

Jaxon clenched his teeth. He could feel pain in his right leg— what a gift! "I've read up on your stem cell research."

"Yes." The doctor nodded as he spoke. "We've had great success with compression- and herniation-based spinal injuries, but the bullet partially *severed* your spinal cord, Mr. Blanchard. Stem cell therapy is not a treatment for your type of injury."

Jaxon dropped his head again and took a deep breath. His mom had tried to talk him out of coming to Houston for this appointment. She'd said they needed to work on accepting what had happened. He'd come anyway—navigated the city himself to be in this man's office. For nothing.

"I very much wish I had better news for you, Mr. Blanchard. I understand how difficult this is."

"No, you don't," Jaxon snapped, then pressed his lips together. "I'm sorry, that was rude, but you *don't* understand, and I am *so* tired of people saying that they do."

The doctor wasn't fazed by Jaxon's rudeness. "You are right, I cannot *fully* understand, but I have a great deal of experience with people in your situation, people who do not deserve to suffer this way and try everything they can to overcome, only to hit a wall."

I'm not at a wall, Jaxon said to himself. *I'll find another doctor.* He raised both hands to his face and scrubbed at his cheeks. He wanted to scream and throw something and . . . run.

Dr. Kubadia continued. "I have seen patients in similar situations go on to live remarkable lives, but I have also seen them give up what life they have left."

"I'm not suicidal," Jaxon said, calming down and putting his hands in his lap. "You don't need to worry about that." Every doctor asked him if he thought about suicide.

"Because you have had hope," the doctor said. "I have just told you that there is none."

Jaxon held his eyes. "My dad was shot, too, in that mall," he said, grateful that he only remembered flashes of what had happened the day they'd gone shopping for his mom's Christmas present. They'd already bought a sweater and were heading to another store for a gift certificate. They were talking about grabbing lunch at the Chinese place in the food court when people started screaming while weird popping sounds filled the air. Jaxon remembered a girl falling on the ground in front of them, blood gushing from her neck while she kicked and screamed with wide eyes, her long dark hair tangling around her face and shoulders as it mixed with the blood like a big paintbrush. He turned back to his dad, but his dad was gone; then something hit Jaxon in the hip. The whole experience felt more like a movie he'd watched than something he'd actually lived through. "Dad didn't make it to the hospital alive. I would never put my mother through another loss."

"Living for someone else will only last so long."

Jaxon shook his head. Whatever. This guy didn't understand.

"You are familiar with the five stages of grieving?" Dr. Kubadia asked. "Depression, grief, bargaining, acceptance."

"That's only four," Jaxon said, trying to remember the fifth one. He'd been taught the theory many times.

"The fifth is denial, and it sometimes takes the form of continued hope even when all options have been exhausted. Denial is a coping mechanism and people can become stuck within that phase to the point that it becomes toxic and prevents them from taking realistic opportunities to improve their lives. Instead, the denial blocks them from the acceptance of their situation that can lead to peace and further development."

"I am not in denial," Jaxon said. "I know what happened to me."

"But you still think you can be cured. That is denial."

Jaxon let out a breath and grabbed his gloves. He was ready

to go. If he got on the road soon, he could get home before dark and save himself the cost of a night's motel room and the inevitable awkwardness of trying to check in. Desk clerks always panicked when they saw him enter. What he wouldn't give to be looked at like a normal person again. How dare this doctor take that wish away from him!

"I would like to invite you to attend an event tonight," Dr. Kubadia said. "It is for spinal cord injury patients like yourself."

"I'm not interested in a support group." He pictured a bunch of people in wheelchairs blubbering about their woes. How did that help anyone? He put on his left glove.

"It is not a support group," Dr. Kubadia said. "It is a fitness group to help people maximize their abilities. The gym was designed by a triple amputee, a former marine, and all the equipment is adaptive to different injury levels. From the looks of your upper body, you have made fitness a priority."

Jaxon paused. He'd set up a home gym, but he hadn't worked out today and had never been to an adaptive gym, though he'd seen a documentary about one in Los Angeles. "They meet tonight?"

Dr. Kubadia nodded. "The gym is available for general use every evening at seven o'clock, and sponsored by the medical department if your insurance won't cover it under physical therapy. If you want to see it first, I can have someone give you a tour—they do specialty sessions during the day."

"Only for spinal cord patients?"

"And amputees," the doctor said. "But everyone who attends has some type of functional disability. There's also a basketball and tennis court available for adaptive matches if you are interested."

Jaxon wasn't interested in wheelchair basketball—he'd tried that back in Dallas and thought it was ridiculous. He hadn't been that good a player before the shooting; he was garbage afterward. But the idea of a fully adapted gym was intriguing. If nothing else, maybe he'd get some ideas on things he could incorporate at home. "I guess it wouldn't hurt to take a look since

I'm here." If he decided to stay, he could manage getting one more night at a hotel. If he decided to leave after the tour, he would have lost half an hour of driving time but could still make it home.

"Very good," Dr. Kubadia said. He picked up the phone and punched in some numbers before talking to someone about meeting Jaxon at the gym in half an hour. He hung up and then handed a brochure to Jaxon. Jaxon frowned when he saw it wasn't for the gym; instead it read, "Stages of Grief."

"Hope for happiness is a good thing, Mr. Blanchard. Hope to overcome obstacles and do the very best you can is commendable and will be an asset to you. Refusing to accept the reality of your situation will prevent you from achieving either. I encourage you to read through this and evaluate yourself honestly."

13

Amanda

A block from the house, Amanda noticed one of the cars that had been parked in front of the house in her rearview mirror. She wove through the streets of her neighborhood for ten minutes and lost the car, but it was waiting for her when she reached Madison Street. She stayed calm, went through an Arby's drive-through—the other car waited in the parking lot—then got on the freeway going the opposite direction from what she had planned, drove two exits, and made a quick dive for the off-ramp before the black car could make the same move. Once she was back on I-90 East, she checked her rearview mirror compulsively for the next ten miles. The black car did not reappear and she settled with more ease against the back of her seat and began unwrapping her sandwich with one hand. Eventually she took the 380 toward Iowa City, determined to put as much time and distance between her and Sioux Falls as possible.

The need for fuel and a restroom finally took her off the freeway near Cedar Rapids hours later. Once out of the car the fatigue hit her with the same intensity that the Iowa winter wind froze her bones. She hunkered into her coat—a paltry defense against the wind—as she filled up her gas tank. The sun was setting. Could she drive a few more hours? Should she?

Her son had died today. She'd packed the last of her house today. *Exhaustion* did not seem a big enough word to describe how she felt. She closed up the gas tank and parked her car in front of the gas station. Robbie used to tease her about how she wouldn't leave her car at the gas pump when she went inside. "You paid for the gas—that earns you five minutes of parking there."

"What if someone needs to use the pump and I'm blocking it?" she would say as she pulled forward to the parking spaces in front of the store.

When she reached the glass doors of the gas station she looked back at the eight fuel pumps, only one of which was occupied— the driver nowhere to be seen. Maybe Robbie had a point. Still, it wasn't hard to drive twenty feet to a regular parking spot. She used the restroom, then stood staring at candy bars for a full three minutes until she decided to do the second half of the drive tomorrow. She'd done enough for today. Her body needed sleep.

She got back into her car and drove toward the Holiday Inn sign that stood bold against the amber-colored sky. A stack of the day's newspapers on the counter drew her attention as the clerk checked her in. MALLORIE PUT TO DEATH IN SD. Amanda looked away from the paper and wondered where Robbie's body was right now, or if it "was" at all. Amanda hadn't liked the idea of cremation when he told her that's what he'd decided. She worried his request was based on some kind of simulation of hellfire he felt he deserved. In the research necessary to make her argument, however, she learned that some private cemeteries refused burial to executed inmates. Headstones were often defaced and destroyed. In one instance, someone attempted to dig up the body of a serial killer from the cemetery of his small town in Georgia. Amanda had withdrawn her objections to cremation.

Several years ago—long before the shooting—one of Amanda's fellow teachers at the high school had taken up genealogy as a hobby and talked about it nonstop for weeks during lunch in the faculty room. She had remarked how irresponsible it was when people weren't properly buried in a place that would keep records. "You have no idea how hard it is to trace family lines

when there is no listed burial marker. It affects generations."
Amanda had nodded in agreement, finding it endearing that this
woman was so passionate for something Amanda had never
thought much about.

At that point in her simple little life, Amanda had fully expected both of her children to be buried decades after her own
passing. Next to their husband or wife, where their own children could visit and leave flowers on Memorial Day each year.
Their generation would follow hers, and their children's would
follow them. Some genealogist down the line would be so grateful for the forethought as they filled out their pedigree chart in a
single afternoon. There was something in the Bible about that—
the hearts of the children turning to their fathers. Robbie would
have no hearts to turn toward him, though. Not in life and not
in death. No headstone, but anyone who wanted to would find
his dead end easily enough. Maybe even be grateful that a monster like him hadn't propagated his broken genetic codes.

"Mallorie?"

Amanda looked up at the clerk staring at her a bit too in-
tently as she held Amanda's credit card and glanced quickly at
the stack of newspapers between them. Amanda usually paid in
cash when she went to brick-and-mortar establishments or went
through the self-check lines. Mostly she ordered online. She'd
tried to get a credit card in her maiden name after a cashier refused to ring her up at a grocery store that didn't have a credit
card machine Amanda could swipe herself. The cashier's eyes
had bored through Amanda with such hatred that day. Amanda
had looked around as though someone might rescue her. A few
eyes darted away from the silent spectacle and then finally
Amanda leaned over, picked up her card from where the woman
had dropped it, and hurried from the store without her tampons
and Rice-a-Roni. The application to get a card in the name of
Amanda Stewartson had been denied, and she'd felt too self-
conscious to try again. She'd instead focused on avoiding situations where she had to hand over her credit card—like at a
hotel.

"Are you—?"

"I'm very tired," Amanda cut in. She put her hand out. "Can I please have my room key?"

The woman's face pinched and Amanda kept her expression impassive even though she was withering internally. *I will never get away from this*, she thought sadly, then felt like a jerk. The families of Robbie's victims couldn't get away. Why should she? After a second or two of standoff, the clerk seemed to remember that she worked in the hospitality industry. She gave Amanda back her credit card and room key and with a flat voice told Amanda there would be breakfast in the lobby from six until ten o'clock the next morning.

Amanda thanked her, dropped off her suitcase in her room, then walked to a burger place across the parking lot. She paid in cash and ate her cheeseburger alone in her hotel room while she watched the first X-Men movie. Neither of her kids had gotten into X-Men and maybe that's why she watched it. She'd indulged in so many succulent memories today, and enjoyed every bite of the past, but, like running a mile after a long, cold winter spent indoors, they were wearing her out. All those moments she'd remembered when she could never have imagined what was coming. So many instances when she'd naïvely believed she had control of her future. That she was a good mother. That her children were safe. That the world was safe from her children. Robbie was dead. She'd wondered again if it would have been better if he'd never been born. The thought still left her hollow inside, mostly because she didn't know the answer.

While changing into her pajamas, she found the class ring she'd put in her pocket earlier.

She lay down on the bed and held the ring above her while one group of mutants battled another group on the TV—she'd lost track of the storyline. She looked at the ring from every angle, as though she might have missed something. She knew some high school rings had the person's signature engraved inside, but this one didn't. Just the name STEVE printed into the thick metal on the outside band. All the same questions she'd had earlier came back to mind. Who was Steve? Why did Robbie have his ring? Why did she care so much?

After a few minutes, she got off the bed and set her laptop on the small table by the heating and air-conditioning unit. Part of the veneer was peeling up on one side. She imagined taking hold of the raised corner and pulling the layer off like duct tape.

Amanda connected to the free Internet on her third try—grateful she didn't have to call the front desk for help—and then typed "Skyline High School" into the search bar. There were several Skyline High Schools across the country: Virginia, Utah, California, Tennessee, South Carolina, North Carolina. She went to the website for each school in turn until she found the school that had a bear as the mascot and the color blue as one of its school colors. "Skyline High School in Decaturville, Tennessee," she read out loud. She felt a tiny thrill of accomplishment for having discovered a clue. But none of her questions were answered. Robbie knew someone from Tennessee? Not just anyone, but Steve, number 76 on the football team who graduated in 1989?

How?

When?

Why had this Steve person given the ring to Robbie? Or had he not given it? Maybe Robbie had simply found the ring. Maybe he'd stolen it. She shook her head somewhat ruefully. Her son might be a murderer, but he was not a thief. How pathetic that the sentiment should give her comfort.

She read everything she could on the website about Skyline High School—recently renovated. Took second in state last year in both football and basketball. They had an excellent theater department, but of course that notice was at the bottom of the page, below all the sports. They were doing *Bye Bye Birdie* this spring. Amanda had helped with the school play every year at Jefferson.

So, how would she find number 76 from 1989? There were all kinds of privacy and protection policies for students—but did alumni fall into that same category? Could finding the information she needed be as simple as asking someone at Skyline High?

"Steve Jones?" she imagined the secretary saying. "Number

seventy-six, sure I know him. My sister married his cousin's neighbor." Was Decaturville a town like that? Was she willing to talk to someone about the ring? Voice-to-voice over the phone? What had been a dislike for phone calls before had become almost a phobia since; these days text messages and instant messaging with her online students made communication so much easier. She often saved up the phone calls she needed to make to insurance companies and utilities for weeks until she would then have to spend a whole morning making call after call. She'd need a Xanax by the end.

Knowing she would never call the school, Amanda clicked on the e-mail address for the vice principal listed on the site and typed "Found class ring" into the subject line before she paused with her fingers hovering over the keyboard.

Sorting that last box had been cathartic. She'd chosen which aspects of Robbie's life she would keep and which she wouldn't, but she'd *known* everything. Every item in there had some connection to him—the little plastic ninja toys the kids got from the dentist office if they had no cavities. The progress report from the year he was in Mr. Burt's class. A participation medal for cross-country. Everything fit into the portion of Robbie's life back when Amanda woke him up for school each morning and told him for the third time to go to bed each night. Everything was familiar in one way or another, except this ring. Sending an e-mail felt like . . . not enough. Maybe the vice principal would e-mail back and say, "Send it here. We'll get it to its owner." Then Amanda would never know why Robbie had had the ring. There might be enough information on this ring that she *could* find the owner. She had his name, Steve. Probably short for Stephen. He'd have probably been born in 1970 or 1971 since he'd graduated in 1989. He played football, which meant he'd be on a team list somewhere. Maybe his name had been published in the paper. Resolving this tiny piece of a very large puzzle could be as simple as finding his last name and looking up his address. She would ask, "How did my son get this ring?" He would answer. The puzzle piece would snap into place and there would be no more mystery about it. It would be setting right something that was bothering her—maybe the only thing bothering her that *could* be set right.

On the other hand, she could imagine going on to her new life in Cincinnati and rediscovering this ring every few months like that proverbial pea under the stack of mattresses. The tiny rock in the toe of her shoe. Something left undone.

She closed the e-mail and typed "Distance between Cedar Rapids Iowa and Decaturville Tennessee" into the search bar. Five hundred and fifty miles from the Iowa interchange to Decaturville—was she seriously considering driving that far out of the way? All that instead of a single phone call? She imagined introducing herself over the phone to the owner of the ring and saying, "Hi, this is Amanda Mallorie. . . ."

"Mallorie?" he'd reply, like the hotel clerk had asked. "As in Robert Mallorie?"

She'd drive a thousand miles to avoid a phone call like that. Besides, there was no guarantee a phone call would work. She could easily get flustered and say things wrong. The more she thought about it, the more convinced she was that it *wouldn't* work. She looked back at the web page. It wasn't like Skyline High School was on the West Coast; there was a direct route to Decaturville from this hotel and it was mostly freeway. It was *almost* on the way, give or take several hundred miles. She leaned in and began typing again, a bubble of excitement catching hold of her.

There was also a direct route from Decaturville to Cincinnati, almost straight north and a little east. If she left early in the morning, she could reach Skyline High School tomorrow afternoon. She couldn't plan much past that since she didn't know what would happen once she tracked down Steve—he could live in New York now for all she knew—but she could probably learn his full name and do some more investigating. Maybe he still lived there. Maybe his family did. This was *way* out of her comfort zone, but she wouldn't let herself look too close. One way or another, she could head to Ohio the next day—Saturday. It would put her just one day behind schedule, though that many miles on the road would be draining.

The bubble popped as the faces of Melissa and Lucy and Paul came to mind. They'd been waiting for her to join their lives for years. The thought stilled the air in the hotel room. Why could she not be the mother Melissa deserved? Didn't she want to get on with her life?

Amanda gathered all her skittering energy together and called Melissa—the one person she didn't dread talking to on the phone, though she still preferred e-mails and text messages. She needed a reality check, and her daughter was the only reality she had left.

"Hey, Mom," Melissa said, an eagerness in her voice that clenched Amanda's chest a little bit. Amanda was rarely the one who called.

"Hey, sweetie," Amanda said, reaching forward and closing her laptop so that the colored route from Cedar Rapids to Decaturville wouldn't distract her. "I decided to stay in Cedar Rapids tonight." She began pacing back and forth across the hotel room in hopes of keeping her anxiety in check.

"Oh good, I didn't like the idea of you driving in the dark." Melissa sounded like the mother. "I can meet you at the condo whenever you get into town tomorrow. I'm so excited for you to see the place. It's so cute!"

"I can't thank you enough for doing all the legwork to set it up for me." Amanda had been in such a fog these last months. Well, years, but especially these last months. When they'd announced Robbie's execution would be in January it was as if she'd stepped out of what life she had left and walked beside her own body as it went through the motions. When Melissa had heard, she'd called and asked her—again—to move to Cincinnati. Amanda had said, "Okay, but I don't know where to start."

"I'll take care of everything," Melissa had said, eagerness overflowing every word. "I'm just . . . Mom, I'm so excited to have you close. So excited!"

Excited? She'd been so *excited* for Amanda to come. And now Amanda was coming and Melissa was so *excited* to show her the condo. Amanda hadn't cared enough about it to even look through all the photos when Melissa sent her the link.

"What if I came on Saturday instead?" Amanda said, stopping to pick at the pulled-up bit of veneer on the corner of the table.

Silence. "Saturday? Why?" That disappointed tone had settled into Melissa's voice—tone was never an issue in text messages. That "Don't you see me?" voice that broke Amanda's heart. Yet not enough to change her mind.

Amanda told her about the ring.

"You want to track down some guy who graduated from some school in Tennessee thirty years ago?"

"Yeah," Amanda said, as though not understanding Melissa's confusion. "I do."

"It doesn't matter how Robbie got that ring, Mom."

Amanda understood the anger in Melissa's voice—Melissa *had* come second and Amanda *had* put Robbie first, but it was the only thing Amanda felt she could have done. She couldn't have gone to Cincinnati and been whole as a mother and grandmother while Robbie was alive and alone in South Dakota. She believed she had saved Melissa from even heavier heartbreak by not trying to pretend otherwise.

Amanda wanted to believe that now, *finally,* she could get close to her daughter again; that they could reestablish the relationship they'd once had, and Amanda could offer the wholeness Melissa wanted from her. But was that a fair expectation? Was it realistic to think that anything Amanda did now could make up for what she *hadn't* done these last years? How did she start? Where would they begin? Would Robbie remain between them even in death? The thought deepened her exhaustion. How was a mother supposed to act when her son was put on death row? Should she have been like Dwight—even Melissa to some extent—and removed herself? Should she have treated Robbie as already dead once the sentence was passed? Should she have lived as though that end had come already?

"I feel like I should go," Amanda finally said, keeping her tone even and unrevealing. "I don't have to log back into work until Tuesday morning, and my furniture won't arrive for a couple of weeks." She paused for a breath and a bit more vulnerability. "Over the last four years Robbie's life has been on exhibit for the world and—"

"On exhibit for the world?" Melissa cut in with biting frustration. "What does that mean?"

For the first time in a long time, the merest hint of confrontation did not shut Amanda down. "It means that nothing was sacred anymore, nothing was just *ours*. His childhood has been combed through in hopes of finding a cause for what he did. His friends have betrayed him. Everyone in the world thinks they know Robert Mallorie—the murderer, the druggie, the psycho, the child killer, the pig. The—"

"Mom, stop," Melissa said, instantly weary.

Amanda stopped. She took a breath. "Everyone thinks they know him, Mel, but they don't. They don't know my son. They don't know your brother. They don't know who Robbie was when his mind was calm and his heart was right."

"Maybe that wasn't ever really him," Melissa said in a sad voice. "Maybe he was always a monster and we just didn't know it."

"That's not true," Amanda said, reminded that her daughter was going through a process of her own. *A process you could help with*, said a voice from inside herself. "And you know it's not."

"I don't know what I know," Melissa said with a sigh. "I can hardly remember him before."

"Then you need to try harder," Amanda said, feeling like a mother. It relaxed her. She sensed that Melissa needed her. She took a breath and opened herself up a little wider. "All day today I have let myself remember *Robbie* and it's been beautiful, Mel. Remember those handprints you two made in the driveway? Or that time we went to the Black Hills?"

Melissa was quiet and Amanda allowed the silence. "That was a fun trip," Melissa said after a few moments had passed. Her voice had softened exactly as Amanda had hoped it would. "I *so* did not want to go—Mount Rushmore sounded like such a dumb trip—but we had a good time. Remember that machine that made eight pancakes at a time on that huge griddle at the campground?"

Amanda hadn't remembered that until now, but she laughed, and they talked about that trip for the first time in years. Melissa didn't remember the rock-bird story but thought maybe she would when she saw the rock. They could be close again, right? They could remember together and love Robbie together and find joy in each other and Melissa's beautiful children. "I don't know anything about this ring," Amanda continued once the conversation cycled back to topic. "Everything else about Robbie and his life has been filleted and served to the world. They have devoured him."

Melissa was quiet, and the warmth of their shared memories faded. "He killed nine people, Mom."

Ten, Amanda thought, thinking of Valerie. "I know." Amanda dropped her chin and felt the horror of it. Ten innocent people dead because of Robbie. Ten sets of parents forever grieving. Twelve other people maimed, injured, or forever disabled by his actions that day. Countless siblings, friends, teachers, aunts, uncles, and neighbors trapped in the tragic loss of someone who mattered to them; someone they loved and needed. Generations thwarted. Lives unlived. It was staggering to think of the ripples of pain Robert Mallorie was responsible for. *Staggering.* "And Robbie gave up ownership of his identity the day he went off his medication and let the crazy take over—I know that. But this ring . . . I don't know anything about it. You don't know anything about it. But someone—this Steve person—knows. I want to find this man and give him the ring in exchange for whatever memory of Robbie he can give me. I'm starving for good memories, Melissa. I want to do this before I start my new life in Cincinnati."

"You don't even know if this man still lives in Tennessee," Melissa said. "You might be wasting your time even if you do find out who he is—he might live in Florida or Rhode Island."

"You're right." Amanda nodded and started pacing again.

"And it might not be a good memory, Mom," Melissa said softly. "It might be something really bad."

"Yeah, I guess it might . . . but I don't think it is." Robbie as a teenager had been . . . whole. "I want to see if I can learn something about my son that no one else has stripped down and diagnosed and packaged up."

"Are you sure this isn't just an excuse to put off coming to Cincinnati?"

Amanda had worried about that, too, but hearing Melissa say it sounded different. "I *do* want to come," Amanda said. "I'm ready to get my life back and be a grandma . . . I've missed you and I want to get to know little Lucy and this new grandbaby who's on his way. I just need one more day."

Another quiet stretched across the call. "I've missed you, too, Mom," Melissa said in surrender. "And if you feel like you need to look for this guy, then go ahead and look. I won't be mad."

"Thank you," Amanda said, not realizing until this moment that she *had* been asking for permission. She didn't want to do anything that would widen the distance she and Melissa had to cross.

They were quiet again. "You know, Paul said something the other day. . . ."

"Yeah," Amanda replied, wondering at the hesitation in Melissa's voice.

"When his brother died—" She paused and Amanda thought about Paul's older brother, killed in a car accident years ago. "He said that for years people would see him or one of his parents and stop them to share some memory they had of Brian. Old classmates, teachers, his T-ball coach. So, the other night Paul and I were lying in bed and he said how sad it was that no one would do that for us. I mean, no one here even knows I'm Robbie's sister."

Amanda hunched slightly at the pain of that, but she said nothing.

"And other than that one article someone did on Paul when he first joined the faculty, no one's made the connection between Robbie and me—the blessing of having a married name, I guess."

Amanda managed a polite laugh, but she was somewhat offended by this. Even though she'd tried to get a credit card in a different name so that she, too, could hide a little bit better.

"But anyway," Melissa continued. "We don't get that, do we? No one is going to take me aside and share with me some sweet memory of Robbie. Even the good ones people have are tainted somehow."

"Yeah," Amanda said, nodding slowly. Over the years there were a few people who had tried to remind her of better days by doing the very thing Melissa was talking about—sharing some happy memory of Robbie. But they could never tell the story without their eyes showing the fear of who he'd become. Especially if the memory was perfectly ordinary. A project at school. A game they'd once played. She could see the ticker tape looping through their mind, demanding, "How could I have been so close to someone like that and not know?" And then there were plenty of people who said they *did* know. "Something was always off with that kid," one of his cross-country teammates had said to a reporter. "He had cold eyes." But he didn't have cold eyes. Not back then.

"I'm sad we won't get that," Melissa said. "Even Paul didn't know Robbie before he got sick."

"We can have it with each other," Amanda said. "We shared a lot of good years with him."

"Yeah," Melissa said. "And maybe you're right, maybe this guy has a good memory we can add to the others. We'll see you on Saturday."

14

Steve

Ten years, five months, two days

It was almost 7:00 when Steve finally got home. He changed out of the Brigham Brothers polo shirt and jeans, and put on an old NASCAR T-shirt and flannel pajama bottoms. He made fried eggs for dinner and turned on the Cavaliers game. It was the second quarter when his phone rang. He glanced at the screen before answering.

"Hey, Rachelle," he said as though they were old friends. Which, technically, they were. They'd been friends before they started dating their junior year. Then lost that friendship somewhere between her telling him a few weeks before high school graduation that she was pregnant, and him throwing up his hands and walking away ten years later. Would he ever talk to her without remembering how badly he'd treated her? He paused the game. "What's up?"

"Well, I hate to ask . . ." She trailed off, not finishing her sentence. It used to drive him nuts the way she'd do that, like she didn't want to *actually* ask for something so she'd set it up so that the person on the other end of her question had to do it for her. Now it was just a quirk.

"Ask," Steve said with a laugh.

"Well, I'm planning out next week and the guest toilet is running and the bottom hinge on my pantry door is stripped out or something. So, I was wondering . . ."

"Could I do it Thursday morning?" Steve turned the phone to speaker and toggled to his calendar. He had the last part of the week off so he could go see his mom for a long weekend—he hadn't taken any time off for Christmas so that his guys could have more flexibility but he'd promised Mom to clean out her basement as soon as he could get away. "I could try and make it over earlier in the week, but I've only got Sunday off before then and I'll be working long days because of the trip, but maybe I could—"

"Thursday is perfect," Rachelle interrupted. "I've been meaning to ask for a couple of weeks and keep forgetting—which is why I'm calling you instead of talking about it at Emma's party, but well . . ."

"I could come by around ten thirty—would that work?"

"That's perfect," Rachelle said, her tone relieved. "I should probably just hire someone for stuff like this, but with Mitch's medical bills piling up and my working extra hours as it is and . . ."

"It's not a big deal," Steve said when he realized she wasn't going to finish the thought again. "How's Mitch doing?"

Mitch and Rachelle had been dating when Steve moved back to Florence just over a decade ago. It was awkward at first even though Steve hadn't come back with the expectation of him and Rachelle getting back together. Rachelle married Mitch a year later. Nine months ago, Mitch was diagnosed with cancer: non-Hodgkin's lymphoma. His chances for recovery were good, but that didn't mean he didn't have a battle ahead of him.

"He gets his treatments on Fridays, and it lays him flat for the weekend," Rachelle said, then must have noticed the heaviness of her tone because it suddenly lightened. "He's usually feeling better by Tuesday, though, and is able to work the rest of the week. It's a blessing."

She'd started going to a new church after Steve had left; that was where she met Mitch. She talked a lot about blessings and gifts from God now, but he knew her faith wasn't dispelling her fear entirely. Mitch was supposed to be her reward for what Steve had done.

"I'll run to Home Depot before I come over and get a new flapper for the toilet. Do you need help with anything else while I'm there?"

"Just the toilet and the pantry door. Max said you're heading down to Decatur. This won't get in the way of your trip, will it?"

"Nope," Steve said. "I'll do it on my way south. Is the spare key still under that same paving stone?" Mitch was an accountant and good at a lot of things, but he wasn't very handy. At family events Mitch would ask Steve how to do something, like re-caulk the sink or fix the clothes dryer, and in the end Steve would offer to come do it and Mitch would say he could probably figure it out. Steve would assure him he didn't mind, and Mitch would relent. Steve would then replace the furnace filter or fix the sticking drawer and feel like he'd fixed something from those lost years too. Dealing with Rachelle directly hadn't started until Mitch got sick.

"Yes, but you're sure you don't mind?" Rachelle asked. "I don't want to mess up your trip—I know you don't get down there very often."

Both he and Rachelle were from Decaturville, and it was where they'd been living when he left her. If she hadn't gotten pregnant in high school, she probably would have gone on to law school and become an attorney. Instead she'd raised three boys, first on his paltry salary, and then on her own paltry salary. Rachelle and the boys had been forced to move in with her parents once he was gone, and *his* parents paid for her to take some night classes so that she could become a paralegal and make more than minimum wage. She was offered a job in Florence once she graduated and moved almost four hundred miles north of her support system. Her family still hated Steve for what he'd done, and he couldn't blame them. She still worked for that law firm. She was good. Really good. But she would never be an attorney. Fixing toilets and pantry doors was a lousy payback for what he owed her.

"I'm happy to do it, and it won't take me long."

"Thanks, Steve. We really appreciate it."

"Of course."

They finished the call and Steve pressed play on the TV. He washed the dinner dishes during the final quarter—the Cavs lost—confirmed with Max via text messages that he'd be babysitting for them tomorrow night, and then got ready for bed. The house was always quiet, but it felt emptier than usual tonight. He thought about his other boys while he turned off the lights and checked the locks. He called Jacob and Garrett every Sunday, since they both lived out of state now. Garrett had had a big project due this week in his domestic economics class. Jacob, his middle son, was living in Virginia and working for a cabinet company. He didn't usually answer Steve's calls, but they had texted a little last week and Steve took that as a good sign. While brushing his teeth, Steve let his thoughts drift to Tara from work. What would it be like to date her? Her kids were young, under ten he thought. He shook his head as though he'd asked a question. He wasn't interested in Tara. He'd gotten a second chance at life because Rachelle had worked with him on payments and because his boys had forgiven him for the turmoil he'd caused. He was happy with things the way they were. Besides, dating a coworker was always a bad idea. Right?

It wasn't until he turned off the bedroom light and was feeling his way to the bed that he thought about that Mallorie guy again. He'd meant to read up on him a little bit. Tomorrow before he went into work, maybe. He got into bed and rolled onto his side, facing the window and listening to the sound of cars going by on the street.

15

Amanda

One day, eleven hours, forty-two minutes

Amanda waited outside of Skyline High School Friday afternoon after having made good time on the drive. According to the bell schedule posted online, there would be a class break in about two seconds. When the mechanical bell sounded, she entered the front doors, blending with the mêlée of students as she walked past the reception area. This situation didn't *necessitate* a conversation with anyone, and therefore she'd planned her entrance to avoid one.

She reached the library a few minutes later—identified via the evacuation maps posted intermittently through the halls—and stepped out of the gurgling mass of students making their raucous way to class. What was it about teenagers that made transitions, which could be carried out in absolute silence, such rowdy affairs? Back when she'd taught in an actual school, she'd had a theory that, for boys especially, their vocal cords were connected to their arms and legs. They could not physically move without making noise about it.

A thin boy with blond hair came careening around the corner, looking over his shoulder to laugh at something. He almost ran into her, except that she stepped to the side, butting her shoulder against the wall.

"Sorry," he said, facing forward and catching her eye. He lifted a hand to push the shaggy hair off his face. For an instant, he was Robbie. She knew he wasn't, of course. He was too tall and this boy had brown eyes and thicker hair. Yet he *was* Robbie, in a sense. Robbie had been young, carefree, happy, and innocent within the walls of a high school not much different from this one. Once upon a time.

"It's fine." Amanda looked away; the eye contact was almost painful. The boy moved forward, his mind already past the middle-aged woman he'd nearly run over. His future was wide open—"As wide as the sky," Amanda used to tell her children when they would stress or strain over some aspect of their future. "There is nothing in your way, your potential is limitless." Then, bit by bit, choice by choice, that sky became a window. Not that every choice was bad, only that choices imposed focus, which in and of itself invoked natural limits. Choosing which college to attend limited the people and ideas they would be exposed to. When Melissa had become Paul's girlfriend, her future, to a point, had become set. She changed her major from Accounting to Elementary Education because a career that would allow her to stay on the same schedule as her no-longer-vague children had become important. Amanda had been proud to have her daughter follow in her footsteps and pursue teaching, proud of Melissa's ability to see her future and plan accordingly, and she was relieved to like the man Melissa was falling in love with. But the choices were limiting all the same. Not every choice led to a better path, the way Melissa's had, and therefore resulting in a lovely window with amazing views. These kids here at Skyline High School still had the sky above and around them. Endless chances to be and do and become. One day—not too distant for some of them—their sky would start becoming a window. And for a few, a very few she hoped, the window would disappear completely. Like Robbie's. Like hers? She'd chosen to love her son to the end, and that choice had made her window very small.

Is that where the analogy ends, she wondered? Or could she bring the sky back into her life? Could new choices usher in an expansion of the view, change the location, and bring the light back in?

The glass-walled library brought her back to the present and Amanda slowed her steps. As she pushed through the doors, she glanced cautiously toward the desk. A black woman—the librarian, probably—and a student, perhaps a library aide, were looking at something on the computer together. A dozen or so students sat or stood in various spots around the room, wrapped in the library hush. Amanda quick-stepped behind a row of shelves in hopes no one would notice her. If they didn't see her, they wouldn't stop her, ask her who she was and what she was doing there. Even a simple interrogation was frightening.

The yearbooks at Jefferson High in Sioux Falls had been kept on the back wall of the school library, out of the way, yet semi-archived and available. The kids liked to go back to old volumes sometimes, usually to make fun of the hair and clothes of yesteryear. This school's library couldn't be that different. Amanda headed toward the most likely place for the yearbooks to be stored—the corner farthest from the doors and tables.

It took a few minutes for her to find her way from where she expected the yearbooks to be on the back wall and where they actually were—on an aisle—but the fact that she didn't have to ask anyone and was still hidden from the reception desk calmed her nerves. The yearbooks went back as far as 1965, and Amanda counted the years in her mind as she moved forward in time. Eighty-five, eighty-six, eighty-seven—the year she'd graduated in Watertown, South Dakota—eighty-eight . . . She used one finger to tip the spine of the 1989 volume toward her, then pulled the book out with one hand. She considered taking the book to a table, where she could more conveniently look through it, but she didn't want the librarian to see her. She also considered sneaking the book out in her purse but imagined the headlines: ROBERT MALLORIE'S MOTHER ARRESTED FOR THEFT.

Amanda had always been someone who bottled emotion until the pressure forced everything out like a flash flood. As a little girl, she'd have her feelings hurt, but not react for days—usually not until she was alone so she didn't have to feel bad about causing anyone else distress. After Robbie's arrest, there had been so much to do that there was no time to give in to the building pressure. Lawyers to meet with. Criminal code to study. Neighbors, family, and friends to suffer with—she'd *had* neighbors, family, and friends back then. They would come over to console her, but they were the ones who seemed to draw the comfort. Not her. She shook inside her own head, counting the minutes until they would leave so she could finish the article on South Dakota's requirements for capital punishment—Robbie met three of them: murder in a public place, murder of a law enforcement officer, and murder of a child under the age of thirteen. Dustin Sommer had been eleven. She'd told herself she needed to be informed, but she had already begun to shrivel up inside; she had felt it day by day.

Then the trial started. Melissa came with her at first. Amanda's mother flew out for a week until she couldn't take it anymore. A few neighbors and friends tried to support her, but there was only so much they could do, especially as she continued to pull further inside herself. Eventually, only Amanda went to the courthouse. It was on one of those days, when she was attending alone with space on both sides of her because no one wanted to sit too close, that Robbie, sporting a fresh haircut, was led into the courtroom with manacles and a broken collarbone from a fight he'd gotten into over the weekend—he'd told her about it during his phone call the night before. He was being held at the jail during the trial, in the general population despite his dire charges. The prison doctor had put his arm in a sling to isolate the fracture, but the authorities still insisted he be manacled. She could tell the chains were hurting him when he met her eyes and gave the same sad, sheepish smile he gave her every day. She'd smiled back, sitting on her hands to keep from leaping the short wall that separated the viewers from the court. "Can't you see this is hurting him?" she wanted to scream at the guards. "Surely you don't think he's going to get violent with a broken collarbone?" But, then, surely no one had expected he would go on a shooting rampage in a mall two weeks before Christmas.

When Robbie had faced the judge, she caught sight of his first prison tattoo—he had not told her about this new development that must have been there before but gone unnoticed because his hair had been grown out. It was a spider on his neck. Anger had begun to rise in her chest—didn't he know that would make him look like a criminal? Didn't he care what she would think? It was a physical representation of how lost he was to her, how not-Robbie he had become, and it sent her mind into a panic.

She'd held herself together throughout the day, then the dam had broken loose on the ride home. *How could everything go so horribly wrong?* The sentence repeated over and over in her head. The emotion built and boiled. She could not do this. She was not capable. She'd thought of pulling off the road when she couldn't get control of herself, but she wanted to go home and lock herself inside and finish her breakdown under her covers. Alone and away from the world. At home she could cry until she fell asleep and wake up the next morning to go back to the courthouse again.

Amid her overwhelming grief and sorrow she'd run a stop sign. There were no other cars in the intersection, no one was in danger, but a cop had seen it and pulled her over. She tried to apologize to the officer despite the fact that she could barely draw a breath. She said something about her son and that she needed to get home. He asked for her license and registration and went back to his car. She hadn't even cared that she might get a ticket; she just wanted him to hurry so she could go home. She'd put her head against the steering wheel and kept crying, unable to stop herself. She kept seeing that horrible tattoo while simultaneously castigating herself for focusing on that. Of everything Robbie had done, was it really a tattoo that she was upset about? A van pulled up behind her about the same time the cop came back, but she barely registered it. The cop didn't say he knew who she was, but he did. He only gave her a warning, and said he'd follow her home to make sure she got there all right. The kindness was so unexpected she'd fallen apart all over again. Eventually she did as he said and drove home, comforted by his presence and forgetting all about that van.

The next day her story was in the paper: ROBERT MALLORIE'S MOTHER ON THE WRONG SIDE OF THE LAW. The article claimed she was pulled over for reckless driving. There were pictures of her car from the back, the officer leaning into the window. In hindsight, she realized there had been a note of compassion included with the article, a reminder that Robert Mallorie had a mother who loved him and was upset as she'd left the courthouse that day. But it had felt like an invasion of her privacy at the time. It made her feel vulnerable and watched and distrustful. She'd wondered if the cop had called the newspaper reporter. Or had the van been following her from the courthouse? Were people watching her *all the time*? Waiting for her to do something the least bit sensational?

Amanda blinked herself back to the present and reminded herself that she wouldn't steal the yearbook so there was no fear of an article showing up in the newspaper about her doing so. *Focus. Look how far you've already come. Everything is fine.* She leaned her back against the bookshelf and opened to the yearbook's index. She looked up "football team" then flipped to page 57 for the team photo. Thirty-some teenage boys looked back at her through grainy black-and-white portraiture and the shaggy hair that was all the rage in the mid-80s. Some smiled but most didn't, attempting, it seemed, to strike a more sophisticated pose. *We are football players. We are too tough to smile for the camera.* Amanda scanned their faces for a moment just in case she might recognize someone, but no one looked familiar. Number 76 was on the first row, second in from the left. He was sitting cross-legged on the ground rather than standing or "taking a knee" like the others. He had a hand on each knee, palm down, his head cocked to the side, and one eye closed as though squinting into the sun. Blond, broad, unsmiling. She scanned through the names listed beneath the photo until she matched the face to the name: Stephen Mathis.

Steve. She'd found him!

The satisfaction of discovery brought a smile to her face and wavy anticipation to her stomach. She went back to the index and looked up the name Stephen Mathis, then turned to the first page listed, which happened to be his school photo printed in full color. He had a nice toothy smile and brown eyes that might be a little too close together beneath his very thick eyebrows.

His jaw was square, his nose wide. She went to each page number listed next to his name in the index, building a more three-dimensional understanding of him in the process. There were pictures of him in the weight room—he was certainly built like a football player, thick and stocky but not exceptionally tall. Another photo showed him at a school dance standing arm in arm with a big-haired girl Amanda suspected had on green eye shadow and navy blue mascara. The girl had chosen heels and stood almost two inches taller than Steve. *I bet he hated that*, she thought.

Steve was in a few action shots, which made her think he was a star player, but the team didn't place in any state competitions that year as far as she could tell. There was another Mathis listed in the yearbook too. Jeremy was a sophomore, and she looked him up as well and compared the photos. They had the same nose and eyebrows, though Jeremy was a freshman in the photo so he wasn't filled out like his older brother.

"Can I help you?"

Amanda fumbled the book before clasping it to her chest and looking up to see the woman she'd noticed when she entered—the librarian. The woman's smile gave a commanding impression that clearly stated Amanda was not supposed to be here. The woman glanced at the yearbook pressed against Amanda's chest and then back at Amanda's face, raising one thin, well-penciled brow, which was full black upon her dark brown skin.

"Oh, um, I was just looking through a yearbook."

"I can see that. Can I ask why you're lookin' through the yearbook?"

She decided to be as honest as she could. "I'm looking for someone, a former student."

"Who are you lookin' for?"

"Steve Mathis."

Here's where the librarian might say she knew Steve Mathis—he lived a few blocks west, across the street from the First Baptist church. Instead, the woman's well-shaped eyebrows pulled together. "Who?"

Amanda released the book from her death grip and turned

the cover so that the woman could see it. "Steve or, well, Stephen Mathis. He graduated in 1989 and I recently found his high school ring. I'm trying to return it to him." It was rather remarkable how normal it sounded.

The woman's eyebrows remained clenched, a furrow etched between them. "Where's your visitor pass?"

Whatever reprieve she'd felt from her continual anxiety closed with a silent snap. "Oh, um, I didn't get one—was I supposed to?" Amanda knew full well she was supposed to have checked in at the office. She blinked innocently, however, and held the other woman's eyes as though she was ignorant of such protocol. As if she hadn't sat through hours of policy meetings in which the importance of every person in the school being accounted for was repeated and repeated and repeated yet again.

"If you're not a student or a teacher, you need a visitor pass from the front office," the librarian explained. "We can't be too careful."

How many times had she heard those words said in the wake of Robbie's crimes? Whether it was about assault weapons bans or security at public places or early intervention for the mentally ill. *We can't be too careful*, they would say, and to her it always sounded as though they meant that *she* should have been *more* careful. When Robbie had made that threat against the university, she should have kept him locked up at home so the world would be safe. She should have known he could never be normal or live a normal life. When he'd dropped out of college the next year and said he just wanted to work for a while, she should have . . . what . . . forced him to go back? He was twenty-one years old. Or maybe when he'd stopped returning her calls, she should have stalked him at his work and apartment complex, forcing them to spend time together. Maybe she should have done those things, maybe everyone was right about her and she'd unleashed a time bomb that only she could have stopped. Maybe she'd done everything wrong.

The thought fell heavy on her shoulders, instantly reminding her of the past days' events and her exhaustion, not remedied by a fitful night's sleep in an unfamiliar bed. She'd woken this morning eager to tackle this task ahead of her, on the verge of . . . excited to find Steve Mathis. And she had found him, or at least his name. Amanda looked away from the woman and slid the book back into the shelf she'd taken it from, feeling wrong. Out of place. "I'm sorry," Amanda said, her anxiety creeping up on her slow but steady. "I'll go."

"Now wait right there," the woman said after Amanda had taken just one step. Her tone struck a chord of fear in Amanda's chest, but she did her best to keep her expression from showing how jumpy she felt. "I'm not kicking you out, just explainin' the protocol. Now, you're lookin' for a former student, is that it?"

Amanda remained cautious, but she nodded.

"A Steve Mathis?" the librarian asked.

"Right. His full name is Stephen Mathis. He graduated in 1989."

"And you have his class ring?"

Amanda pulled the ring out of her pocket and handed it to the other woman, who took it carefully and then turned it to inspect it much as Amanda had. "It's from Skyline all right," the woman confirmed. She looked up and met Amanda's eyes again. "And you're lookin' to return the ring to him?"

"I am." Was this woman going to help her or somehow hold her back? Could Amanda trust this woman's help if she offered it? Could anything Amanda did or said be used against her somehow?

"Where'd you get it?"

Amanda looked at the ring and thought of the last two days, shaping and forming what "was" into what could be explained. "My son . . . died and I found the ring amid his possessions. I wanted to return it to its owner and perhaps find out why my son had it in the first place. I'd never seen it before."

"I'm so sorry for your loss," the woman said with compassion as the last of her hardness disappeared. Her big brown eyes became sudden pools of sympathy.

Instant tears pricked Amanda's eyes, taking her off guard. She thought of what Melissa had said about their not getting the typical compassion other people received when someone they loved died. Even though the woman's sympathy was based on Amanda's misrepresentation of Robbie's death, she gathered the commiseration as though it were gold and held it tight. "Thank you," she said softly.

"When did he pass away?" the woman said.

Amanda paused. "Pass away" was such a gentle phrase. It made Amanda think of dandelion seeds on the wind, of someone closing their eyes and peacefully letting out their final breath, like when her dad had died. Robbie had been lying on a table when he "passed away"—did it have a thin mattress or was it cold metal?—with tubes in his arm and a strap around his chest as poison was dripped into his veins. He'd stared up into fluorescent lights while people on the other side of the glass cheered silently that the world was nearly rid of him. "Yesterday."

The woman's eyebrows pinched, alerting Amanda to her mistake. Under normal circumstances a bereaved mother wouldn't be tracking down the owner of an anonymous ring the day after her son's death. "He'd been ill for a long time," Amanda said in another misrepresentation. Robbie *had* been ill—mentally ill—and in a sense his illness *had* caused his death, but it wasn't from some random and undeserved disease besieging him. Or maybe it was, only his disease had taken nine innocent people's lives along with his own because he hadn't chosen to manage his illness the way he should have. Could have. Ten victims counting Valerie. Was Robbie as much a victim as they were? Amanda gave herself a mental shake—he was a victim, yes, but *not* like they were. Not anything like they were. He was the only one of the dead who could have prevented each death, including his own. If he'd stayed on his meds, if he'd kept seeing his therapist and not turned to self-medicating in ways that further unbalanced his mind, all of them would be alive today. As fatal as whatever switch had been flipped at two o'clock yesterday morning, Robbie's deciding not to take that daily pill had changed everything.

The woman nodded slowly but wasn't fully relieved of her confusion.

"I'd better go," Amanda said, straightening the strap of her purse on her shoulder. This was why she didn't talk to people.

This was why she always reminded herself that people were watching her, whispering about her, wondering about her. So that she would keep her guard up. Protect herself. "I'm sorry about not getting that visitor badge."

"Wait," the woman said, pivoting to keep watching Amanda as she headed toward the doors. "Don't you want help findin' him? All you've got is a name—that won't get you very far."

Amanda stopped and turned, something in the woman's voice pulling at her flight reflexes. "You'll help me?"

The woman shrugged, the confusion dropped from her expression as though she'd made peace with Amanda's story in the space of three seconds. "I can try."

Amanda had to consider the woman's offer for a few moments to feel assured there was no trick involved; then she nodded and followed the librarian to the desk. "I'm Margo," the woman said as she moved to the interior of the U-shaped desk and woke up the computer, which was showing a slide show of dark-faced children—Margo's children? An older teenage girl and two younger boys. Three kids with futures as wide as the sky.

"I'm Amanda." Margo wouldn't ask to see ID, would she? And if she did, would she realize who Amanda was and withdraw her help? Amanda rolled her shoulders, trying to fend off the increasing tension. She glanced through the glass doors and reminded herself of the way out of the building should she need to make a run for it.

Margo tapped at the computer, then called someone in the front office, then called one of the teachers, and then called *another* number that teacher had given her. "Old football coach," Margo said after punching the final number into the phone. Amanda watched the events unfold as though she were starving and Margo's calls were for food. That tingly feeling was bigger and stronger, almost frightening. She'd felt so dead inside for so long that this new play of emotions left her dizzy. She realized she was clenching her hands tightly into fists and pressing them against her thighs. Margo couldn't see from the other side of the desk, thank goodness, but Amanda tried to relax anyway. *She's helping you,* she told herself as part of the talking-down process. *She doesn't have to, but she is.*

Amanda could hear the slight burring sound as the phone rang on the other end of the line. Five, six, seven. Margo frowned and hung up. "He didn't answer," she said. "And no voice mail."

Amanda trapped her disappointment into a bubble and set it aside. She'd come in with very few expectations and already had learned more than she'd have ever guessed. "Thank you for trying."

"If it weren't the weekend, I'd tell you to come back tomorrow."

Amanda nodded, feeling an odd sense of embarrassment, though she was unsure what it was for. Wasting this woman's time, perhaps, but more likely that she'd dared hope this old football coach would answer the phone. Now what?

"You feel okay callin' him yourself?"

Amanda looked up at a note the woman extended toward her.

"It's not like his number is unlisted or anything."

Amanda reached for it slowly, as though afraid Margo might pull it away at the last moment. She didn't, though. For a brief moment, they both held one side of the paper, Margo's dark fingers with purple acrylic nails contrasting with Amanda's thin white, unpolished fingers. Amanda used to paint her fingernails, which grew out rather well when she let them. She couldn't remember the last time she'd done it, though. It would have been years before Robbie's sentence; maybe even fifteen years ago. Melissa used to paint them for her on Sunday afternoons at the table in the kitchen. They would talk about normal things like boys and school and makeup. How long had it been since Amanda had remembered that?

Margo let go of her side of the note and the paper was all Amanda's.

"Thank you," Amanda said, looking up and forcing herself to make eye contact with this woman. "I really appreciate your help."

Margo's look was searching.

"I better go." Amanda folded the paper and put it in her purse.

"Y'all call me if you need anything else, okay? Mrs. Hovely. I'm here in the library every day school's in."

"I will, Mrs. Hovely. Thank you very much."

The librarian gave a final nod; then Amanda pushed through the glass doors, trying not to walk so fast that she might look suspicious. She couldn't shake the feeling that Mrs. Hovely was following her. When she reached the stairs, she finally dared glance over her shoulder. The woman wasn't there; she'd likely gone back to work as soon as Amanda left the library. Amanda sent a silent "thank you" and continued down the stairs and out the front doors.

Once in her car she locked the doors and looked at the paper in her hands. *Coach Chris Miller* it said before the number, which must be local since Mrs. Hovely hadn't written down an area code. What if the coach was out of town? Was Amanda willing to wait all weekend for him? How would she explain that to Melissa?

She bit her lip and took a breath, not knowing what to do. She had wanted the yearbook to give her everything she needed, and even though she knew that was a silly expectation, she lacked the ability to think of her next course of action. There was no one she could talk it through with, the way she would have years earlier when she'd had friends. She'd even had a *best* friend, Brenda. They'd called each other all the time about what they should make for dinner or how they should handle something at work. Brenda had been the receptionist for a financial planning office. Like Amanda, she was a single mom, though her kids were younger. They went to lunch once a month and made promises to each other about getting into shape. After Robbie, well, things changed. They weren't equal anymore. Amanda's problems were so much bigger than diet plans and that power bill that didn't get paid the month before. Confiding in Brenda felt like opening a jar of honey over her friend's head, getting Amanda's problems all over her and leaving a mess almost impossible to clean up. And how could Brenda possibly have any advice to give Amanda?

Over the course of those first nine months their friendship went from texts and lunches, to awkward conversations when Amanda would finally answer Brenda's call after five or six tries. Brenda offered help that Amanda turned down over and over. Finally, Brenda stopped calling. Amanda had seen her at the grocery store a few months ago. Amanda was checking out at the self-service register when Brenda walked past with her bagged groceries already in her cart. Her daughter Lilly, who must be fifteen now, was with her.

"Amanda," Brenda had said, her face lighting up as though they were still friends even though they hadn't talked for almost two years.

Amanda had looked up, a box of pasta in her hand ready to be scanned. They'd held each other's eyes for a moment. "Hi, Brenda."

"Hi." They'd stood there a few more seconds and Brenda's expression went from excited to cautiously polite. "It's been forever. We should . . . we should go to lunch or something."

"Oh, that would be great." Amanda was lying, but then so was Brenda. They wouldn't go to lunch. Couldn't go to lunch. Mothers of mass shooters didn't do lunch; it was one of the rules in the book that no one had ever written.

16

Margo

One year, eight months, thirteen days

Margo Hovely pulled into the carport and shut off the engine. She brought her purse with her from the car and opened the side door to the sound of boisterous boy noises. She smiled despite the fatigue their energy brought on. "I'm home!" she called out. A hundred feet came scampering around the kitchen wall, or, well, six.

Hugs and kisses and "How was your day?" and "Where's your homework?" abounded for a few minutes, until twelve-year-old Damon and ten-year-old Mario were at the kitchen table doing worksheets. Cambian had disappeared back into the living room and Margo went to find him. When she sat on the couch, he climbed up into her lap and molded himself to her as though he belonged there—all without taking his eyes off the TV. He put two fingers in his mouth like his mother used to do when she was little. Margo knew she should make him take them out, but she didn't. Instead she stroked his fluffy hair and let their bones settle in together for a minute. In moments like this he felt as much her son as the two in the kitchen were, but she was not his mother and should not be pretending that she was. Not a day went by that she didn't think about her Cherie and wonder where she'd gone wrong.

After Margo's own mistakes, she'd been determined to do better by her little girl. She'd gone to college, she'd worked hard, she'd taken her baby to church every Sunday. Russell had been an answer to her prayers—a daddy for Cherie and a husband for Margo. He was fifteen years older than Margo and a diabetic, but he'd wanted more children just like she did and so they'd had the boys and made themselves a real family. Cherie had brothers and everything seemed perfect . . . for a while. Then Russell's foot got infected. Three sectional amputations followed. The medications ruined his kidneys. Looking after her husband took Margo's attention off Cherie, and the girl-child ran with it. By the time Margo tried to pull in the reins, Cherie was three months' pregnant. Russell was dying.

Cambian was born in September and Russell lived two more weeks. They buried him a week before Cambian's dedication at church. Cambian's father didn't do much for his son, and Cherie tried to be the mom for a while, but she was only eighteen years old and nurturing came so much easier to Margo. Cherie got to where she was living like a teenager again while Margo let that baby fill all her empty spots. When Cambian was eighteen months old, Cherie met some white guy online and moved to South Dakota. She'd come back for Cambian as soon as she was settled in, she said—Tony was going to be a great dad. "Over my dead body," Margo had said, and she meant it. If that boy would take her away from her child, he'd never do right by either of them. Margo got state-appointed guardianship of her grandson after six months and tried hard not to resent her daughter for not doing better with the life Margo had worked so hard to give her. "You're a damned fool," she said every time she hung up after a phone call with Cherie, which was once a month or so. She'd stopped asking for money now that she had a job, but she'd been gone longer than she'd ever been a mother to her son—twenty months now. Almost two years.

"How's my baby?" Cherie would ask each time she called, and Margo would try not to grind her teeth, then ask the Good Lord to forgive her for being so angry. It had been long enough now that Margo needed to start the process to officially adopt

Cambian. It would be best if she could have it all squared away before he started kindergarten in a couple more years. Life sure didn't turn out like you expected sometimes.

The boys finished their homework and Margo's moments with Cambian came to an end as they all started wrestling and taunting each other. Margo took that as her cue to get started on dinner—a good chicken stew would be perfect. Maybe she'd whip up some brownies too.

She was dicing celery when her phone rang. She wiped her hands on a dishrag as she crossed to her purse and pulled out the hot-pink phone. She raised her eyebrows when she saw it was Cherie—they'd talked a few days ago and Margo didn't expect to hear from her for a few weeks at least.

"Hey, baby girl," she said in the falsely chipper voice she tried to use to cover her frustrations.

"Hey, Mama."

There was something wrong, and Margo turned to lean her hips back against the counter. "What's goin' on?"

Cherie sniffed.

"Cherie?" Margo asked, her voice a little more demanding. "What's going on?"

"Can I come home, Mama?"

A bubble of hope rose into her throat, but she forced herself to take a breath and keep her perspective. Wouldn't do any of them any good for her to get too excited. "You know the conditions."

"I'll go to school," Cherie said. "And I'll live clean . . . I . . . I just really need to come home." Her voice caught.

"What happened?" Margo asked.

"He hit me again."

Again? Margo felt the hair on the back of her neck stand up. That boy was hitting her baby girl? Lord have mercy.

Cherie took a breath and it all came tumbling out. How Tony had convinced her that the first time was the last time, how she'd so wanted to make this work, how she'd known for months that she didn't want to be with him, but she didn't want everyone to be proven right about her having been an idiot for being with him in the first place. "I'm sorry for being so prideful, Mama, and I'm so sorry I've stayed away from my baby for so long."

"He's not a baby anymore, Cherie. He's three years old and he barely remembers you." Cherie hadn't visited, not once. She always said she couldn't afford the gas, or Tony had just started a new job. "It's not gonna be an easy road."

"I know."

Margo almost laughed out loud—Cherie didn't know *anything*. She opened her mouth to say so and then remembered the woman who'd snuck into her library this afternoon. She'd lost her son . . . yesterday. Margo couldn't make sense of what she was doing trying to find the owner of that ring instead of planning her boy's funeral, but there was something haunting enough about the woman that Margo hadn't pressed. She'd felt like she should help her, and so she had. That's what Christian women did. And Christian mothers did not stop loving their children because those children were idiots.

"We all get a few chances in our lives to choose different," Margo said, keeping her voice calm and feeling the truth of those words and how they had played out in her own life. "I will do everything I can to help you, but you're the one who's gonna have to make better choices—the freeing kind of choices that keep your future open instead of slammin' doors on you. You can come home—I'll even send you the bus money if you need it—but this is the only second chance I can give you. If it don't work, I'll adopt Cambian and raise him as my own 'cause he needs a stable place. Do you understand?"

"I understand, Mama," Cherie said, sounding relieved. "And thank you. I'll make you proud."

They talked a few more minutes to iron out the details; then Margo went back to making dinner, humming a hymn and making a plan.

17

Amanda

One day, twelve hours, two minutes

Amanda looked at Coach Miller's phone number on the paper in front of her, letting the wish for a friend to talk to fade as it always did. Friends were too hard. She started her car and headed toward a gas station, where she had to ask for a phone book from the clerk—were there truly no pay phones anymore? The headlines of the Tennessee newspapers next to the cash register didn't say anything about Robbie and that helped keep her breathing in check despite feeling like everyone who came into the store was looking at her as though they knew she didn't belong here; didn't belong anywhere.

There were three Christopher Millers in the Decaturville area, but matching up the phone numbers showed which one was the former coach. She scribbled down the address and thanked the clerk, who gave her a bored smile, probably annoyed that Amanda had troubled her for the phone book and not even bought a candy bar. Amanda had almost reached the doors before she turned back and picked up a Kit Kat from the rack.

Once back in the haven of her car, Amanda typed Coach Miller's address into her GPS and ate two of the candy bar segments. Once her phone had the address loaded, she followed the dictated route to a neighborhood of older homes and mature trees that shaded the street. It was warmer here than it had been in South Dakota or Iowa, but it was still winter. Feeling a little tipsy from both the sugar rush and growing eagerness, Amanda got out of her car and walked up the sidewalk, noting that the flower beds had been overgrown before winter had mangled the different plants, perennials mostly, into crooked, nasty-looking tentacles of varying shades of brown and black. It seemed that at one point the landscaping had been well tended, but a year, maybe two, had gone by since someone's green thumb had run out. There was a broom, snow shovel, and baseball bat leaning against the corner of the porch, as well as a mangy-looking wreath that hadn't come down after Christmas.

Amanda rang the doorbell and waited. No one answered, and the failure threw her into another spin of uncertainty. Hope was dangerous—she'd known that all along—and now it had abandoned her and she felt foolish. She shifted her weight and took note of the spider webs in between the bricks in the corner.

How long would she wait for him? Melissa was expecting her in Ohio. Perhaps she could find this Stephen Mathis without the old coach's help. Yes, that was it. This was a sign that she'd gone the wrong way on this crooked path. She was acting rashly, not thinking things through. All she needed was a motel room and her computer; that was how she'd find Steve Mathis, right? It was an oddly regretful sense of relief that kept step with her off the porch and down the walk while she began planning her on-line search. And why hadn't she looked up Stephen Mathis when she had that phone book? He might be only a few blocks away.

She had just reached the curb when an old yellow pickup truck turned onto the street. She was about to open the door of her car when the truck slowed to a stop beside her, leaving her trapped in the four-foot section of road between the other vehicle and her driver's door. An old man was looking at her from the driver's seat. He motioned her toward him, but she didn't know what he was trying to indicate until he'd done the waving gesture three times. Did he want her to open the passenger door of his truck? She looked up and down the street as though she might need to call for help. Who would help her? She walked forward and pulled up on the old silver handle. The heavy door squeaked open on what were likely original hinges from the late seventies.

"Looks like you're coming from my place, young lady. What can I do you for? Windows on this old clunker ain't automatic, so I can't roll that one down from my side."

Amanda blinked at the man, who had to be in his eighties but had a large build that hadn't entirely given way to his age. "I'm looking for Coach Chris Miller."

"Ho," the man said with a laugh. He had a full head of white hair, pulled into a ponytail at the base of his neck, and, she realized for the first time, he was wearing a Pink Floyd T-shirt with jeans and black Velcro shoes. "Been twelve years since I deserved that title, but I sure don't get tired of hearing it." He slapped the seat with his hand. "Sit on down and you can drive with me the rest of the way."

The rest of the way was about twenty yards into the driveway, but Amanda didn't want to hurt the man's feelings so she climbed up into the cab of his truck, careful not to kick either of the two grocery sacks on the floor. She pulled hard on the door so that it slammed shut—her dad had had a truck like this for years and years. There were few things more embarrassing than his showing up to pick her up from some activity in Old Belle. More than once she'd told him she'd rather walk.

Amanda felt as though she should say something by way of introduction, but her atrophied social graces got the better of her. She remained silent and imagined this man's face turning red if he learned who she was and that he'd let her sit in the front seat of his truck.

"There's a chance of a storm tonight," Coach Miller said as the engine growled and the truck moved forward ten feet to his driveway. He pushed a button on a garage door opener connected to his visor and waited as the garage door was slowly pulled upward. "Didn't want to be caught without some staples, so I went to the store. Glad I caught you before you left."

Amanda looked at him, certain her expression reflected her confusion. "You don't even know me." As soon as she said the words, she flushed, embarrassed to be so bad at making simple conversation.

He smiled at her, the skin of his face folding into a hundred wrinkles that hadn't been there a moment earlier. "At my age, when a pretty young thing comes knockin' at your door, you don't ask too many questions."

Amanda looked down but couldn't suppress a smile. She'd turn fifty next year and she wasn't pretty or young, but the way he said it made both feel possible.

Once he came to a stop in the cluttered garage, he shifted into park while Amanda looped the handles of the grocery sacks in her hand. "I'll bring these in for you." Only after she said it did she realize that she'd invited herself into his house. Her face turned red. She wasn't fit for association with people. She was making a mess of this!

"Lucky indeed that I came home when I did," he said as he took off his seat belt and pushed open his door—it was better oiled than Amanda's side had been. Maybe he didn't get many passengers.

She considered pulling back her assumption that she'd go into his house, but he didn't seem nearly as affected by her poor manners as she was, so she waited for him to lead the way inside. She tried not to look at the mess. Cardboard boxes, an ironing board, tube-style television, and various odds and ends were stacked haphazardly next to the door that led from the garage to the interior of the house. He looked over his shoulder in time to catch her perusal. "Every few months I pay the neighbor kids to clear all this junk out—'til then I just throw stuff I don't need out the back door. Guess I'm due to help them earn some video game money, ain't I?"

"It's fine," Amanda said, embarrassed to be seen as judgmental and desperate enough to try to cover it to attempt something she wasn't sure she could do anymore—small talk. "Have you lived here long?"

"Kate and I bought this place back in seventy-five—same year as that pickup." He nodded toward his truck while holding the door open for Amanda. "That was a really good year." He continued grinning and she smiled back while she passed him in the doorway. The house was in nearly as bad shape as the garage, and she looked around the cluttered kitchen for somewhere to put the bags.

"Just put them on the floor by the fridge and come set down and tell me what you're here for—I'm a lonely old man but won't be so rude as to take your entire afternoon, I promise."

Amanda did as he asked, putting the bags down on the dirty linoleum and following Coach Miller through an archway and into a living room stacked with newspapers and magazines. There was an old leather recliner with his imprint in it and he settled himself in before he waved her toward a velvety brown sofa. There was just enough room for a person to sit down between the stacks of newspapers and books.

"Now, what can I help you with?"

Amanda wondered if there were names carved into any shelves in this house, or a doorway used to measure the height of his children or grandchildren. She envied him the sense of belonging he had within these walls; it made her miss the home she'd left in South Dakota. She forced herself to get to the point.

"I'm looking for one of your former students—a football player. Stephen Mathis. He graduated in 1989. The school thought you would know how I could get in touch with him."

"Number seventy-six, tight end."

"Y-yes," Amanda said, even though she didn't actually know about the tight end part. Come to think of it, she didn't know what a tight end was. Robbie hadn't been into football so Amanda hadn't learned much about the game. "That's him."

"He's not in some kind of trouble, is he?"

"No," Amanda assured him. "I found his school ring and want to return it to him, that's all."

Coach Miller looked relieved, making her wonder why he'd jumped to the conclusion of Steve Mathis being in trouble. "Glad to hear he's keeping his nose clean. His class ring, you say?"

Amanda nodded and pulled the ring out of her pocket. She

handed it to him and he looked it over. "Wonder how he lost it," Coach Miller mused, then passed the ring back to Amanda.

"I think he gave it to my son nine or ten years ago," Amanda said, still looking at the blue stone. "My son . . . died recently and I found this among his things."

"Ah, I'm sorry about your son," Coach Miller said. Amanda refused to meet his eyes and simply nodded, still staring at the ring. "It's a bittersweet thing to love so well."

Amanda knew exactly what he meant but only nodded again, afraid to speak for the way his sympathy drew on her emotions. He was the second person to console her in the last hour. She suspected that he'd lost his wife—Kate, whom he'd mentioned before—and knew firsthand the agony of death, but her loss was so different. So deserved, in a sense. Not like the loss of a sweetheart—an innocent. "I was hoping you might know how I could contact Steve," Amanda said. "Does he still live in Decaturville?"

"He hasn't been around here for a while, but he stops in to see me from time to time—his mama's still here. I got a Christmas card from him last month." He used the armrests of the recliner to push himself onto his feet. He went to a desk fairly overflowing with papers he sorted through. Amanda stayed on the couch, unsure what to do and worried it would take hours for Coach Miller to find the Christmas card. Her fingers fairly itched to start straightening the disorder. Her mother had always said, "A cluttered house is a cluttered mind. Want to think clearly, then clean your space." Her mom had never been able to wrap her mind around what Robbie had done. She passed away last summer and by the end they didn't talk about Robbie, which meant they didn't talk much at all. Amanda had gone to her mother's funeral that had been in Sioux Falls even though Mom had lived in Arizona the last five years, remembering that she had a brother and cousins and family friends as they came up to say hello. She kept a distance from every one of them and escaped back home as soon as she could.

"Steve had some tough times after high school," Coach Miller said, though his back was still to her while he rifled through the desk. "Some kids seem to peak out in high school and the reality of adulthood sends 'em running with their tail between their legs, if ya know what I mean."

"Yes," Amanda said, staring at a spot on the carpet and thinking of that cross-country photo she'd decided to keep. If anyone had told her that would be the peak of Robbie's life, she'd never have believed it.

"Steve moved around a lot for a while," Coach Miller continued. "Took him longer than it should have to settle into his responsibilities, but eventually he did—ah, here it is." He turned back to her and held out a red envelope, the paper jagged across the top where he'd ripped it open. He handed the envelope to her and returned to his chair, which rocked slightly when he dropped back into it.

Amanda held the envelope and blinked at the obviously male handwriting—blocky and efficient. She looked at the return address—handwritten. "Where's Florence, Kentucky?" Kentucky was north of Tennessee, but how much farther out of her way would Florence be? She hated that she was going to have to face this choice all over again and wished she could make sure finding Steve Mathis was worth the extra miles and hours it would cost her.

"Oh, well, Florence is a good way north of here, four hundred miles or so."

"East or west side of the state?" Amanda asked. Her route back to Cincinnati took her right through the middle of Kentucky.

"Midland," Coach Miller said with a shrug. "You take the 65 most of the way, head through Louisville, and then ride 71. My wife's sister lived in Cincinnati, so we made the drive a few times a year. Not bad, as far as drives go."

Amanda felt her eyebrows lift in surprise. "Cincinnati? That's where I'm headed. I'm moving to be closer to my daughter."

"Florence is, what, fifteen or twenty miles south of Cincinnati, just west of the Ohio River."

The coincidence unnerved her, but heightened her anticipation. She would be driving right through Florence. Steve Mathis *lived* there. She looked back at the envelope in her hand and had the strangest feeling. Why had she found the ring? Why did she care so much about it?

"Miss?"

Amanda looked up at him. When had she last been called "miss"?

"I just now realized I never asked your name."

"Oh, I'm sorry, my name is Amanda."

Coach Miller nodded. "Right pretty name."

Amanda's blush surprised her and she looked back at the envelope again.

"You planning to drive on to Florence, then?"

Amanda shook her head, then paused. "Am I so easy to read?"

He laughed a low chuckle that ended in a cough. "Well, you best get going, then. Four hundred miles is four hundred miles after all."

Amanda looked up at him again, then let her gaze move past him to the kitchen, where it lingered for a moment before she looked back at him again. The success of the last few moments washed her with boldness she didn't recognize in herself. "When did your wife pass away, Coach Miller?"

It was a presumptuous comment to make and took Amanda off guard that she had asked it. Part of not putting herself in a position to be asked any questions was making sure not to ask questions herself. Especially personal questions that could create attachment and intimacy. Coach Miller, however, barely reacted, though his smile softened. "Comin' up on two years," he said, then lifted a grizzled eyebrow. "Am I so easy to read?"

For whatever reason the comment made tears come to her eyes along with a thought that she rolled around in her head for a few moments before she dared say it out loud. These last years—nightmares every one of them—had pushed her away from people, connections, relationships, and anything other than the most basic of interactions. She had no friends. She had pulled away from family. She asked nothing of anyone, but in the process, she gave nothing to anyone either. It was too risky. Fear of either rejection or publicity had driven her into herself, hiding and fretful and selfish. But the woman she'd once been had taken meals in to new mothers at church, helped shovel snow for a neighbor woman after she broke her hip, donated to causes, walked in fund-raisers, and generally lifted the hands that hung down. How long it had been since she'd felt the sweetness of those things; how long it had been since she'd dared to risk. Even now it scared her. What if Coach Miller discovered who she was? He might reject her as so many people had.

But what if Coach Miller didn't find out? What if she were just Amanda, a pretty name for a pretty face who could help this man who exuded loneliness? And what if she could leave his home an hour from now, maybe two, having done something for someone other than her son or herself? What if his day could be made brighter through her—the mother of Robert Mallorie? Hadn't Mrs. Hovely at the library already helped Amanda? Hadn't this man helped her too? Wasn't it only right that she try to return the favors of their assistance?

She'd been quiet too long before she accepted her idea as having merit and met his eyes again. He had a patient look on his face and she remembered that the last thing he'd said was that his wife had passed away. She hurried to catch up with their exchange of dialogue. "I'm so sorry about your wife, Coach Miller. I guess you know firsthand that bittersweetness of loss you mentioned earlier."

He inclined his head in acknowledgment but still looked at her with an air of expectation.

"I am eager to meet Mr. Mathis. I want to know how my son got his ring and return it to him."

Coach Miller nodded again but continued to leave the talking to her.

"However," she said, taking a breath for confidence, "I've been traveling for a couple of days now and I'd been packing for several days before that, leaving me to forage for my meals amid cereal boxes and soup cans rather than waste time cooking."

Now he was still, as though he knew what she was going to say next.

"I know you don't know me, but I'm a pretty good cook and if you don't mind a little company, it's been a very long time since I've shared a meal with . . . well, anyone."

"You're asking me out to dinner?"

Amanda blushed at the coy smile that spread across his face. "Well, actually, I was asking you *in* to dinner." She nodded toward the kitchen. "I'm sure I could find something to make a meal out of, but I might have to do some dishes along the way."

"You, young lady," he said, making her smile again at his insistence on seeing her as a girl, "have got yourself a deal." He pushed himself up and out of his chair again while Amanda got to her feet and put her purse on the couch as though it belonged there somehow.

"I bought some hamburger and there's any number of other odds and ends in the cupboards, though you'll want to check the expiration dates. If you're as good a cook as you say you are, I expect to be very impressed."

18

Coach Miller

Two years, one month, four days

While this Amanda woman cooked, she cleaned the kitchen, and even though there were few things Coach liked less than cleaning—to which the current state of his house could attest—he couldn't very well sit in his chair and watch TV while she cleaned up after him. Kate's voice sounded in his head as it often did: "If you can lean you can clean." Then she'd hand him something to put in the garage, or a broom to sweep the floor. Amanda, though, wouldn't tell him what to do and so he had to come up with tasks on his own. Considering the mess he'd let grow around him these months, he had plenty of starting places to choose from. He hauled newspapers out to the garage, put all the books back onto the shelves, and then disappeared into the bathroom when he realized she would likely need to use it at some point, and wouldn't he be embarrassed then? There was something mysterious about this woman, a secret bubbling under the surface like that time on the field when the sprinkler had broken and created a pond under the sod. The team had run out to practice, broken through the grass, and ended up in mud to their knees. He didn't expect Amanda to reveal her secrets—he was still a stranger—but he had the oddest sense that her being here was . . . helping her with it somehow. If Kate were here he could discuss the idea with her and she'd either laugh and shake her head or nod thoughtfully and say, "That's something to chew on, isn't it?"

With the bathroom garbage bag in hand, he went into the kitchen and gathered up the garbage that had fallen around the edges of the garbage can.

"You and your wife lived here for forty years?" Amanda asked as he sat on a chair so he didn't have to bend as far to pick up the wadded paper towels and eggshells. What a slob he'd become.

"Yes, ma'am, it's the only home we ever owned and we paid a whopping twenty-five thousand dollars for this place." He slapped his hand against the side of the cabinet by where he sat—original to the house, which had been built in the 60s. He'd replaced the hinges, and Kate had repainted them a decade ago, but the actual cabinets were the same ones. Sturdy. They didn't sell this kind of think at IKEA. No sir.

She laughed, then caught herself and blinked as though she didn't know where the sound had come from. He reached for an empty clam chowder can.

"How did you two meet?" she asked.

"Belmont," he said. "We were both working on our teaching degrees and ended up teaching each other a thing or two." He grinned broadly when she looked at him. She shook her head the way his daughter did when he said outrageous things.

"And how many children do you have?"

"Four," he said, looking away and using his foot to pull an empty cereal box closer to him. Being this close to the garbage can alerted him to the smell—atrocious. "Carl and Kevin both live in Memphis, the other two are out of state now."

"None of them are close by, then."

"Nah," he said. "They come to visit now and then, but they've got families of their own—all but Kevin, who I have finally accepted doesn't like girls—and they're all busy, busy, busy." He didn't try to hide the bitterness in his voice; he'd expected better from all of them, but they seemed pretty content to live their lives without him. At least Linda called him once or twice a month. Kevin stopped by when work brought him through town.

"Have you ever thought of moving closer to them?"

Coach shrugged. "I'm not sure any of them want me to."

"I'm sure that's not true," Amanda said while finding room for just one more plate on the drying rack. Coach was glad she hadn't asked when he'd last washed dishes because he couldn't remember. Sometimes he'd rinse something and put it back in the cupboard, but mostly he just piled them up and then wiped off what he needed when he needed it. Kate would be horrified, but then she'd been doing that sort of thing for him for almost sixty years of his life. He didn't know how to live without her, so he stagnated and marinated in misery and moved in and out of depression, wishing he was dead even on the good days. She'd be disappointed by that, too, but then she wasn't the one who was left behind, wondering what her purpose was and what good there was left in living.

"Kate was the one they came to see. Now that it's just me, there's not much incentive. Darryl used to live just a few streets over." He pointed with his thumb over his shoulder toward the neighborhood to the south. "But he got a new job and I barely even talk to him anymore." He shrugged as though it didn't matter, but he could tell she wasn't buying it. He'd have considered himself closest to Darryl before he took the job with that fancy-schmancy law firm in Sioux Falls just months after Kate's funeral. Coach had needed that relationship more than ever, and Darryl just up and left, took the kids with him, and left Coach to rot. Thinking on it made his chest heat up. He deserved better than what he'd got.

"You and your daughter must be close for you to be moving near her," he said to change the subject.

"Not really," she admitted after several seconds. "We've had some really hard years, and I'm worried that her expectations are higher than I can meet."

"Maybe that's better than her having expectations that are too low," Coach said, thinking of his own kids, who never asked for his help or his opinions. Maybe because he tended to think there was only one way to do a thing, and they always tried to do it differently. When Kate was here she softened the edges, helped them find common ground, and offered a bridge for everyone. He felt rejected and lonely when he allowed himself to remember that there were people out there with some of Kate in them who didn't care enough to keep in touch. "Parenting is tough work."

She nodded and lifted the lid to the pot on the stove.

"Smells good," he said.

"It's nothing fancy, hamburger gravy over rice."

"Beats soup from a can," he said, and went into the living room to straighten up in there.

By the time Amanda announced that dinner was ready, he felt a little sheepish—it hadn't taken much to fill up a garbage bag with crap he didn't need and take dishes into the kitchen. The kitchen looked like it had back when Kate was here. It had taken, what, an hour? Which meant that a few minutes a day over the course of years could have made a substantial difference all this time. Or he could hire someone like Linda had suggested a dozen times.

Coach pulled out the chair set for him at the table. Amanda slid into her chair—Kate's chair—after setting down the pan on a trivet, something one of the grandkids had made for Kate a few years ago. Did they miss their grandma as much as he did?

They served up dinner—gravy over rice with a side of canned green beans—and savored a few bites before Coach asked a question. "Do you have any other children, beside your son who passed—sorry about that, again—and your daughter?"

"No, just the two." She stared at her plate a moment and shifted uncomfortably. There was a tightness in her answer that kept the rest of his questions about her son to himself. They took a few more bites and against his preference, he decided to talk about himself again. She was more open when the focus wasn't on her.

"What do you think I should do about my kids, Amanda?"

She looked up, her fork caught halfway between her plate and her mouth. She sat back in her chair and lowered her fork to her plate as though he'd asked a gripping question that required a lot of thought. He was content to wait her out and took another bite. The meal was simple, but delicious. He really should have learned how to cook.

"Oh, I really don't know, Coach. I'm no expert."

"You raised two kids," he reminded her, watching the way her eyes moved to a spot on the table and stayed there. "You've got the same training any of us have."

"Raising kids is only one piece of parenthood," she said while straightening the silverware next to her plate. Even though they were only using forks, she'd set out all three utensils.

"True," Coach said, taking another bite. "This is excellent, by the way, best meal I've had in I don't know how long."

She smiled tremulously and picked up her fork again.

"I'd still like your opinion," Coach said.

"I'll think about it," Amanda replied.

They ate the rest of the meal in silence. Then she did the dishes while he cleared the table and wiped everything down with a wet rag. She'd filled a mixing bowl with soapy water she put in a corner of the farmhouse sink to make it a double. They had a dishwasher—a Christmas gift to Kate a decade ago—but it was broken and Coach wasn't handy with stuff like that. He started drying the dishes beside her with dishtowels he realized Kate must have washed before she'd died. He tended to use the paper variety. He was tempted to lift the dishtowel to his nose and smell the detergent she'd used. He'd recently realized that what-ever he was buying wasn't the same brand. Nothing smelled like her anymore.

Amanda cleared her throat in a "I have something to say" kind of way. He turned to look at her, but she kept her eyes on the dishes. "My parents would come and see me when my kids were small, and I loved that. My dad would take . . . my son fishing and Mom taught Melissa how to knit. Those were things

I didn't have the patience to do, but they were retired and better at sitting still than I was."

"I don't really know my grandkids very well," Coach said. Darryl's had been so little when they'd lived here, or at least they'd seemed so little.

"That might be the key right there, then," Amanda said, sounding more confident. "I loved seeing my parents with my kids and it brought us all closer."

Coach nodded. "Is that what you'll be doing in Ohio, being a grandma?"

Amanda nodded, looking nervous as she rinsed the final pan under the tap. "Might be easier said than done, but I'm going to try to do my best. Lucy is two and I've only seen her a handful of times. Melissa's pregnant with a boy now. I'll actually be there to help when he's born. I'm looking forward to that."

"All any of us can do is our best, right?"

Amanda nodded, then glanced at him as though she was going to say something, but turned forward and began wiping down the sink.

"Spit it out," he said. "I can take it."

"Well, I was going to suggest hiring someone to come in and clean once a week—if you can afford it. You don't seem to like housework, but it might make this place a bit more inviting." Her cheeks colored. "That was rude, what I meant was—"

"Not rude," Coach said. "It's a valid point. My daughter's said the same thing. And maybe I *should* go see the kids instead of waiting for them to come around. I don't like to travel much, but I'm getting awful lonely knocking around here by myself."

"Is there a senior center in town?"

He acted offended. "And hang out with all those old farts?" He laughed and she smiled. "Maybe my pride is cutting me off from some opportunities—is that what you're saying?"

"My dad took an art class at the senior center and ended up with a group of men who would golf once a week. It was really good for him—that's all I have to say."

"I'll think about it."

She nodded, then dried her hands and glanced at the clock before turning to face him. "Thank you," she said with sincerity that touched him.

"It's my house that's clean and my belly that's full. Thank *you*."

"Well, thank you for letting me. It's been . . . a while since I've been able to take care of someone. Not that you need to be taken care of, that's not what I meant, only that—"

"It's been a while since anyone has taken care of me, and it's pretty nice. You brought me some sunshine today, Amanda, and I appreciate it. The leftovers should make me a happy man for a few more days."

"I'm glad." She retrieved her purse from the living room and he walked her to the door—it was full dark and he considered inviting her to stay in one of the extra bedrooms, but he'd be basically asking her to clean out a place for herself, and, well, call him old-fashioned, but it wasn't appropriate to have unmarried men and women under the same roof.

"Amanda," he said, his tone a bit more serious as his thoughts turned to what had brought her here in the first place now that their odd meeting was coming to an end. She turned to face him and adjusted the strap of her purse on her shoulder. It hadn't started raining yet and he hoped she would get some miles under her tires before the storm hit. "I told you that Steve had some trouble after high school."

Amanda's expression became serious, as though she, too, had just now remembered the reason she'd come. She nodded.

"He had a hard go of things for a while and it wasn't just circumstances. Do you know what I mean?"

Amanda pondered on that for a moment. "You mean that he's responsible for the hard go of things."

Coach nodded. "I get the feeling that you want to find him for more than just returning that ring."

Amanda shook her head quickly. "I only want to return the ring, really."

"I just want to ask that you give him a chance to be more than he was."

Her cheeks flushed. "Oh, Coach, it's really not like that."

"Maybe it is and maybe it isn't, but promise me that if you get the chance, you'll *give* him a chance to be more than he was."

Amanda paused, then nodded. "Okay, I promise, but—"

He put up his hand to stop the argument. Maybe he was a hopeless romantic now that his own sweetheart was gone, but it had felt right to speak his mind. He lowered his hand. "It was lovely meeting you, Amanda, and I wish you the very best on your journey. Tell Steve hi for me and ask him to stop by the next time he comes to see his mom."

She agreed, thanked him, and then went into the cold night. He watched until her brake lights disappeared and then closed the door and went back inside. Instead of turning on the TV, he sat in the silent house for a few minutes, reviewing the evening. He appreciated what Amanda had said, even the stuff she had been embarrassed about. He could afford to pay someone fifty bucks a week to straighten up, and he'd seen the expressions of people when they came to the house. Truth be told, he kind of liked that they could tell how broken up he was by the way the house was falling down around his ears, but that was pretty pathetic, wasn't it?

He picked up the cordless phone he always kept next to his chair. It was dead—when had he last used it? He went into the kitchen and picked up the corded phone from the cradle on the wall, then had to go through a stack of papers to find Darryl's new cell number—his wife, Clara, had sent it with a card a few months ago when they moved into their new house; there was a picture of it on the same card. It was a mansion, but he ought to stop being so judgmental about that. Darryl was an attorney and being rich wasn't a sin. He punched in the number and wished he didn't feel so nervous.

"Dad?"

It unnerved him how people knew who was calling before they answered their phones these days.

"Hey, Darryl, how are things?"

"Things are . . . good, Dad. Everything okay?"

He thought Coach was calling because something bad had happened. Coach deserved that.

"Things are good here in Decatur," Coach said. "But I was thinking of taking a little road trip—what are you guys up to next weekend? Would it throw you off if I dropped in to say hello?"

Darryl was quiet for a few seconds and Coach tensed. What if Kate was, literally, what had kept them a family for so long? "I don't mean to impose and understand if—"

"Actually," Darryl cut in, "would it be okay if we came down and saw you instead? Clara and I were just talking about it—the kids have that next Monday off, so we could come for a long weekend if you'll have us."

Coach stared at a spot in the worn-out carpet, surprised at the way his throat got thick. "You want to come here?" He looked up from the filthy carpet to the piles of yet more newspapers in the corner and thought of the guest rooms upstairs that had become catchalls for anything he didn't want to bother putting away.

"If that's all right," Darryl said. "This job up here isn't working out as well as we'd hoped and we're exploring some options."

"You're moving back?" The enthusiasm in his voice was as genuine as it had ever been.

"Well, assuming I can join a firm down there, and we've got to sell this house and . . ." His voice trailed off in a way that spoke of being overwhelmed and anxious about the details. Coach had worked at the high school for nearly thirty years; he didn't know what it took to pick up one life and set it down somewhere else.

"I've sure missed you guys," Coach said with rare vulnerability. "Hasn't been the same since you left." It hadn't been the same since Kate died; that's what he really meant. She'd been sick for a year, and yet it wasn't until she was truly gone that life had lost all its color.

Darryl was quiet again. "No, it hasn't," Darryl admitted.

They sat in silence for a few seconds until Coach spoke. "I would love the family to come stay—I'll have everything ready for you. Next Friday?" He'd hire a cleaning gal as soon as possible. Kate's friend Dorothy would know someone, wouldn't she? He'd have plenty of time to get those guest rooms cleared out.

"Yeah," Darryl said, sounding a tiny bit relieved. "We'll see you Friday. Thanks, Dad."

19

Amanda

One day, sixteen hours, twenty minutes

Amanda stopped for gas on her way out of Decaturville, surprised at how light she felt—how could she feel so good when
Robbie was so dead? But helping Coach and sharing a meal had
awakened something in her, as though another layer of her defenses had fallen and she was closer to the person she used to be
than she'd been in a very long time. While filling up the tank,
Amanda saw the boxes in the back seat and decided to finally
get rid of the ones full of garbage. She drove around the back of
the gas station, shifted into park, then looked about to make
sure she was alone. When she was certain no one was watching,
she threw the three boxes into the open Dumpster. She stared at
the Dumpster for another minute. Did she feel anything, having
gotten rid of those report cards and trophies and outdated elec-
tronics? Was her burden lighter now that she'd disposed of
some of this minutia?

With a sigh, she realized the burden had never been the boxes.
They held the dregs, easy to discard. The coach had lifted some of
her burden, though. She got back on the road and reviewed her
time with him and what he'd told her about Steve Mathis. Coach
seemed to think she had some . . . romantic intentions. She
shook her head and felt her cheeks flush as they had when he'd
said as much. Nothing could be further from the truth, but the

coach's assumption made her wonder if other people might assume the same thing. Melissa, perhaps, and even Steve himself. Some of her confidence waned as she practiced what she would say to him. Would getting his ring back resolve the awkwardness of her showing up out of the blue?

Maybe Amanda could go to Cincinnati first, move into her condo, and then take the ring back over the border in a few weeks with Melissa as her sidekick. But bringing Melissa would interfere with the fresh start she wanted to make. Steve's ring was connected to Robbie's past and Amanda was trying to move forward. She had to return the ring before she could feel truly free. She rolled her eyes at her own dramatics, but she also confirmed her decision—she would return the ring on her way to Cincinnati; Florence was oddly right on her way. She would cross the border to Ohio without it.

Her thoughts turned toward what she knew about Steve, or perhaps what she didn't know. Coach Miller had said that Steve had a hard time after high school—what did that mean? Should she be worried? She sat with that thought for a minute, but realized that she wasn't worried . . . which was odd; she worried about everything. But today, she'd driven through two states by herself, successfully asked for help from two strangers, and received it. She'd cleaned the kitchen for an old man she would never see again. For a woman who had come to view everything with skepticism, these events were of no small consequence. Kind of like the ring. So small and yet it had held enough information that Amanda had tracked Steve Mathis down and was on her way to meet him. In the process, she was feeling strong again, self-assured, and capable. Of no small consequence, indeed. But it didn't keep her from obsessing.

Would he be home on a Saturday? Was he married? Coach Miller wouldn't have encouraged her as he had if Steve were married, and it was only his name on the return address now safely stored in her phone's notes. What if he had a live-in girlfriend? If Amanda showed up and he wasn't there, would she leave the ring with her?

Amanda's thoughts suddenly stilled and her enthusiasm turned brittle. She had wanted the connection to Robbie that this ring held, but she hadn't considered Steve's reaction to the fact that mass murderer Robert Mallorie had possessed his school ring. Robbie had been all over the newspapers she'd seen these last two days—what if everything went horrible?

Amanda didn't sleep well at the motel she checked into around ten o'clock. She and her bundle of firing nerves were wide-awake by five. She showered, fixed her hair, dressed in jeans and a pink button-up top, and went downstairs for a complimentary breakfast in the lobby while the morning news droned on in the background. The bagels were dry. Her spoonful of cereal stilled halfway to her mouth as Robbie's picture filled the center of the television screen. Or, rather, Robert Mallorie's picture did. An instant later she put the pieces of information together and realized that it was a news segment on the death penalty.

As the most recent execution in the nation, Robert Mallorie was the current poster boy for the topic of capital punishment. Was it right? Was it wrong? Was it fair? Amanda felt every muscle in her body tense as she methodically went back to eating the breakfast she could no longer taste. Her eyes stayed glued to the television.

"Protesters claim that allowing Robert Mallorie to choose not to file the appeals granted to him through the Constitution of the United States denied him his rights to a fair trial." A young black man flashed onto the screen, dressed in a very lawyerish suit with a U.S. flag pin placed in the center of a yellow tie. "Mallorie is a perfect example of accelerated timeframes to execution that disallow the discovery of additional information and possible accomplices. Now that Mallorie's execution has taken place, the opportunity we have to learn additional details about his crime or possible other crimes he committed prior to the Cotton Mall shooting has now been denied the American people. I don't call that justice; no, I do not."

Amanda took another bite and chewed slowly. Suspicion that Robbie had committed other crimes wasn't new—during his initial confession to the police he'd claimed to have robbed a dozen banks, killed a cop, and planted a bomb in Air Force One. He was in a state of florid psychosis at the time, unmedicated, high on some type of opiate and bloodlust, and reeling in the attention the police were giving him. Each of his claims was investigated and found to be unsubstantiated, but the possibilities that there could be some nugget of truth within his rambling continued to circulate and gave fodder to those who wanted to use his story as a way to press their personal agendas.

Robbie had been restored to sanity by the time he was on the stand thirteen months later and tried to explain what it felt like to be in a state of psychosis—how real things seemed and how ideas became reality so quickly he'd forget they were ever ideas at all. He'd said it as a way to explain that he wasn't in full control of himself when he went to the mall *or* when the police arrested him and he made his crazy confession. The prosecution, however, had pointed out that he'd taken the gun three weeks before the shooting, that he'd purchased the military-themed clothing in the days prior to the shooting, and had left a suicide note for his roommates in which he said he'd thought long and hard about what he had to do. "If innocent people must die to protect so many others, then they must die." The prosecution claimed that if he were so aware of what psychosis was and could so clearly see the differences between psychotic and normal behavior, why would he knowingly go off the medication that kept it at bay?

His attorneys had struggled to prove him mentally incompetent under the legal definition of the law due to his premeditation, and no one was surprised when the jury found him guilty. Not even Amanda. Horrified. Not surprised. Amanda thought of Robbie on the day of his sentencing, standing in front of the judge with a chain running from his cuffed hands to bound ankles. His head had been shaved and he was so raggedly thin. He had additional tattoos by then, and it seemed to her that he belonged to the prison now; it was marking him as property. How she'd wanted to hug him, to look into those big blue eyes and tell him that everything would be okay. Instead, she'd sat on the bench behind his attorney—Robbie hadn't made eye contact with her when he came in—and sobbed as quietly as she could while he asked to be sentenced to death. "I deserve to die for what I've done, and the families of the people I killed deserve to know that I'll never have the chance to hurt anyone ever again," he'd said. "For the good of everyone, I should be given the death penalty." Several people in the courtroom cheered and Amanda realized how alone she was. Everyone else watched with varying levels of acceptance of the inevitable and "right" decision. Only she seemed to feel the shards of the sentence pierce her skin and eyes and heart; only she felt the tragedy that at some point in the future, after her son was allowed to rot in prison, someone would kill him. And on that day, more people would cheer.

Someone else was talking on the television now, and Amanda looked up to get a visual of the new voice—it was the same middle-aged white man who had started the segment and Amanda pulled back the top of her yogurt. Blueberry, Robbie's favorite. "The cost of incarcerating death row inmates is atrociously high, adding the insult of higher taxes and bogged-down judicial processes to the injury already inflicted by the accused. If I had it my way, I would make execution mandatory within three years of a conviction."

The black man spoke again. "What about the staggering numbers of inmates who have been found innocent after years in prison? The overturned verdicts are unprecedented, and no one knows how many other innocent men and women are yet awaiting their own acquittal. With the progress that's been made through DNA technology in recent years, one can't help but wonder if future discoveries will increase our ability to acquit even more."

"But not every death row inmate is innocent," the original commentator said. Amanda took a bite of her yogurt but found she couldn't swallow it. "Mallorie confessed to his crimes and *asked* to be put to death, yet it still took almost four years for that to happen and cost the U.S. millions of dollars in the meantime—never mind that he was forced into the direct appeal even though he didn't want it. That the execution happened at all is certainly worth celebration, that it happened faster than most death penalty cases is worthy of even greater acclaim, but that it took *four* years to kill the man after he murdered nine people in a matter of seconds is deplorable."

No longer able to eat, Amanda picked up her Styrofoam dishes and threw them away with the last of her breakfast. She tried to sort out her feelings on her way back to her room, but she'd been trying to do that for so long she didn't know where her feelings began anymore. Her inability to be objective made her opinions meaningless anyway, because she was in the position no one else was—she was Robbie's mother. No one else knew what that felt like. She didn't want exceptions made for him. She didn't want him free to hurt anyone else. She didn't hate the judge or jury that had sentenced him or feel that anyone was wrong, but he'd been dead for forty-eight hours. When did his resting begin? When did hers?

After packing her suitcase, she bundled up as much for comfort as for warmth and went out into the blustery morning. She drove straight through the rest of the way to Florence and arrived in the small town around 9:30 Saturday morning thanks to her GPS. She parked in front of a small condominium not so different from the one she would be living in soon. It was beige, the bottom half of the first floor brick, then stucco on the top half. It matched half a dozen other condos on one side, and three on the other side—the garages must be attached to the back of each unit. There were a couple of feet of flower bed separating the dead brown lawn from the condo itself. Some of Mr. Mathis's neighbors had made the most of this decorative opportunity, although their plants were dormant now. Mr. Mathis's border looked very much like Coach Miller's flower beds, tended once but neglected since. Two half circles of cement curbing made a circle halfway between the sidewalk and the porch. A tree had been planted inside the ring, but all the leaves were gone this time of year and so the stark branches added nothing to the overall ambiance, which was neither spectacular nor squalid. A gust of wind blew and the tree shuddered, but stayed remarkably steady despite the look of frailty. Amanda wondered if a leaf from that type of tree was in Robbie's leaf book.

Amanda pulled the ring from her pocket while the usual butterflies she felt when she had to interact with people invited a thousand of their friends to make chaos. High hopes, desperation, and an odd sense of nostalgia had sustained her through most of the journey, but only the satisfaction of accomplishment drew her up the walkway right now.

The door was painted a shade darker than the beige stucco with a white frame and a gold knocker she knew from a glance was only for show—it was too small to make the resounding noise necessary for it to be better than Amanda's knuckles. She knocked three times. Maybe Steve Mathis worked Saturdays. Would she have to come back another day?

The creak of the door hinge pulled her out of her mixed hope and fear that no one was home. When the door swung open she closed her fist around the ring and then stared at the man framed in the doorway. The hair wasn't blond and shaggy as it had been in the photograph. Instead, it was gray and sandy blond, not thinning, but cut short. His hair melded into a neatly trimmed beard and mustache, full gray under his chin. He looked respectable. The bulk of his football-player days had turned into an overall thickness. He smiled politely. "Can I help you?"

His voice had a rich timbre to it and she imagined that when he laughed, you could feel it through the walls and floors. She didn't think, however, that he laughed very often. When she didn't answer his question right away, he lifted his eyebrows, which weren't as thick as they had been when he was in high school. She reviewed half a dozen explanations and introductions in the space of a breath. When none of them seemed quite right, she simply lifted her hand and opened her fingers to reveal the ring resting in her palm. She watched a look of confusion pull those eyebrows together. They both stared at the ring, then dawning recognition smoothed the lines of his forehead.

Steve reached toward the ring, but then paused and met her eyes, his hand hovering a few inches above her own. A gust of wind sprang around the side of the house, sending Amanda's hair whipping around her face. "Is that . . . my high school ring?"

"Are you Steve Mathis?" Amanda asked in return. She used the hand not holding the ring to push her hair from her face. His hand continued to hover; his eyes were locked on hers, though. Kind eyes. Confused eyes. Wary eyes?

"Yes, I'm Steve Mathis."

She lifted her hand higher, toward him, urging him to take the ring. "Then this is your ring."

He held her eyes for a moment longer, then looked back at the ring and carefully picked it up. He held the band between the thumb and forefinger of both hands as he turned it back and forth, inspecting every detail. He tried to put it on the ring finger of his right hand, but it only went to the first knuckle. "Damn," he said under his breath, then moved it to his pinkie and slid it on. "Fits that one." He looked up at her and smiled.

Amanda smiled back and the butterflies began to settle until she remembered the next part of why she was here at the same moment he did the same thing.

"Where did you get this?"

Did his question mean that he hadn't known what had happened to the ring? Butterfly spasms. "Um, I found it in my son's things."

Another gust of frigid wind that took her breath away seemed to remind him of his manners. "I'm so sorry—would you like to come in?" He stepped to the side, ushering her in.

She didn't move, and shook her head while pushing the hair out of her face again. Her nose was numb. "No, thank you," Amanda said, needing the space and the close proximity to her car to keep her courage. Besides, it wasn't fair to go into his house without his having full knowledge of her identity. The mother of a murderer. Even as she thought this she realized she'd gone into Coach Miller's house without revealing herself. But that was different. Yet it wasn't.

"Are you sure?" he asked, pushing the door open a bit wider. "I've got some coffee on."

For an instant, she imagined accepting his offer. Walking into his condo, looking around. Commenting on the décor. She would follow him into the kitchen as though she went into other people's kitchens all the time. Not counting Coach Miller's, she couldn't remember the last time she'd been in any other kitchen but her own. What if they sat down across from each other? What if she could talk like a normal person? What if he found her engaging and interesting?

She shut down the fantasy that had broadsided her, embarrassed to have thought it. Coach Miller was to blame; he'd planted the seed that Steve Mathis might be more than the owner of a class ring. She would not allow such a thought. She couldn't. "I can't go in." The honesty of her answer was sad. She truly could not go inside. Nothing could make her accept his invitation.

He cocked his head to the side slightly, and concern entered his eyes. He had very telling eyes. She looked away from them and pretended to straighten the hem of her coat around her hips. "I'm afraid you have the upper hand, ma'am. You know my name but haven't told me yours."

"Amanda," she said, not looking up. His hand appeared in her line of vision and she had to think a moment before realizing that he was requesting a handshake. She took it. His hand was warm and large, and folded around her smaller hand quite comfortably. She shook his hand once, then pulled away quickly and pushed her hand into her coat pocket. She didn't touch people in this life she lived, no one except Melissa and her family twice a year. And Robbie three days before he died.

"Thank you for returning my ring, Amanda. But you say your son had it?"

Amanda nodded and felt her anxiety building now that she was on the cusp of learning how this man knew Robbie, or if he knew him at all. "I don't know why he had it, though." She eyed him carefully—waiting for him to remember. Did he already know Robbie was Robert Mallorie? If he did, wouldn't he have said so by now?

He looked confused. "Did you ask him?"

"My son is dead," Amanda said with a stoicism that she despised even though that flatness had been a close friend for some time now. "I found the ring among his things—I'd never seen it before. I wanted to return it to you, but I . . . also wanted to know why my son had it."

Steve looked at the ring and kept his own thoughts for several seconds. Amanda would have found it awkward if she weren't so used to long silences of her own. Finally, he met her eyes again. "You're Robbie's mother?"

Amanda blinked quickly, surprised by the effect the sound of the "before" name on someone else's lips had on her. *He doesn't know.* She nodded.

"He . . . died?"

She opened her mouth but was afraid of what she'd say. She closed her mouth and nodded again. Steve looked at the ring again, then at her. "He was a great kid. I'm so sorry to hear that he died. He had to be, what, only twenty-five or so?"

"Twenty-six," Amanda said. He'd turned twenty-six the first week of November. His execution date hadn't been announced yet and she'd hoped they would wait until after Christmas. They did. She had put extra money in his prison account so he could buy a honey bun from the commissary on his birthday. When he called her the next week, he'd thanked her for it. He'd sounded like her son that day. Sounded like Robbie. She'd missed him so much.

Steve tsked, a sorrowful expression on his face. "I'm so sorry," he said again, his eyebrows pulled together in sympathy. "*So* sorry. What happened?"

Amanda shook her head and looked down in hopes of communicating that she wasn't prepared to talk about it. That wasn't necessarily dishonest—she *wasn't* ready to talk about it. She took a breath and looked up at him again. The eyes that had been too close together in that high-school yearbook picture didn't seem that way now—he'd grown into his face. He was pleasant looking, comfortable. He was two years younger than she—in his late forties. "How did you know my son?" She'd meant the question to be a bit more casual and soft, but the words had popped out like those pressurized biscuits in a can. She was on borrowed time now. He didn't know Robbie was Robert Mallorie. But he might figure it out. And when he did . . . would he yell at her? Would he back away slowly? Would he hedge and shift and try to give the ring back as though it were tainted? Cursed? Would he withhold what he knew? She couldn't stand the suspense.

She saw the embarrassment on his face, making her doubly regretful having asked the way she had. Would he allow her to make another attempt? "I'm sorry, Mr. Mathis," she said, forcing calm into her tone. "I didn't mean to sound accusatory or . . . I just . . . I miss my son." Her voice caught. She cleared her throat. "I would love to know how you knew him and whether or not he touched your life in some way." He could hurt her with the wrong answer.

Mr. Mathis's expression softened. "Call me Steve," he said. "And he definitely touched my life. He was a remarkable kid."

Amanda knew her eyes had turned pleading—or begging really—she saw it reflected back at her in the minute shift of his expression. "*Please* come inside."

She'd already refused the invitation but was aware of how odd it was that she would ask him for something but not enter his house. She swallowed her fear—or some of it anyway—and nodded. He looked relieved and stepped to the side, holding the door open for her. She smelled his aftershave as she passed him and wondered when she'd last been that close to a man. Other than Robbie, whom she had hugged just five days ago and would never hug again.

She stopped in the middle of the living room. A doorway led into the kitchen—a similar layout to her condo.

"Have a seat," Steve said, waving her toward a chocolate brown leather sofa that faced a flat-screen TV mounted on the wall of the narrow room. She tried to smile politely and sat on the very edge of the very end of the couch. He didn't sit; instead he shifted his weight from one foot to another. "Hang on just a sec," he said, then turned and headed up the stairs set against the west wall. Amanda let out a breath slowly, trying not to let the panic take over. What was she doing here? Alone with a man she'd never met. She stood up and turned toward the door, thinking maybe she should go back outside after all. Mounted on the eighteen inches of wall between the door frame and the window was a photo. The young man in the picture—a father— looked a lot like the yearbook photo of Steve Mathis. He was holding an infant in one arm while his other arm was wrapped around the shoulders of a dark-haired woman who was holding a tow-headed little girl. Amanda stared at the photo. At the man who was the sort of man she'd expected Robbie would be one day. A wave of jealousy rose up inside her.

The vibration of footsteps on the stairs broke her spell and she started as though she'd been caught doing something inappropriate. She wondered if she should hurry back to the couch so he wouldn't know she'd nearly left; then realized she couldn't make it in time.

"Sorry," he said, smiling sheepishly. "I should have told you what I was doing. I'm just . . . shocked by all this, I guess." He held his hand out to her as though to give her whatever was clasped in his fist. After staring at his closed fingers a moment, she put her hand out to receive.

He opened his hand and a plastic coin dropped into her palm. She didn't pull her hand in for a few seconds. Not until Steve had dropped his arm back to his side. Then she drew it in and looked at the object more closely. He must have seen the question in her eyes when she lifted them to meet his.

"I thought maybe you'd recognize it," Steve said.

Amanda shook her head.

"Oh." He sounded disappointed. "Well, see, Robbie and I made a trade. My ring for this token."

Token? Amanda looked at it a bit more closely and realized that it was the green 90-day sobriety token Dwight had given to Robbie during that summer visit. Robbie gave it to this man in exchange for a high school ring?

Amanda looked up at him, her anxiety growing—she couldn't stay here much longer. "How did you know Robbie?"

"We, uh, worked on a landscape crew together a few years ago—well, I guess almost ten years ago, now."

"In Sioux Falls," Amanda said.

Steve nodded. "He . . . well, he helped me get perspective on some things going on in my life." He ducked slightly, smiling with another kind of embarrassment tinged with regret. "I know, how is it that some teenage kid could make such a difference, right? But he was a pretty insightful kid."

Insightful. She pulled the word tight to her chest. Robbie *had* been insightful once. She remembered. "Why did he have your ring?"

"Well, when I decided to come here—to Florence—I gave him my high school ring; it was kind of a symbol of what I was holding on to, or wishing for, or missing, or something." He shrugged. "Sounds a little melodramatic when I say it out loud, but I asked him to hold on to that ring until I was ready to accept high school as a part of my life rather than the *best* part. I got so busy putting my life back together that I didn't give much thought to the ring, which I guess proves I was able to leave high school where it belonged." He shrugged, giving a half smile that spoke of his own vulnerability. "My son graduated a couple of years ago and got a class ring of his own, and I put some thought into getting mine back, but I . . . I couldn't remember Robbie's last name." He looked down as though embarrassed by this. He pushed his hands into the pockets of his jeans. "We were all being paid under the table, ya know, so we weren't on more than a first-name basis with one another. Not a bad job for a high school kid. Kinda pathetic for a man in his late thirties."

His expression became a bit more contemplative and his glance more direct. He cocked his head slightly as he continued to look at her. "Did we meet back then?"

Amanda closed her hand around the token. She still didn't know why Robbie had given it to Steve. "Well, I, uh, brought him his lunch a few times. Maybe we met then." But Amanda had no recollection of Steve. If they *had* met back then, it wasn't impactful enough for her to have any memory of it.

"Robbie," Steve repeated in a musing tone, still looking at her with a thoughtful expression. "Will you wait here for just another minute?"

Amanda nodded nervously and clenched the token even tighter in her hand as he went into the kitchen and disappeared to one side so that she couldn't see him from where she stood. She'd returned the ring and she'd received a nice memory in return. He'd said Robbie was insightful and she would treasure that. She should go. Avoid any potential ugliness. She looked over her shoulder at the door and was beginning to turn when she heard him coming back to the living room.

Steve returned with an iPad he was swiping his finger across as though scrolling through information. Her anxiety began to peak, and with it a muddling of her thoughts. She should have left.

It was good she'd stayed.

This was risky.

Act normal.

After a moment, he paused and typed something in. Then he looked at the screen, looked at her, and looked at the screen again. His expression, which had been so easy to read, suddenly went neutral. She'd waited too long, and the hope of having this moment free of Robert Mallorie sputtered away.

"Is this you?" He turned the tablet to face her and she tensed as she looked at a photo of herself wielding a sledgehammer over a corner of her driveway. It was more of a close-up than she'd expected; she could see the black hair tie she'd used for her braid that day and the way her neck strained with effort. Her expression was determined. She looked crazy and felt her cheeks heat up.

"That's me," she said in the barest of whispers, taking another step back and putting her hand on the doorknob. She should go. Now. Run.

"So Robbie is . . . Robert Mallorie?"

She turned without looking at the censure she was sure would be on his face and pulled the door open. In two steps, she was off the porch and hurrying toward her car, the speed of her steps increasing the farther she got from the gaze she could feel on her back. With a little luck the shock of uncovering her identity would keep him in place long enough for her to get out of here before he said anything else that might ruin their meeting.

She was walking around the front of the car and frantically digging in her purse for her keys when Steve said, "Wait."

She looked across the top of her car as he walked toward her. He was dressed in black jeans, a polo shirt with some logo in the corner, and house slippers—had she caught him right before he went to work? Her hand settled into her purse and she closed her fingers around the boondoggled key ring Robbie had made in Scouts. She'd found it a couple of years ago in a drawer and replaced the key ring she'd gotten from the used car dealership. No one knew Robbie had made the boondoggle. Even Melissa didn't know.

They held each other's eyes; she saw the conflict rising up in his. He didn't know how to act toward her. Did he look pale behind his beard, or was she seeing things? He opened his mouth to speak, but nothing came out. What could he say to the mother of Robert Mallorie, who he'd just realized was the same boy he'd known as Robbie?

"Thank you, Mr. Mathis, and . . . and I'm sorry." She pulled open the door and slid into the driver's seat. He stayed where he was. The wind blew her car door shut and the slam seemed confirmation that she'd overstayed her welcome. His hair, short as it was, hardly ruffled.

Within seconds she had started the car, checked her mirrors, and was pulling onto the road. She risked a single glance out the passenger window. Steve held the iPad at his side, watching her, eyebrows pulled together. He raised a hand to wave goodbye. The ring she'd brought all the way from Sioux Falls was still on his pinkie finger.

Her heart was racing, which was ridiculous, and it was a few minutes before she was breathing normally and remembered the token. She patted her pockets and looked around the car as best she could without driving off the road. Where was it? She pulled over and got out of the car. It wasn't in any of her pockets. It wasn't on the floor of the car or on the passenger seat. She dumped out her purse on the back seat—it wasn't there either. A second search of every potential place she could have put it confirmed it was gone. Had she dropped it?

Hot tears rose in her eyes while a gust of wind sent her hair into a flurry around her face. This shouldn't be upsetting—it was Dwight's token that Robbie had given to Steve, not a connection to her in any way. But it had been Robbie's and was therefore a connection to *him*. It was part of a good memory she hadn't had this morning and could now add to the others she'd allowed out of their hiding place. It was . . . something amid a whole lot of nothing, and she'd lost it. Steve had kept it for ten years; she hadn't managed to hold on to it for ten minutes.

She blinked away the tears as her awareness of being on the side of a road on a blustery day returned. Someone might notice her and pull over to see if she needed help. She got back on the freeway and reviewed the exchange over and over and over again as she crossed the Ohio River without the token and whatever it might represent. "Get over it," she told herself out loud. She'd expected nothing, so there wasn't anything she should be disappointed about. And Steve had said kind things about Robbie before he'd realized who he was. *Remarkable. Insightful.* That's what she'd wanted. It was all that she wanted and now that she'd completed the task, she could move forward to the next phase of her life.

Amanda would start back to work on Tuesday, at the computer in the new condo she'd never seen except for pictures. Maybe she would babysit Lucy once or twice a week. Maybe they would go to parks. Swing on swings. Make cookies. The thoughts overwhelmed her, as though she didn't know how to do any of those things anymore. She would take one step at a time. One day at a time. One box. One goal. Maybe she would make a list so she could check things off as she went. There were no guidelines about how to move on after your child was executed. She would have to make things up as she went along, but she was freer than she had been in such a long time and she could finally mourn her son. And herself. And everything that had changed so horribly.

And Mr. Mathis . . . Steve, had his ring. Some measure of order in this chaotic world had been restored. It was a starting place.

20

Steve

Ten years, five months, four days

"What's that ring?"

Steve held up his hand as though he wasn't aware that he still had the ring on, then looked across the pink plastic tablecloth that matched the balloons that matched the plates that matched the Barbie cake that was prominently displayed on top of the fridge where Steve's grandchildren could be driven crazy with the wanting. Steve made eye contact with Max, his oldest son and the parent of said grandchildren. Eli was almost two. Emma had turned four today, hence the Barbie cake and the small gathering of family. "It's my high school ring," Steve said, shrugging as though it weren't a big deal. As though he hadn't relived Amanda's visit over and over while he'd worked today. Amanda? Mrs. Mallorie? Robbie's mom?

Robert Mallorie's mother.

"No way," Max said, putting out his hand. "I haven't seen this for years."

Steve twisted the ring off of his pinkie finger and handed it across the table, watching as Max turned the ring in his hand, reading the different designs and insignia that encompassed the identity of Steve Mathis in 1989. Max put it on his ring finger; it fit. "That's awesome, Dad," he said, then took it off and handed it back across the table.

"What's awesome?"

They both looked up to see Rachelle sit down with a plate of loaded baked potato. She looked between them expectantly with those same brown eyes Max had inherited; Emma too. Mitch was still sick from yesterday's chemo, so he wasn't at the party.

"Dad's class ring," Max said, waving toward Steve. Steve had already put the ring back on his finger.

"You still have that?" Rachelle asked, picking up her fork and spearing a bite of potato.

"I, uh, just found it." He didn't want to tell them how he'd gotten the ring back. The encounter felt . . . sacred and . . . confusing to try to explain. But he told the truth these days. To everyone. Come what may. But did he tell the *whole* truth? Had he told the whole truth to Amanda? Mrs. Mallorie? Robbie's mom? Robert Mallorie's mother? "Actually, a lady brought it to me this morning."

Kassie, Max's wife, called Max to help make Eli a plate. "Be right back," he said, popping up from the chair and moving toward the kitchen counter, where the items for tonight's dinner had been laid out. Steve had brought shredded cheese, sour cream, and Oreo ice cream—items easily picked up at the store on his way from work to here; Rachelle and Kassie's mom had helped with the dinner portion. Two of Kassie's sisters were here as well, one with her two kids. Steve watched his son bend to little Eli's level and ask what he wanted. Max was a good dad.

"Some woman found your class ring?" Rachelle asked, drawing Steve's attention. "Where?"

Steve looked back at the ring and twisted it so the blue stone was centered on his finger. "I gave it to her son back in Sioux Falls. She found it in his stuff." Still not the whole truth.

Rachelle was quiet and he looked up at the anxious expression on her face that reminded him why he wasn't telling everything, even though part of him wanted to divulge. If he explained it out loud, maybe they could sort through it like receipts at the end of the year or coins from the cup holder in the car. Maybe someone else could make sense of what had happened this morning and how he should feel about it. Rachelle, however, got a particularly strained look anytime Steve talked about the years he'd spent hiding from everything but the one thing he wanted distance from the most: himself. They didn't talk about those years very often, not since the family therapy they'd attended after he came back. Every Thursday night for four months after his return, he and Rachelle, and the boys sometimes, met with Dr. Gary, who helped them sort through the years of history they shared, then plan for the future they would also share. Rachelle had raged in those sessions when the boys weren't there to overhear—had he any idea what he'd done to them? Hadn't he ever wondered how she took care of three boys by herself? Didn't he care how much his boys needed their father? His defenses were small and sickly. *I was drinking too much. I was depressed. I was selfish.* Eventually the anger was spent and the therapist was able to build from where they were. Steve became a dad again. Rachelle forgave him. The boys had been old enough to know he'd left them. He'd had a lot of work to do to earn back their trust. Still did. Always would.

Max slid back into his chair, slightly out of breath but with a plate of food in his hands. Eli was seated at the plastic picnic table Max had brought in from the patio earlier. He had a pile of grated cheese, three tortilla chips, and half a banana on his plate. He ate the cheese one shredded particle at a time while eyeing his cousin across the table as though afraid he might want Eli's cheese. "You'd better get some dinner before it's gone, Dad."

"Yes, I should—it smells delicious. You guys did a great job."

As Steve stood, Rachelle leaned into Max, so easy and sweet and comfortable. The liberties of a mother who had never left and therefore had earned the right to be affectionate on a whim. "I love to do it."

Max turned his head and kissed his mom's temple. "You're the best."

"Thanks."

Steve smiled, grateful to be a part of this. Max had forgiven him. Steve's youngest son, Garrett, had also allowed Steve to prove himself dependable again. Steve had coached Garrett's flag football team for three years before Garrett moved on to the junior division. They'd come together through their love of sports, especially football, and Steve had found a place in Garrett's life. Garrett had graduated from high school last summer and accepted a scholarship to the University of New Mexico. Not on football, but academics. He got his smarts from Rachelle. Jacob, their middle boy, had been suspect of Steve's return from the start. He resisted visitation, didn't invite Steve to his events, and still kept Steve at arm's length. The therapist had told Steve he couldn't force it, so Steve had stopped trying, but Jacob was a reminder that not everything can be fixed.

Steve went to the food table and chatted with Max's wife, Kassie, while he dished up his dinner. He liked Kassie, and she seemed to like him, but he didn't have much in common with a twenty-five-year-old mother of two and they ran out of topics pretty quickly. Steve had thought Max and Kassie too young to get married five years ago, when Max was only twenty-two and Kassie only twenty—two years older than Steve and Rachelle had been. But Max was different. He wasn't restless and burdened by his family; he adored them and worked from home half the week as a software developer so he could eat lunch with his little family on Tuesday, Wednesday, and Friday. Steve was so proud of his son.

Steve loaded his potato with chili, cheese, broccoli, and onions, then grabbed a root beer from the bucket of drinks moved onto the counter so the kids wouldn't throw ice at each other. There used to be beer at these family gatherings—before he'd left anyway. The new church Rachelle had joined didn't sanction drinking, so he'd come home to teetotalers, which was a relief. He hadn't had a drink in almost a decade and although he couldn't blame his leaving on the booze, if he hadn't been drinking he'd have come back sooner. Years sooner. It had only taken a couple of months after abandoning his family for the reality of what he'd done to hit him in the chest like a battering ram. You left them. You *left*. Another beer. Three more. A whiskey chaser. Make it a double.

Liquor softened the edges of his regret. It softened the lines on the hard-living women he met in those bars. It bought him one more day. Day after day. Running. Hiding. Coward. It was only when he stopped drinking that he finally dared go back to the life he'd turned away from. It was when Robbie reminded him of his sons and gave him his father's token as a symbol of change. Steve hadn't told Robbie's mother that. Amanda. Mrs. Mallorie.

Steve returned to the table, catching sight of his class ring still on his finger as he put down the plate. Would Rachelle or Max resurrect the topic? Did he want them to? Could he talk about the strange meeting this morning and get clarity, or would talking about anything from the lost years cast a pall over the evening? There was still a fragile edge to each of the relationships and he was very careful to focus on the people he loved and how he could make their lives better—not how they could take care of him. He needed them, not the other way around.

The cake was cut. The presents unwrapped. His bouncing granddaughter raced from room to room, high on gifts and sugar. Steve talked basketball with Kassie's dad while they did the dishes. Max took the kid-sized picnic table back outside. Eventually everyone began making their goodbyes. Steve thanked his family for the meal and then drove the eight minutes from their house in a suburban neighborhood to his condo by Walmart.

He entered through the garage door and flipped on the kitchen lights. Mrs. Mallorie had come inside when he'd invited her the second time. She'd stood right there in the living room. He moved to the doorway between the living room and kitchen and stared at the spot where she'd waited while he'd gone upstairs. He guessed Mrs. Mallorie was about his same age—Robbie had been a year younger than Max when Steve had known him. Robbie. Robert Mallorie. That prickly feeling ran down his arms and legs again, the way it had this morning when he'd made the connection and each of the five hundred times he'd re-

membered the moment throughout the day. He could not reconcile the awkward teenage boy he'd known with the tattooed
face he'd seen on TV, but must have recognized him somehow.
He still wanted to argue that it was impossible for Robbie and
Robert Mallorie to be the same person, but Mrs. Mallorie had
confirmed it by coming here. Steve had assumed the parents of
people who committed such depraved acts were angry and broken and raising broken human beings who were destructive and
volatile. Mrs. Mallorie didn't seem like that. She looked like . . .
Rachelle. A middle-aged mother with a no-fuss haircut and a
Lands' End coat. She drove a Toyota, but he wouldn't hold that
against her. He knew from what Robbie had told him all those
years ago that she was divorced and her ex-husband was an alcoholic. Robbie's dad had visited that summer—that was how
Robbie had the token—but he hadn't been a regular part of
Robbie's life back then. Steve hadn't looked for a wedding ring
on Mrs. Mallorie's finger, but he sensed a familiar loneliness
that told him she hadn't remarried. Or, if she had, that it had
ended badly too.

During his thoughts, he had removed his coat and hung it by
the door, filled a glass with water, and now sipped it while leaning against the sink. That his eyes kept going to the laptop,
closed on the counter, was almost unnoticed. How much did he
want to know about the man Robbie had become?

Steve had *known* Robert Mallorie. He'd shared lunches with
that kid, dug trenches, and showed him how to wire a sprinkler
timer. Robbie had become Max that summer and given Steve
the motivation to go back to the people he'd left behind. Steve
had given his high school ring to Robbie. And Robbie had given
Steve that chip and said he should hang on to it until he had one
of his own. Had his dad stayed sober, Steve wondered? Had Mr.
Mallorie ever asked his son if he still had the chip?

Steve put the glass down on the counter and turned toward
the stairs. After returning from South Dakota, he had started attending AA meetings. He'd hated being lumped in with a bunch
of addicts who had made a mess of their lives. In the beginning

he'd attended to prove to Rachelle that he was serious about giving up the bottle for good. In time the steps became more than words on a paper, though. The people at those meetings turned out to be parents and children desperate for salvation from the vices that had nearly destroyed them too. Instead of weakness he saw strength, and instead of keeping a death grip on willpower he found reason and purpose and hope. He didn't go to meetings very often anymore, but he thought about the steps a lot. Lived them. Praised them for what they had given him.

"My dad gave me this," Robbie had said, reaching into his pocket and pulling out the green token. "It's proof that he's gone three whole months without a drink. He's never gone that long." Robbie had smiled, proud and hopeful. "It's proof, Steve, that people can change and be better."

A few days later, and two full weeks without a drink, Steve made his decision to go home. On the last day that he and Robbie had worked together, Steve gave him the ring. It had felt necessary to separate himself from that carefree jock who felt he had the world by the tail in high school. A kid who was convinced he'd be somebody. In high school, Steve had raced motorcycles on the weekends and thought he might go pro. Get sponsors. Meet bigwigs. He sweet-talked his girlfriend into going further than she wanted. A dozen times. He'd felt invincible, with this simmering potential that was ready to burst forth into the brilliant light that would be his future. High school would only be the start of what he'd thought would be a life full of accomplishment, and he'd bought the ring to represent how far he'd already come in what would only be the first arena of success. He'd been a boy who expected to make everyone proud. A boy who might or might not spend his life with Rachelle Anderson, but would enjoy his time with her while it lasted.

Instead of greatness, he'd become a statistic. A has-been before he was nineteen. While his friends went on to college, he worked in a carpet factory. When other friends went to bonfires and spring break trips to Mexico, he tried to figure out what he was supposed to do with a baby on the nights when it was his turn to be in charge. By then the ring had become a reminder of better days. Days he felt robbed of and would do anything to return to. Robbie had been part of Steve's realizing that leaving had fixed nothing. So, he'd given the ring to Robbie, who was the right person at the right place at the right time to help Steve break out of his self-pity and be the man he should have been already.

More than once Steve had felt bad for having kept the sobriety token. It was Robbie's, a gift from his father. But Steve had held on to it anyway. When Steve got his ninety-day chip, he'd given it to Max and kept Robbie's in his pocket. He'd given his 180-day chip to Jacob, who had left it in the kitchen of Steve's apartment when Rachelle had picked him up later that night, and his one-year token to Garrett, who had been so proud of him.

Steve entered his bedroom and turned on the light. It was sparsely furnished, with a full-sized bed, an overflowing laundry hamper, a nightstand, and a dresser which held an old TV and a jar half-filled with change and some crumpled-up receipts. There was no woman's touch here, no sir; all he needed was function. He walked to the dresser and pulled the top drawer out, none too smoothly. It was on wooden tracks, rather than rollers or ball bearings. The top drawer was narrow, possibly meant for handkerchiefs and ties.

He had a tie tack his mother had given him, still on its plastic backing since Steve didn't own a tie. Some pictures of the kids and a stress ball he'd never gotten the hang of. There was a Led Zeppelin CD case, some safety pins, and a Ziploc baggie full of his sobriety chips. A rainbow of colors, but no green. Not now that he'd given the green one to Mrs. Mallorie. He fished out the one-month token, gold. It hadn't felt like long enough to brag about back then, which was why he hadn't given it to one of the boys. Once he hit three months he'd felt as though he'd accomplished something.

Steve put the token in his pocket, even though he hadn't kept a chip on him for years, and headed back downstairs—today had come with a lot of reminders about who he'd been and he needed some fortifications to help him remember who he was now. He turned on the TV in the living room for company, grabbed a bag of pretzels from the kitchen, and planted himself on the well-worn center cushion of his couch—the only piece of furniture he'd ever purchased new from an actual furniture store. He put the laptop on the coffee table and flipped open the lid.

21

Amanda

Three days, twelve hours, forty-seven minutes

Amanda returned to Melissa's at 3:00 on Sunday afternoon, just as she'd promised the evening before after they'd had dinner at a local restaurant, Randal's Diner. Paul had said it had amazing corn chowder and he'd been right, but she'd been relieved when she was alone in the unfamiliar condo later that night. It was hard to be with people. Now, standing on her daughter's doorstep, Amanda clenched and unclenched her fists in an attempt to release the tension. It didn't go away.

The door swung open and Amanda smiled in time for Melissa's greeting. "Mom," she said, and stepped onto the porch to give Amanda a hug. Amanda hugged her back, but she couldn't relax. The last three days kept cycling through her head, and over and over she would ask herself if it had all really happened. Was Robbie really dead? Had she really driven to Tennessee? Had she run away when Steve recognized her? She could still see his face, pale with realization. "I'm so glad you're here," Melissa said, a huge grin on her face that was overwhelmingly expectant.

"Me too," Amanda said in a voice that didn't sound like hers.

"Lucy just got up from her nap and is begging to go to the park—do you mind if we do that?"

"Of course not."

"Great, I just need to find her shoes and coat."

Amanda had been to this park on other visits; it was only a block away and a better option than having to sit across from Melissa and make small talk. She'd already prepared a list of topics that could keep them from talking about anything too emotional—how behind she would be at work when she logged back in on Tuesday, when the moving truck would arrive, details about the condo and how much she loved what Paul and Melissa had found for her. She wanted to make sure she was super positive.

Lucy came running in as soon as the front door shut, but then stopped as she looked up at Amanda with big blue eyes and took hold of Melissa's leg.

"This is Grandma, Lucy," Melissa said with a laugh. "You saw her last night, remember?" Lucy put her arms up without taking her eyes off of Amanda and Melissa picked her up, holding her on her hip, Lucy's left leg draped casually over Melissa's rounded belly.

"Hi, Lucy-Bell," Amanda whispered, coming closer. Lucy's hair was untamed and completely enchanting. She had a big purple flower tacked onto an elasticized headband that did not match the pink top and pants she was wearing. All of a sudden Lucy leapt from Melissa's arms, causing both women to gasp and Amanda to quickly catch her. Lucy giggled as wild as her hair. Amanda laughed nervously as Lucy threw her arms around her neck and gave her a squeeze. Melissa shook her head with the look of a bemused parent.

"Apparently, she remembers you after all," Melissa said. "Let me find those shoes."

The afternoon was nice, if a bit stilted. Exactly as it had been on prior visits, but with the added weight of knowing this was something she would have to do over and over again. Would it always be this way?

Amanda squatted at the bottom of the slide to catch Lucy while Melissa took a phone call from a friend of hers who wanted to know how Melissa had made homemade Play-Doh. Melissa gestured while she talked, then rested her hand on her belly, then laughed. So natural with a friend. Amanda turned back to Lucy, who was babbling about something as she climbed the ladder to the slide again, and realized she was . . . jealous of Melissa? She turned and looked at her daughter again and felt the confirmation. Jealous of the ease Melissa could have with people and jealous that Melissa had found a way to still be herself, whereas Amanda had had to put up barriers and checkpoints. And then another thought came to mind. Was she also jealous of Melissa on Robbie's behalf? Jealous that Melissa had done everything right while Robbie had done everything wrong.

Amanda shook her head. It was cruel to hold any of that against Melissa.

"Everything okay, Mom?"

Amanda started, realizing that she'd lost touch with the present again while Lucy played with a plastic pirate wheel that had distracted her on the way to the slide. She was singing to it. Amanda blinked at Melissa and put her plastic smile back in place. "Yes, of course. Sorry."

She turned away and headed for the bottom of the slide so she'd be ready when Lucy descended.

"Are you . . . thinking about Robbie?"

I'm always thinking about Robbie, Amanda thought. She shook her head, however, uncomfortable with the intimacy of the question and sensing that Melissa would disapprove if she were to say the answer out loud. "Lucy?" she called up the slide. "Grandma's ready to catch you."

Lucy looked through the slats of the play area, grinned, and scampered to the top of the slide.

By the time they had arrived home, Amanda had exhausted the topics of conversation she'd been prepared to discuss and could feel her nerves frazzling. She tried to act happier in hopes of covering her increasing anxiety but knew it came off false.

Paul came home from a meeting at their church and helped diffuse the guilt-inducing tension. Amanda and Melissa made dinner together—grilled cheese sandwiches, tomato soup, and peach cobbler made from preserved peaches Melissa had put up that summer. Amanda hadn't known that Melissa home-preserved foods, and asked how Melissa had gotten interested in it. Melissa's answer filled up the space between them for a full fifteen minutes until the cobbler was in the oven.

Amanda kept smiling, but all she could think about was going back to her condo. It was more than exhaustion and awkwardness that made her long for isolation; it was that she was so much more aware of her exhaustion and awkwardness than she'd been before. She hated seeing that they had become a mother and daughter who could not connect despite the daughter's attempts. A family in mourning, and not just for Robbie. For everything they'd lost when he did what he did. A daughter who had left her brother behind for her own sanity. A mother who was disappointed that her daughter's life could be so good. It was so wrong and horrible, and yet rather than put down the plates she was drying by hand and say "Melissa, can we talk?" she kept drying the dishes and letting Paul and Melissa talk about everyday things that required limited answers on her part. She kept seeing Steve's pale face. Was that the reaction she could expect from anyone who learned who she was here? Had she been better off in Sioux Falls, where she didn't have to inform the people she met? Where she didn't have to manage a mother–daughter relationship.

Amanda put the final dish in the cupboard, then hung the damp dishrag over the edge of the counter to dry. "Well," she said with forced cheerfulness that drew Paul's and Melissa's attention from where they were sitting on the other side of the counter. "Thank you so much for the lovely afternoon and dinner, it was all just perfect. I think I'll head home. I'm exhausted and need to plan out my errands for tomorrow. I start back to work on Tuesday and want to have everything done by then."

"Oh, that's right," Paul said with a smile and understanding as his tone. "Back to the grindstone."

"Oh my gosh," Melissa suddenly broke in. "I didn't even ask you about giving that ring back to that guy. How did it go?"

"It went . . . fine," Amanda said, but she felt her voice waver and sensed an internal alarm going off. Today had been *a lot*, what with trying to be comfortable in this new role of three-block-away mom and grandma while running through the last few days and continually thinking about the blood draining from Steve's face when he'd learned who she was. "He was very gracious about the whole thing." She started walking toward the living room, where she'd left her coat. She could sense a breakdown coming and she needed to go before it happened here. No one saw her in her raw form. Ever.

"Did you find out why Robbie had it?" Melissa asked, following.

"Um, yeah, he worked with Robbie one summer on that landscape crew and gave it to him."

"Just like that?"

No, not just like that, but she hadn't stayed to hear anything else and she couldn't stay to explain that right now. She needed to go back to the condo, fall apart, and then put the pieces back together.

Steve Mathis was nothing to her. She needed to focus on her new life in Ohio, and she was scared to death that she wouldn't be able to be everything she needed to be now that she was here. That she and Melissa would never connect, that they would never talk about Robbie or Robert Mallorie or anything of substance. "Just like that," Amanda lied.

Melissa stopped in the doorway between the kitchen and living room. "Oh, good." She sounded disappointed, as though she knew Amanda was running away from her.

"Thanks again for everything," Amanda said. "It was all so great. This is going to be really fun being so close."

"Yeah," Melissa said, but her sad tone cut through Amanda, causing more feelings to bubble up, which leaked more panic into Amanda's system. Too much, too soon. What had happened to all her strength and resolve? How could she be so certain about the importance of finding the owner of a stupid ring and so uncertain of how to connect with her daughter? She heard Melissa take a breath and for a moment Amanda thought she was going to get angry. Stomp her foot and demand that Amanda stop running away. Stop letting Robbie, even in death, be the only person in her world. Did part of Amanda want

Melissa's rage? Because it would help shake Amanda into this new reality, or because if she raged then Amanda could be angry in return?

"You're sure you need to go? The cobbler will be out in another ten minutes, then ten minutes to cool and, shazam, we have dessert." Melissa's smile was a little bit wobbly, a little bit pleading as she tried one more time to say what she'd tried to say a dozen times today. *I need you. I want you. Please be here with me.*

Amanda had to pretend she didn't notice, as she had done a dozen times today. Melissa deserved more than this and they both knew it. More time. More truth. More effort.

I'm not ready yet, Amanda told herself as she picked up her coat from the back of the chair. But couldn't she be a little bit honest? Didn't Melissa deserve that much? She imagined that after she left, Melissa would turn to Paul and cry. He'd hold her and assure her that things would get better, but Melissa would be sad and disappointed and, maybe like Amanda, worry that it wouldn't get better.

Amanda took a deep breath and chose just a little bit of courage. "I'm sorry, Melissa." She raised a hand to her head and rubbed her forehead. "I'm just . . . overwhelmed. It's been so long since I've talked to people, or spent time with anyone I care about and then I miss Robbie and . . ." Her voice was shaking as the words tumbled out and her anxiety spiked. She couldn't fall apart here. Not like this. She didn't look at Melissa as she put her hands through the sleeves of her coat. She looked at the toe of her leather shoe, where there were two dark spots from where Lucy's apple juice had spilled earlier. *I'll be what you need me to be, but not tonight. Not yet.*

When? a voice asked. *Why not now?*

Because it's too soon. I'm not ready, and neither is Melissa, whether she thinks she is or not. We need to get to know each other. We need time to be comfortable again before she sees how broken I really am. Better yet, maybe I can be all healed up and perfect before she ever has to know.

"Lucy, come say good night to Grandma."

Melissa wasn't going to fight her on her escape. Amanda let out a relieved breath and turned toward the kitchen doorway, where a pink shooting star with a big purple flower in the center of her forehead dashed through, her arms wide open and her feathery brown hair floating around her head as though she were in water. Amanda barely made it to one knee before Lucy jumped, fully expecting Amanda to catch her for the second time that day. The little girl wrapped her arms around Amanda's neck. It seemed natural for Amanda to embrace her tightly, but then she closed her eyes, and *felt* the absolute love this little girl had for a woman she'd really only just met. The sensation rippled through Amanda, reminding her of the pebble in a pond analogy she'd thought of so many times with Robbie. This time Lucy was that pebble and the ripples were the kind you wanted to savor one by one. Amanda inhaled the scent of grilled cheese sandwiches, a walk to the park, and strawberry baby shampoo. Lucy. With her big blue eyes, wraparound heart, and future as wide as the sky. Unlimited potential and eternal greatness were within this tiny body even though Lucy could not tie her own shoes or understand the concept of what it meant to need redemption. Everything perfect and innocent and wonderful. Something shifted inside Amanda's chest and she stopped fighting the emotion she didn't want anyone to see. She had been stuck for such a long time, but there *was* more. More now. More later.

Okay, she said to herself, knowing that welcoming acceptance Melissa was extending to her now wouldn't be open forever. If Amanda insisted on hiding, Melissa would start protecting herself. The awkwardness would stay. The hurting would continue. They would be physically closer but just as far apart as they had been these last four years. Robbie would continue to keep them apart. That *something* shifted again, cracked, began to splinter. The shaking she felt was a sob from deep inside of her, bottled but bursting. The choking sound she made caused Lucy to relax her squeezing and pull back. Amanda blinked through the tears, but the face of her granddaughter would not come into focus. She felt a tear slide down her cheek. This wasn't the kind of fun-grandma impression she wanted to make. Lucy was going to be scared.

Except Lucy wasn't scared. She lifted her chubby little hands and patted Amanda's teary cheeks. She grinned widely and then flung her arms back around Amanda's neck. Amanda looked past Lucy to see Melissa, still standing in the doorway with big blue eyes full of tears and a wraparound heart all her own. Amanda reached her hand toward her daughter with equal parts apology and invitation. "Melly," she said in a whisper. Melissa crossed the room and came rather awkwardly to her knees behind Lucy. She leaned over her pregnant belly and two-year-old daughter to embrace her mother, who was finally *here*.

22

Steve

Ten years, five months, six days

"You look like hell."

Steve turned to give Kyle a flat look. "Gee, thanks."

Kyle grinned, then sat down at the other computer and began updating order statuses. Steve focused on one of his Monday morning tasks, reviewing the day's service schedule and managing the outgoing parts order—ongoing stock items like filters, oils, and O-rings that were used on a regular basis. He took another swallow of coffee—his second cup and it wasn't even eight o'clock. But then he didn't usually stay up until after midnight, eyes glued to his computer. Eyes now scratchy and burning in protest.

"Looks like they didn't send that muffler," Kyle said absently from where he reviewed the order sheet from receiving. "We might have to send someone over the river for it. Hey, what's that?"

Steve followed Kyle's gaze. "It's my high school ring." He twisted it off and handed it over while trying to hide how closely he was watching Kyle inspect it. He didn't know whether or not to be surprised that Kyle had noticed it—so had his family. Apparently a blue stone the size of a marble got people's attention.

"Man, I wanted to get one of these my senior year," Kyle said wistfully, turning the ring this way and that. "Football, huh?"

Steve nodded, feeling pride in his accomplishments on the field for the first time in who knew how long. "Tight end."

"Awesome." Kyle handed it back. "I only played my sophomore year until I blew out my knee. How come we've never talked football days before?"

Because I had to cut out that part of my life to have this one. "We should start."

Kyle grinned and then swiveled his chair back to face his portion of the counter. "So, back to the muffler—whatddyawannado?"

"Ty comes in at noon—maybe he could pick it up on his way," Steve said. "I'll text him."

Kyle grunted in a kind of ambiguous agreement to the plan. Both men fell silent save for the tapping of their keys for a few minutes longer. Tara came over to wish them a good morning. Steve made eye contact only long enough to return the greeting. She leaned forward with her elbows on the counter and asked how the day's schedule was looking. Steve kept his eyes on the computer, though he was pretty sure he could look down her shirt if he wanted to. He suspected she knew that. "Busy in the morning, easing up in the afternoon, though scheduling will probably fill the open spots."

"So, you mean we might actually get a lunch break today?" Tara asked, lifting her eyebrows. She had dark hair, dark eyes, and full lips. She was pretty. Young.

"I hope so," Steve said, politely. "Might be the only one this week, though. Things are stacked in pretty tight for the remainder."

"You picked a fine time to leave us, Steve-o," Kyle sang out.

"Oh yeah, you're heading out of town this week, huh?" Tara made a pouty face.

"Thursday through the weekend," Steve said.

Tara laughed as though what he'd said was terribly funny. "Maybe you and I can run over to Wendy's for lunch then, since you won't be around later in the week."

Steve's hands paused on the keyboard and he met her eye. She'd never issued a direct invitation before. His mouth went dry and for an instant he imagined her as a partner in life. To have her sitting on the couch next to him, helping him decide how best to manage his 401(k). To take her to the movies and call her to see if he should pick up milk on the way home. The momentary longing made his chest soften and shift, like frosting on a warm day. He'd never had that kind of partnership. He and Rachelle were eighteen years old when they had tried to make their marriage work, and it never really had. She had cried, a lot. He stomped around feeling sorry for himself in equal proportion. And then they were parents and life was going a hundred miles an hour. The moments of blissful ease were so few that it was hard to stop his mind long enough to believe they had really been there at all. Rachelle had that ease with Mitch now, and Steve would often try to ignore the envy he felt when she would snuggle into Mitch's side, or he would give her hand a squeeze. Not envy because he wanted Rachelle—that ship had sailed—but the desire for . . . someone. The idea that Tara could be that person burned out before he could turn it into an aspiration. "Thanks for the invite, but I brought something from home."

"Surely it will keep. That's what the employee fridge is for, right?"

Her boldness surprised him, but he turned back to the screen as though he hadn't noticed. "Thanks anyway," he said with finality. "Kyle, what's the ETA on the transfer case for that Dodge? By noon, I hope."

Kyle answered him. Tara left. Steve felt like a jerk.

Once she was gone, Kyle let out a breath. "Seriously, Steve? When was the last time you got an offer as good as that one?"

"And how about that transmission—it'll be here in time for the two o'clock, right?"

Kyle was quiet in a way that said too much. "Yeah, I expect both of them in the ten o'clock shipment."

They didn't talk about it anymore and ten minutes later the doors were unlocked and Monday officially began. Steve put in an order for some seat covers and replaced the battery in an old woman's key fob. He pulled parts as needed by the service techs, checked off the second morning shipment—a full set of tires hadn't come in and he spent half an hour tracking them down at a dealership in Cincinnati. Ty agreed to pick up both the muffler and the tires. The day marched on. Kyle took the early lunch and Steve took the later one. He ate his tuna sandwich in the employee break room while scrolling through more articles about Robert Mallorie, even though he was pretty sure he'd read them all over the weekend. He'd found pictures of Amanda at Robert Mallorie's court hearings. Mentions of her in several articles. Then she was front and center when she argued against Robert's decision to fast-track his execution. He'd found a news clip where she addressed the press in a shaky voice, her strawberry blond hair pulled back from her thin face. The press had eaten her alive for her stance, and as quickly as she'd come out of the shadows to fight for her son's life, she'd retreated back into them. Steve pulled up the article he'd used to identify her when she'd shown up at his door Saturday morning—he couldn't believe now that he hadn't made the connection between Robert Mallorie and Robbie when he'd read it the first time on Friday morning.

"... in a dramatic display, Amanda Mallorie wielded a sledgehammer early Thursday morning, just hours after Robert Mallorie was pronounced dead from lethal injection by the state of South Dakota. According to sources, the purpose of her act was to destroy a set of some type of impressions made in the concrete there many years earlier—one neighbor claimed they were handprints belonging to Robert Mallorie himself. Why she would want to publicly destroy such a thing is a matter of speculation."

Steve shook his head and only just held back a snort. She wanted to destroy the handprints to keep someone from cutting them out of the driveway with a cement saw and selling them on eBay. Why did she obliterate the cement in front of the cameras, though? For a woman who had been so private for so long, it seemed out of character. He wanted to ask her. To know how she balanced the son she'd raised with the man he'd become. She seemed so normal, and Robbie had seemed so normal. Those two things put everything he'd ever believed about killers on its ear. He didn't understand, but wanted to.

He pulled up another article—each one might have a line, maybe two, about her, then go on to talk about Robert Mallorie. Of course, he understood why Amanda wasn't the focus of the articles, but he wanted to know more about her and had to read five articles to get five tiny details. So far he knew that she'd been born and raised in South Dakota, in the town of Watertown. She'd attended USF and married Dwight Mallorie, who now lived in Pennsylvania. Robbie had an older sister. Steve had the vaguest memory of Robbie having talked about her once or twice. Amanda had been a teacher at the same high school Robbie had graduated from, but she'd resigned after the shooting. She must work now—someone had to pay for that Lands' End coat—but he couldn't find anything about her current occupation. Her hairdresser, Robbie's prom date, a Sunday school teacher, numerous members of the faculty at the high school where she'd worked, and half a dozen family friends had put their two cents into the fray at some point or another. He read what they shared with a wince, all but certain that Amanda would have felt betrayed by these people even though he did not know Amanda. At all.

"Whatcha reading?"

Steve blinked back to the present; the austere employee lounge that smelled like metal and oil and tuna because of his sandwich. Tara blinked at him from the other side of the Formica-topped table, her long nails tapping the Diet Coke can in her hands. He put his phone down as though she might read it from three feet away. "Just catching up on some articles."

"Oh yeah, articles about . . . ?" She cocked her head prettily to the side and smiled at him as though genuinely interested.

Why not tell her? "Robert Mallorie."

Tara drew her eyebrows together, then lifted them in understanding. Her forehead moved funny and didn't wrinkle the right way—Botox? "That guy who was executed last week?"

Her familiarity caused Steve to perk up. "Yes," he said. "What do you know about him?"

Tara pulled back slightly. "Um, well, I know what they said

on the news. That he shot up a mall in South Dakota." She paused and smiled. "I didn't even know they had malls in South Dakota."

"I've, uh, been trying to follow his case. I didn't pay much attention to the shooting when it happened."

"But now you're all interested?" She smiled again, flirty and carefree. She was the kind of girl who would want to go get sushi. Steve had never had sushi.

"Yeah, I guess I am."

"Don't tell me you're one of those anti–death penalty types?" Tara said, taking a sip of her Diet Coke.

Steve just shook his head. A week ago he'd have said he supported capital punishment. Now he felt sure he didn't know enough about it. "His mom tried to stop the courts when he dropped his appeals," Steve said, still grasping for . . . something. Information? Opinion?

Tara laughed in a single breath. "Maybe she should have tried harder to keep him from shooting a bunch of innocent people." She shrugged. "A little late to start fighting to save his sorry ass, if you ask me."

Steve stiffened and looked back at his phone. "I guess she moved after the execution—like the day of." He'd learned that from the sledgehammer article. None of the articles seemed to know where she'd gone, though.

"Huh, well, anyway. I was wondering if you have plans tomorrow night. My sister's got some extra tickets to the Wildcats game."

The hopeful look on her face helped Steve focus on this moment and he wished he dared ask her why she'd set her sights on him. There had to be a hundred forty-something men in a one-mile radius who would welcome her attention, many of them far more handsome and financially stable than he was.

"Ah man, thanks for thinking of me, but I've got a bunch of stuff I've got to get done before I head out of town to see my mom for the weekend. I'm really sorry." But he wasn't sorry and the lie clawed at him. Part of his sobriety was telling the truth, all the time, and he'd been fudging the last few days. It was dangerous.

"Oh, that's okay," she said with forced ease. Her eyes had left his, though, and she turned the can in her hands nervously. "It was just a thought."

He should say "Another time" or "I'll be back on Monday—maybe we could grab dinner instead." He could feel her waiting for it. Instead, he pulled back the top of his pudding cup—tapioca.

"Well, I think it's awesome you're going to see your mom," Tara said, extracting herself from the chair. It scraped across the floor when she pushed it back under the table. "I guess I'll see you when you get back."

He looked up, smiled carefully, and nodded. "Yeah, I guess so."

23

Amanda

Six days

Amanda went back to work Tuesday morning, relieved to have a lot to do—online teachers didn't get substitutes, they extended deadlines and got caught up on their own time. Amanda was grateful for the familiar inbox within this new and unfamiliar life she was living. Sunday had been emotional; Monday was exhausting. Amanda and Melissa talked all day about feelings and hurts and memories. It was cathartic and good, but over-whelming. They agreed that when Amanda needed space, she'd say so, and Melissa would do the same. They were going to be pragmatic, and Amanda was relieved that she wasn't expected to step into June Cleaver's sensible heels and pretend the last four years hadn't happened. She wasn't the same woman she'd been before, but she loved her daughter, and both of them wanted a future in each other's lives.

Tuesday evening, she pulled her garbage can out to the street for her first Cincinnati garbage day and the inevitable happened.

"Hi, you must be the neighbor."

Amanda looked up like a deer in the headlights as a plump redhead crossed the street toward her wearing purple velvet sweatpants and a matching jacket. *Don't panic,* she told herself while digging deep for her best polite-but-uninterested-in-friendship smile. It was out of practice and hard to find.

"I'm Emily Shaw," the woman said. She waved over her shoulder. "My husband Joe and I live in number 16."

Number 16 looked exactly like number 21, which was Amanda's.

"I'm Amanda Stewartson," Amanda said, taking the woman's hand. "Number, well, you probably already know, number 21."

Emily laughed for what seemed to be no reason at all. "Of course, I know," Emily said. "I know pretty much everything that goes on around here. For instance—" She leaned in and proceeded to share gossip on her neighbors. Those two were getting a divorce, that one drank too much on the weekends, and that one had a whole litter of puppies in her upstairs bedroom she was trying to keep under wraps until they were old enough to sell—the HOA said you could only have one pet per unit. She would be fined "up the wazoo" if management ever found out. She was lucky Emily knew how to keep a secret. In exchange for a puppy, of course. Laughter.

Amanda kept smiling, but her knees were wobbling by the time Emily ran out of things to talk about and said they would have to go to lunch one of these days—Emily knew the cutest place. Amanda gave a noncommittal answer, then bolted the door as though the woman would come in after her. She tried to buoy herself up with the reassurance that the encounter was now over and she could learn to avoid this woman. And everyone else. Right?

She took several deep breaths, trying to get the panic to go away, and then had a thought she hadn't had for years—*I should call Melissa.*

"Hi, Mom," Melissa said on the other end of the line.

"I just met a neighbor."

Melissa paused for a moment. "Oh, really? Is everything okay?"

"I was stuck outside talking to her for twenty minutes."

"The redhead?"

Amanda paused. "What? You know her?"

"She came over when we were looking at the condo."

"And you didn't warn me?"

Melissa laughed and it loosened up the tension coiled in Amanda's chest. She dared a smile. "I can't believe you didn't warn me."

"Well, I didn't want you to change your mind," Melissa said. "And, well, I hoped maybe she would spare you."

"Are there more of them in this complex? I need to know what I'm up against."

Melissa laughed again—this was exactly what Melissa had wanted when she'd invited Amanda to move to Cincinnati. Amanda had met her daughter's expectation. Even Emily Shaw couldn't take that away. They chatted a few more minutes and then Melissa had to go—she was finishing up dinner. She didn't invite Amanda to join her, and Amanda was relieved. This was her first evening alone and she needed to get centered, so she put on her coat and gloves and hat and went for a walk through her new neighborhood. People waved, and once she realized they were waving to her, she waved back.

She found a pizza place around the corner and ordered a small black olive pizza. During the ten minutes it took for the pie to bake, she walked through a strip mall, pausing outside a gym. It had machines in the front and then a floor area surrounded by mirrors at the back of the narrow space where a yoga class was taking place. Amanda had liked yoga once—she and Brenda went every Tuesday night—yet it made her chest tingle to imagine going to a class again.

"Hi, what's your name?" the cute, fit instructor would ask.

"Amanda," she would say as she rolled out her mat, looking around nervously in case anyone had recognized her. Could she do sun salutations as though she were just another middle-aged woman wanting to get in shape? Could she interact with the same seven people every week without telling them anything about her life? It would feel like she was lying to them.

"You coming in?"

Amanda took a startled step back from the window and looked at a woman in her thirties with her hair up in a messy knot on her head. She wore flip-flops and capris—a huge down coat made up for the exposed skin.

"They've only just started," the woman said, nodding toward the class. "You coming?"

"Oh, um, no. Thank you." She turned and fairly ran back to the pizza parlor. Her heart was still racing as she left with her pizza in hand and headed straight home. She watched *Gilmore Girls* on her laptop while she ate and reviewed the evening. What if she went to that class next week? She got anxious thinking about it, but excited too. It would be something new and different. Then she instantly felt guilty and laid down her pizza. Robbie was dead—tomorrow it would be a full week. She was starting over without him and it made her heart ache in her chest. She'd already made too many changes; she wasn't ready to make more.

She turned up the volume on the show and took a sleeping pill so that it would kick in by the time she retired to her inflatable bed.

24

Steve

Ten years, five months, ten days

"Stephen? Phone."

Steve looked up the basement stairs of his mother's house Friday morning. "Coming!"

The old, cement-enclosed basement was filled with twenty-year-old jars of peaches—at least he thought they were peaches—and something dead in that east corner behind bins of who knew what. Steve was making his way in that direction, but had already hauled up four loads of garbage—he'd have to borrow some space in the neighbor's can for the rest. If he'd thought ahead he could have ordered a Dumpster.

He wiped his dusty hands on his shirt while walking up the stairs that creaked beneath each step. If they hadn't always creaked this way he'd be concerned, but they'd sounded just like this when he was seven and weighed fifty pounds. He wondered during his ascent how much longer Mom would be able to stay in the house. She was seventy-six and every time he saw her he was surprised by how much she'd . . . diminished. She was getting smaller, her skin thinner, her hair fluffier. Dad had been gone a full ten years now—he'd died during Steve's lost years and Steve hadn't found out until after the funeral.

At the top of the stairs, Steve turned right and moved past the circa 1950 built-in shelves and drawers set into the hallway.

Mom had remodeled the kitchen a few years ago and while it was nice—with granite countertops and recessed lighting—the modern lines didn't fit the rest of the house, which hadn't been updated in sixty years.

Mom had left the phone—a curly corded thing that had been on the wall for at least three decades—on the kitchen counter and gone back outside, apparently. She wanted to prep her flower beds since today was warm. The cycling of Steve's thoughts hadn't even brought him around to think of who could be calling him at his mother's house until he was lifting the phone.

"Hello, this is Steve."

"Hey there, number seventy-six!"

Steve paused just a moment and then smiled, leaning his shoulder against the wall. "Coach Miller," he said with a bit of a laugh in his voice. "How's my favorite teacher?"

"Still kickin'," Coach said, then added, "well, shuffling I guess. Can't kick much of anything these days."

"Oh, I bet you kick up plenty of trouble," Steve said. "How are you?"

"Good, good. Heard from your sister you were visiting when I went into Millie's this morning for coffee. Thought I'd see how you're doing."

Steve paused. Had Coach ever called to see how he was doing on prior visits? Steve didn't think so. Once a year or so Steve would stop in on his way out of town after visiting with his mom and catch up with the coach over some diet root beer— Coach knew Steve's history and was one of those distant supporters who were safe and comfortable. They would talk old days and new days, and Coach always told Steve he was proud of him. More than once Steve had wondered if Coach was the only person who was. "I'm doing well, Coach. Better than I deserve."

"Ah, don't talk like that. The kids are good?"

"Yeah," Steve said, then gave a quick rundown on his boys.

"Well, that's just wonderful," Coach said after Steve told him about Emma's birthday. "Grandchildren are the payoff for raising up your own kids. Or, well, so I hear."

"Everything okay with you, Coach? I was planning to stop in on my way out of town Sunday morning. Will you be around?"

"Sure, sure, I'd love to see ya. When I heard you were in town I was hoping you'd planned to stop, but then I couldn't keep myself from calling anyway. I wanted to hear how things went with Amanda."

Time froze and seemed to hitch backward a step. "Amanda?" Steve repeated, an odd sense of vertigo causing him to lean more heavily against the wall into which the phone was set. "Amanda Mallorie? How . . . how do you know about her?"

"Didn't she tell ya she stopped by here? I gave her your address so she could drop off your ring."

Steve blinked again. *What?* Several seconds of silence lapsed. "Sorry, Coach, but you've got the better of me. *You* gave her my address?" Steve hadn't even thought about how *she'd* found *him*. Why hadn't he wondered about that?

When Coach spoke, his tone sounded dejected. "I guess she just dropped off the ring and went, then. Is that it?"

"What else would she have done?" Steve asked, but his thoughts still felt disordered. "She came to *you*? I'm so confused."

"I'd really hoped she'd have told you all that, preferably over dinner," Coach said. "I just had this feeling . . ."

Steve's chest prickled and a rush of heat or anticipation or something washed through him. He hadn't been able to stop thinking about Amanda or looking up articles about Robbie, and the more he looked the more he realized that he wanted to find her. Talk to her. Return the sobriety chip he'd found in the grass by the curb. But he'd hit a dead end trying to find her and convinced himself it was because he wasn't supposed to. Instead he needed to focus on real life. Yet here she was again. In spirit, at least, and there was a whole story about her search for him that he didn't know. His ears felt warm. "You home right now, Coach?"

"I am."

"I'm on my way over."

Steve hung up, slid open the back door, and called to his mother that he was leaving for a bit but wouldn't be long.

"I used up the last of the bread this morning—pick some up on your way home?" she called back.

"Yep." Steve slid the door shut, considered changing into a clean shirt, and grabbed his keys off the hook instead.

Steve didn't realize that he'd been slowly leaning forward throughout Coach's narrative about his encounter with Amanda until he lost his balance and pitched forward a fraction of an inch. He caught himself from face-planting into the brown carpet that had probably been here when Steve was a member of the Skyline High football team. Coach paused while Steve sat back in his chair and wiped his sweaty palms on the thighs of his jeans. Coach finished explaining how Amanda had cleaned his kitchen and made him dinner. "Some kind of hamburger gravy she served over rice, good stuff."

Steve nodded, tensely primed to hear more until several seconds passed without additional information and he realized that Coach was done. Steve looked up and met Coach's eyes. "She never told you who she was." It wasn't a question. Coach would have included the info if he'd known it. To Coach, she was just a woman who'd lost her son and who was looking for the owner of a ring she'd found. And made him dinner.

"She was Amanda," Coach said with a grin. Steve envied him the comfort of such simple information.

"Amanda *Mallorie*." Coach shrugged as though the emphasis on her last name meant nothing to him. "Her son was Robert Mallorie. He was executed last week in South Dakota."

Coach pulled his bushy gray eyebrows together, then shook his head in disbelief. "Nah."

Steve got up and went into Coach's kitchen, where a cardboard box held several weeks' worth of newspapers, some of them still in their rubber bands. He shuffled through until he found one with the right date, still rolled up. With a snap, he released the rubber band and turned back to the living room, where he smoothed it out on his lap. It wasn't the lead story— Kentucky politics held that spot—but it was on the front page, bottom left corner: ROBERT MALLORIE'S FAST TRACK TO EXECU-

TION COMES TO A DEAD END. Steve cleared his throat and started reading the article, having to turn to A7 to finish it.

"Well, I'll be," Coach said when Steve refolded the paper a few minutes later. "What on earth did he have your class ring for?"

Steve explained, sticking to the details he'd given Amanda. It seemed unfair to share more with someone else. He thought of the sobriety chip now on top of the dresser back at his condo. Had she dropped it on purpose?

Coach took a turn staring at the carpet now, absorbing this new information. Reassessing. After nearly a minute he looked back up at Steve. "That explains her . . . reticence, I guess. Got better as the afternoon wore on, but she seemed nervous and never did talk about herself much. I asked about her son a few times and she shook her head or directed the conversation a different way. I'd never have guessed."

"Who would?" Steve looked past Coach into the kitchen that Amanda had cleaned a week ago. Things had been hard on the coach since his wife had died. Steve often took out the garbage after his visits, and he'd mowed the lawn last summer when he stopped by to find it mid-calf. It gave him a funny sort of connected feeling to think that Amanda had seen a similar need and addressed it. Steve pulled himself away from visualizing her scrubbing out Coach's coffee mugs.

"You said on the phone that you had a feeling. What did you mean by that?"

For perhaps the first time since Steve had known this man, Coach got a sheepish look on his face. He looked away from Steve's gaze and picked at where the leather was cracking on the arm of his recliner. "Maybe the romantic in me got the better of common sense," Coach said with an embarrassed shrug. "But I thought about how much Kate would have loved a story about a woman tracking down the owner of a ring—sounds like a book she'd have told me about during one of our Sunday drives."

"I never pegged *you* as a romantic, Coach."

Coach smiled with half his mouth. "Well, I have my moments and, you know, I'm getting old. Old men tend to get softer. In the head and in the heart both, I suppose."

"And, so, well, now that you know who she really is . . ." Steve couldn't finish and felt a flush in his cheeks. Steve cleared his throat. "I mean, now that you know the truth of it, you don't still have a . . . a feeling." He was careful not to phrase it as a question; he didn't want to encourage any particular direction for Coach's answer.

"Honestly, I don't know." Coach leaned back in his lounger and it rocked slightly. "But the more I think on this, the more I wonder why her son should have anything to do with my feeling." He paused as though considering his own words and when he spoke again his tone was a bit more animated—the way it would get when he told the team about an upcoming game against a school he knew they would beat. Eager. Anticipating a win. "She was a nice woman; a good woman. I sensed that in her and when I learned she was looking for you, I had this kind of feeling like—*Isn't fate a funny thing?* I thought about how long you've been alone, Steve, and how hard you've worked to get your life back but how there's something missing. Surely you feel it."

Steve looked away from those eyes that locked on to him. Steve found himself staring at the newspaper he'd put on the ground. The tattooed face of Robert Mallorie looked back at him. He couldn't find Robbie in that face no matter how many times he saw it. "What I feel," Steve said, his tone thoughtful, "is regret for what I've done to the people I love."

"Still?" Coach said in surprise. "After all these years?"

Steve was surprised at the other man's surprise. "I can never make up for having left, Coach. Never."

"No, you can't. That's what forgiveness is for, and you've got that. You can't make what you did right when it was wrong, but the fact that you've done such a solid job of being there since you came back says more than your failure."

Steve kept staring at the newspaper. The tattoos on Robert Mallorie's—Robbie's—face blurred together.

"Remember how hard it was in football to change course?" Coach continued.

Steve looked up.

"You'd be running full out down the field, then have to take a sharp turn—that's when most runners lose balance or slide out or whatever—most injuries happen then too. There's science to support this, I'm sure, but basically whatever direction we're going is the one that's easiest to keep. It's the turning or, bless us, going back the way we came that's so daunting. But that's what you did. You saw your mistakes—that's humility—and you stopped making them. That's the first step toward redemption." He paused and an unexpected smile lit up his face. "Wouldn't Kate be proud of me for all this church talk."

Steve smiled, too, still reviewing the words.

"You took a hard left and changed your course and then worked harder in that new direction than you ever had before, and you've kept it up. You should be proud of that."

Steve nodded. "I am proud of that." *But . . .*

"And stop thinking that if you do it well enough, you can fix the years you were gone. You can't fix them, Steve. It requires mercy on the part of the other people for those years to be made right. You can only do what *you* can do."

Steve nodded, but he still felt uncomfortable.

The coach leaned forward. "The point of all this is that I hope you're not putting your future on hold for the past. That would be a shame."

Steve sat with that a moment. "I don't think that's what I'm doing, Coach. I'm just trying to live in the now, ya know? I just want to live one day at a time and really *be there* for it, so that it doesn't slip away again."

"But I bet you're avoiding things that might make you happy, aren't you? Are you seeing anyone? Have you dated at all since you came back?"

Steve wanted to lie, but he didn't dare—slippery slopes and all that. He shook his head. He had gone out a handful of times, usually at the suggestion of someone who knew *just* the right woman for him. But he hadn't had a single second date. He told himself it was because the woman wasn't right or he wasn't ready, but he knew it was more than that. The future scared him. What if he made a choice that ended badly? What if he created a relationship with one of these women and ended up making her miserable?

"You're still a young man, Steve. You shouldn't give up on yourself."

Steve glanced at the newspaper again, then met Coach's worried expression. "I appreciate that, Coach. And I'm touched that you thought Amanda might be a fit for me, but now that you know who she is, you can surely understand why that's out of the question."

"Maybe that makes her exactly what you need."

Steve laughed, in part to cover his nervousness and in part to react to the absurdity of this situation. "She's the mother of a mass shooter—he killed nine people that day." Yet he was also Robbie. She was Robbie's mother too.

"Well, she's a good woman from the impression she made on me. She's got some baggage, sure, but so do you and . . . and maybe she's looking for a new start herself. She said she was moving to Cincinnati to live by her daughter. They haven't had much contact in several years—probably because of her son."

Steve shook his head again; this was so ludicrous, and yet he grabbed hold of the confirmation that Amanda had moved to Cincinnati. Fifteen minutes away from Florence. Seriously?

"She's certainly not going to judge you," the coach said. "And she seemed like a decent woman to me, a woman in need of a second chance just like you are."

Suddenly Steve remembered something Robbie had said about his mom one day—she and Robbie had gotten in an argument the night before about him not telling her where he was and Steve had pointed out that she must really care about him to be that worried.

Robbie shrugged. "I guess."

"You guess? What if she didn't come home when she was supposed to and you didn't know where she was or who she was with? Wouldn't you be worried about her?" Oh, the irony of his saying that to someone else's kid when his own kids had no idea where he'd been for years.

"I'd figure that she could take care of herself."

"Really?" Steve had said, giving Robbie a hard look, and after a few seconds, Robbie had dropped his gaze. Steve nodded toward the lunchbox open on Robbie's lap. "She make you that? Even though she was mad at you last night?"

Robbie nodded and Steve had felt the shift.

"She must love you a lot."

Robbie nodded again and picked up his sandwich. "My mom's really great," he mumbled, as though not really wanting to say it out loud but unable to help himself.

"Yeah, I bet she is."

And Steve had believed that was true. He'd imagined Robbie's mom being a lot like his mom—kind, hardworking, dependable. When Steve had returned after ten years of deadbeating, his mother had hugged him, cried, and then told him to sit down and explain himself. She was the kind of mom to chew him out in the evening and make him a lunch the next day. The kind of mom he knew would still love him, no matter what he'd done. If Amanda were that kind of mom, what had it cost her to love her son these last years?

Steve didn't know how long he'd been lost in his thoughts, but when he looked up, the coach had laced his fingers and rested them on his belly as though content to wait all day if necessary for Steve to plug back into their conversation. "You've given me a lot of food for thought, Coach."

"I know a change of subject when I hear one," the coach said, smiling again. He looked to his right at the clock by the kitchen doorway and pushed himself up from his chair. "And, well, I gotta get to the store and fill these cupboards before Darryl and his family get here so that my son doesn't know I've been living off of canned soup."

Steve smiled as he got to his feet. "I hope I didn't set back your day."

"Nope," Coach said with a shake of his head. "They're flying in to Nashville in about an hour, then renting a car to drive down here. His fancy-pants job has its perks, I guess. I don't expect them until about five, and it's always a pleasure to see you."

They'd reached the door and Steve stepped outside before

turning to face the old man. "Well, thanks for calling, Coach. You gave me something to think about."

"Good," Coach said. "And don't give up so easily."

Steve smiled, nodded, and then headed back to his car, but stopped partway across the lawn and turned back. Coach was still standing on the porch, and Steve decided to confess. "I've been looking for information about Amanda for almost a week now, Coach, and I had no idea where she was until you told me she was going to Cincinnati."

Coach's face lit up as though Steve had divulged a secret. "Have you now?"

"She dropped something when she was at my place. I just wanted to get it back to her, but I think she's maybe gotten used to hiding. She didn't leave you with a forwarding address, did she?"

Coach's expression fell. "No, she didn't."

"Phone number?"

"I didn't even have her last name."

Steve kept his smile in place, not wanting Coach to feel bad. "Well, I'll keep looking, but maybe it's just not meant to be."

Coach smiled back. "And maybe it is."

25

Clara

Thirteen years, ten months, thirty days

After the four-hour flight to Nashville and then a two-hour drive to Decaturville yesterday, Clara had expected to sleep late, but she was up with the birds—*birds*! The morning sounds in Sioux Falls had gone south months ago. Maybe they all came to Decaturville, which at fifty degrees felt like a tropical paradise compared to South Dakota. She smiled at the thought, then slid to the side of the lumpy full-sized mattress in her father-in-law's guest room. Darryl didn't stir as she shuffled around for the running clothes she'd brought—she hadn't run outside for months. Two weeks ago, she didn't think they would make it to their fourteen-year anniversary; now she hoped they would be house-hunting back here in Tennessee by then. If she'd ever doubted that God answered the prayers of desperate wives who pleaded for their husbands, she would never doubt again.

She tiptoed out of the surprisingly clean house, careful not to wake the kids, who were cocooned in sleeping bags throughout the living room, then texted Darryl when she got to the car so that he'd know where she was when he woke up. It made her nervous to leave the kids at the mercy of Darryl and his father for breakfast, but she thought two grown men were capable of cereal and milk. And it would be good for all of them to see Darryl involve himself more than he had been doing. She headed for her favorite section of the Tennessee River Trail, letting the crisp-but-not-cold morning air, flowing river, and Southern charm infuse her with confidence. They could make this work, couldn't they? Come back to the life that had once felt provincial and take hold of the beautiful things they could now appreciate? Darryl could be happy working contract law again with the occasional litigation to keep his skills sharp? A middle-class life in a middle-class neighborhood where the kids chose one activity a year would be all right, wouldn't it?

She knew she'd make any trade necessary to have Darryl a part of their family again, but would he? She wasn't so naïve to think that the effect of that man's death could change everything, and yet she wanted to believe that the humility she'd seen in Darryl's face the morning of Robert Mallorie's execution was real. She needed to believe that, like her, he realized how truly broken everything had become and was desperate to fix it.

When she returned to the house, red-cheeked and invigorated, the chaos was in full tilt. Apparently, Coach had decided the kids needed eggs and bacon. Something had burned and the windows were all open while the kids flapped cookie sheets to help move the smoke out of the house. They were in their element, Darryl looked frazzled, and Coach was trying to find a new pan. Clara expertly put herself between the men and the stove and put them to work cracking eggs and preheating the oven—she always baked her bacon these days. Forty-five minutes later, they were seated at Coach's table with the chrome legs and eating a real family meal. As an actual family, instead of pieces of what used to be one. *This can work*, she told herself, catching Darryl's eye across the table. He smiled at her—a real smile.

It was another hour before Clara was showered and the kids were dressed. Coach had a treehouse in the backyard and even though she'd always seen the thing as a death trap, the boys couldn't be kept out of it. They'd be filthy in no time, but she told herself that was okay. She didn't have brand-new wool carpets to protect from dirty shoes here.

"Well, I'm off," Darryl said, coming into the kitchen where Coach and Clara were finishing the dishes—the dishwasher was broken. He kissed Clara on the cheek.

"Good luck," Clara said while offering a prayer that the lunch date with his former boss would be everything they'd hoped. He'd need more money than he'd made before, but then he had two years' high-level experience to use toward convincing Jason it was a worthwhile investment on behalf of the firm.

"I sure do hope this works out," Coach said after Darryl had left.

"So do I, Coach," Clara said, feeling nervous again. What if Jason wasn't interested? But then, would he have agreed to a lunch on Saturday with only two days' notice if he weren't? She heard her phone chime from the counter and pulled her hands out of the water before drying them off.

It was a text message from Darryl.

Darryl: I meant to grab a package from my laptop bag. Are you going to be running errands? If so, could you take the package to the post office for me?
Clara: Sure thing
Darryl: I should have mailed it days ago
Clara: Better late than never. I'll drop it off. Good luck!
Darryl: Thanks. Love U

She put down the phone and retrieved the package from the guest room upstairs, a bubble mailer filled with who knew what. She read the name on her way down the stairs and felt her steps slow. Amanda Mallorie?

"Everything okay?" Coach asked when she came back to the sink.

"Yeah, Darryl just needs me to run a package to the post office." She paused. There were confidentiality issues involved, and yet this was Darryl's dad and she wanted to talk to someone about everything that had happened these last ten days. "Did Darryl tell you about the death row case he's been working? I think that's a big part of why we're here—he witnessed Robert Mallorie's execution and it really shook him up."

Coach turned to her a bit more abruptly than she'd expected, startling her enough that she dropped the bowl she was washing back into the soapy water.

"Mallorie?" Coach said, his eyes moving past her to the package on the counter. A sly smile lit up his face. "Oh, Clara, darlin', I want to hear all about what you have to say and then do I ever have a story for you."

26

Amanda

Twelve days

Amanda peeked out of her blinds Tuesday morning to make sure her nosey neighbor wasn't already outside. Seeing that the coast was clear, she hurried to her mailbox, retrieved the mail, and then hurried back into her condo.

It wasn't until she was safe inside that she realized she had more than just the letters forwarded from her Sioux Falls address. She put the envelopes aside and looked at the bubble mailer with her Cincinnati address on the front. A quick glance at the return address of the law firm in Sioux Falls sent a rush of anxiety through her—she'd had an e-mail last week asking for her address so they could send the personal effects the prison had given them. She'd been anxious about receiving this package while at the same time pushing it out of her mind. It was the clashing of old life and new life all over again.

Now she went into the kitchen and sat down at the counter—she'd bought two bar stools at IKEA. She took a breath and then tore open the top before upending the envelope and letting the items slide onto the counter.

There was a biography about President Eisenhower she'd given him for his birthday, a stack of letters Amanda had sent over the years held together with a rubber band, a deck of cards, a few photographs she looked at, and then an envelope with

Mom written on the front. She picked up the envelope with one hand. Robbie had written her a letter. The last words she'd shared with him were not his last words after all.

Once she felt ready, she turned the envelope over and ran her finger beneath the flap. She extracted a single piece of plain copy paper, both sides covered in Robbie's familiar script. She just looked at the letters and words without reading them for a few seconds and thought of the urn now on her mantel that held what was left of the man who had written this.

Mom,
It's Monday night, you left a few hours ago, and I can't stop thinking about you. I thought I had said everything I needed to say, but it's really starting to hit me that I'll never get another chance. First, I need you to know that I stole fifty bucks from your wallet when I was in the seventh grade. I wanted this video game and Grandma had sent you some birthday money and I took it. When you asked me, I lied about it, but then didn't dare bring the game home so I left it at Justin's. I'm really sorry about that. Also, I'm sorry that Melissa and I fought so much, and that I was such a jerk to her once I got here. It was always just the two of us, and we should have gotten along better and I feel really bad that I messed everything up. Will you tell her how sorry I am about everything? I'm really proud of the way she's lived her life, I envy it so much, and hope she knows that I really did love her.
Whew, I feel better. ☺ But that leaves me with what I need to say to you. I know I've said I'm sorry a hundred times, I've meant it, and I know I've told you I love you and thanked you for being here for me when I totally did not deserve it. I want to say all those things again, but there's some stuff I haven't said. As you left today you told me that you loved

me—like you always do—and I said I loved you too—like I do when I'm in a good place. But what I wish I'd said is that I know you always loved me. Even when you were sad or mad or depressed or miserable, you always loved me. When my head was a mess and I couldn't make sense of what was real and what was not, I knew my mom loved me and that you worked really hard to see the best in me. If you'd loved me less, maybe you'd have found more peace than you have. But I'm selfish enough to be grateful—so many guys in here don't have anyone.

I don't know what's waiting for me on the other side, but you taught me about God and I've been going to services here. I'm gonna see if there's anything I can do to make up for what I did. I don't see how that's possible, and maybe I'll go to hell all the same, but I want you to know that I remembered what you taught me and I'm gonna try.

I also want you to promise me something, even though you won't be able to say it to my face. Promise me you'll live your life. Go to a therapist if you need to and maybe meet other moms like you— there's got to be some out there. I would like you to fall in love again, with someone better than Dad was, and travel the world and join a book group. You're beautiful and smart and good. I want you to live the life you deserve, even though I screwed everything up.

There are a lot of people who probably count the days of their lives from what I did that day, and I think you're one of them. Those reset moments in life don't just come from bad things, though— Melissa probably counts the days and months since she married Paul, and this guy in high school counted the time from the day he took first place in State Cross-Country. I really hope you find a day when you can start counting all over again, forget how long it's been since I did such a horrible thing, and forget the day that I met justice for my crimes. I want you to live a beautiful life and count many beautiful moments ahead. Thanks for everything. Thanks for loving me so good.

    Love you,
    Robbie

27

Steve

Ten years, five months, sixteen days

Steve stepped out of his car and wiped his palms on his jeans. He couldn't believe he was here and yet after Coach had found Amanda's brand-new address, he couldn't *not* come. Steve had still taken a few days to make sure he was ready, but when he'd woken up this morning—his day off—the first thing he'd thought of was whether or not he should go to Cincinnati. He needed closure if nothing else. But closure wasn't his only reason.

The condo wasn't much different from his. The roof was a bit more pitched, the front window bayed rather than flat. Instead of brick skirting, it was stone, and instead of brown tones, gray. But similar and familiar. Perhaps he and Amanda were stereotypical single middle-aged Americans who wanted a home without too much yard or too much space, something they could pay off before they took retirement in fifteen years and could navigate until their knees gave out.

He knocked on the front door. The trim was peeling and he lifted a hand to tap a curling flake of paint. It broke off and fluttered to the cement. It wouldn't take long to scrape off the flaking paint, apply a primer coat, and then a top coat. Maybe one full day, start to finish, so long as the weather held. It wasn't optimal painting weather today, too cold, but come spring . . .

He felt the vibration of footsteps coming toward the door and his eyes snapped ahead. The footsteps stopped and he looked at the knob, expecting it to turn, but nothing happened. He looked back at the door itself. Peephole. Amanda must be looking through it and wondering what he was doing here.

He lifted his hand in a little wave and smiled, though the nervous gesture reflected his anxiety more than he'd have liked.

The dead bolt clicked. There was the sound of a chain being pulled back higher on the door. He looked at the knob while it turned. The door opened slowly, creaking in a way that made him suspect she didn't use the front door often. Like him, she probably came in and out through the attached garage—hers was at the side of her condo as opposed to the back like his. He could fix that hinge in less than a minute with a little powdered graphite.

The door stopped when it was open about ten inches. Amanda stood to the side, not completely revealed through the gap. It was three o'clock in the afternoon, but she wore purple flannel pajama pants and a black sweatshirt, bunched up at the elbows. Her reddish-blond hair was pulled up in a sloppy bun on top of her head, bits sticking out in all directions. Her eyebrows were pulled tightly together. She wasn't wearing any makeup.

He smiled at her.

"Mr. Mathis?" She did not smile back.

He nodded, keeping the smile in hopes it would help ease the wariness in her expression. "Hi, Amanda, or, uh, Mrs. Mallorie."

Her expression didn't soften, but she looked past him to the street and then up and down in both directions before meeting his eyes again. "Wh-what are you doing here?"

"You dropped the token." He held out his hand, where the green chip rested in the center of his palm. "Maybe you did it on purpose, and if that's the case I don't want to—"

She opened the door all the way, her eyes focused on his hand until they flitted up to meet his. The wariness had softened into surprise, and maybe gratitude. "I tore my car apart looking for it—I felt terrible for having lost it."

He pushed his hand closer to her and she took the chip, turning it over so that she could look at every side. "It was in the grass by the curb," he explained. "I found it a few days later."

She closed her hand around it and held it against her stomach. "Thank you," she said softly. "But . . . but how did you find me?" A bit of that wariness came back.

"Coach Miller called me and gave me your address, but he said he couldn't tell me how he got it so I wasn't to ask."

She opened her hand and looked at the token again.

"I didn't come just to return the chip."

Her hand closed and she looked at him again, hesitant yet curious.

"I owe you the whole story about how Robbie affected me back then and why that chip was important to him and then to me. Can I tell it to you?"

She blinked, but the lines of her face were caught somewhere between fear and hope.

Something wet hit his cheek at the same time he felt a drop on his head. He looked up at the steely gray clouds that had added to his earlier assessment that today was not a good day to paint a door frame. Another drop hit his face. Three drops landed simultaneously on his shoulders.

She looked at him, then at the ground that was becoming spotted with rain, and finally up at the clouds.

"Would you like to come in?" she asked, nervously polite.

"Thank you." Once he was inside, he stepped to the side of the doorway so she could close the door. The small living room had a couch, a bed frame leaned against a wall, and stacks and stacks of boxes. In the center of the mantel was what looked like a black vase with a lid—an urn?

He looked away, but his gaze landed on a box labeled "Robbie" set on the floor not far away. He looked at her and knew she'd seen him notice. She was rubbing the sobriety coin with her thumb, her other arm crossed over her stomach.

"The moving company delivered everything just yesterday and I only worked on the kitchen," she said, waving toward the boxes. She picked up a throw from the edge of the couch and draped it over the box with Robbie's name on it. "Sorry it's such a mess."

He laughed, and she looked up sharply at the sound. Jumpy.

"You don't owe me an apology, Mrs. Mallorie. I'm the one who showed up on your doorstep uninvited. If it makes you feel better, I'd have called if I had your number, but that wasn't the information Coach tracked down."

She smiled and smoothed some escaping tendrils of hair behind her ear. "Please call me Amanda."

"Okay, Amanda. I hope you'll call me Steve."

She nodded that she would. Silence prevailed for a few seconds and he realized he had better get to the point.

"Well, to get started, nothing I told you that day was untrue, but I didn't get to some things I think you deserve to know." She relaxed. Just a little. "Robbie *did* help me with my perspective and to make some important choices, but that's not the only reason I gave him the ring."

Amanda continued to watch him, but she said nothing. He opened his mouth to speak again, determined to say this as a monologue if he had to, but then she lifted a hand, her palm facing him. "Where are my manners—would you like some coffee?"

He was transported back to that day when she had come to him and he'd invited her inside, knowing she didn't want to accept. Now he was in her house. This was all very strange, but her invitation stripped away some of the tension. "I have to admit it's a little late in the day for coffee for me, but I would love a glass of water."

She smiled and even though he didn't know her beyond what was available in the public domain, he could tell it was a real smile. The kind that didn't show up in pictures unless the photographer caught you unawares. She ducked her head and turned to the kitchen, which was just beyond the living room. She waved for him to follow and he did. There were more boxes in here, but the bar portion of the counter was clear and there were two black backless bar stools tucked underneath. It wasn't hard to picture her sitting at that counter alone. Eating. Reading. Whiling away empty hours. He had a bar just like it, only his had a granite top and hers was something that was meant to look like granite, but then he didn't have a gas stove like she did.

She nodded him toward one of the stools before opening a well-stocked cupboard of glassware.

"I have juice," she said. "V8 or cran-grape."

"I love cran-grape."

The fridge had an automatic dispenser, and she filled the glass halfway with ice, then proceeded to extract the jug of juice and fill the glass.

"You aren't going to join me?" Steve said as he took the cup she pushed toward him.

She shook her head, but was smiling somewhat shyly. He took a sip.

"Well, where to start," he said.

"I think the beginning is standard," she said, and he looked up at her. She was making a joke? This was going better than he'd hoped.

"Well, then, I guess we start with high school a million years ago." It wasn't hard to go back in time to those years of his life. He told her about his glory days, his hopes for the future, and the way it all changed when Rachelle got pregnant. He told her about the shotgun wedding, the carpet mills, the baby and then the next baby and then a third one. "All of a sudden it had been ten years and we barely talked to each other anymore. I was working a different dead-end job, had a growing alcohol problem, and hated my life. I woke up one day and decided to walk away from it."

Amanda showed no reaction to his story, but he felt no judgment, which surprised him. He *should* be judged. He deserved it. But she just continued to watch him. "I realized pretty quick that if I moved around often enough, the courts never caught up with me for child support." He paused for a breath and shook his head. He hadn't realized before now that he'd never told this story before—not like this at least. "I would touch base with my kids now and then and promise my ex that I'd get caught up, but I never planned to and I kept moving around. Kept staying away from my kids. Kept wishing I were number seventy-six on the football team again and had no idea what being an adult was really like. Eventually, that brought me to Sioux Falls, where I got a job working with a bunch of high school kids mowing lawns and fixing sprinklers." He attempted a shrug and a smile, neither of which he pulled off very well. "I was the oldest guy on the crew and most of the kids ignored me, but Robbie and I worked together a few times—he was good at following directions and easy to work with. Robbie was funny and hardworking and accepting of this old guy who ought to have made more of his life than working on a landscape crew."

Amanda blinked quickly—was he upsetting her? He paused, but she waved him to continue.

"One morning he found me in my truck, hungover from a bender the night before and sick as a dog. He bought me a Coke at a gas station across the street and told me I had a problem—smiling the whole time, which, let me tell you, pissed me off to no end." He smiled and to his relief, Amanda did too.

"I told him to F off and though he left me alone that day, after that he always seemed to work close by, asking me how I was doing, or asking me about my life, which I was sure he didn't care anything about. This went on for a week or so until he finally confided in me about his father's drinking problems and how he'd moved out of state after you two divorced. He told me how much it sucked, that even a crappy dad was better than no dad at all—his dad had come for a visit recently and apologized. Robbie had been able to forgive him, he even showed me an AA token his dad had given him—he carried it in his pocket all the time as a good-luck charm." Steve paused for a breath. "He reminded me of my oldest son, Max." Steve had to stop in order to swallow the rising lump in his throat. "And I wondered if maybe I could go back and make things right. Maybe I could choose different than I'd been choosing. I called my kids for the first time in almost a year—my youngest son broke down on the phone and asked when I was going to come see him. One of my older sons invited me to a car show he was going to the next week as though he expected me to come." The regret and shame flooded through him, but Steve let the feelings come. They kept him humble. Kept him trying. Amanda watched him carefully. "I had all this back child support to pay and so many years to make up for, and it just seemed impossible that I could go back to that. I told Robbie, and he said I should go anyway. I should go to this car show and tell my kids I was sorry. Easy as that. He said . . ." Steve paused, transported to the exact moment when he and Robbie had sat next to each other under a tree, eating their lunches, and Robbie turned to him and said the words that tipped Steve over the edge of the fence he had still been sitting on. "My dad could be as good as my mom if he wanted to be."

Steve had found the comment naïve when Robbie said it, but he hadn't been able to dismiss it. Steve had chosen to leave and he was still miserable. Could he choose to go back and be happy? Could he be as good a parent as Rachelle was? What Robbie had said felt like truth. Felt possible. He turned his cup a quarter turn. "I called their mom and she agreed to let me see my kids—she said we'd work out the child support, but my kids needed me. I'd never been much of a dad, even before I left, and I was scared to death that I would make a bigger mess than ever, but Robbie had made it seem simple, and if I could enjoy hanging with my own kids as much as I liked hanging with *your* kid, well . . ." He looked at the ring on his finger again. "Robbie had teased me about the ring from the start. He said rings were for girls and why was I still wearing that girly thing, but this ring was pretty much the only thing from my past life that I still had. I think I was hoping something would come my way that would restore me to that carefree football player who didn't have any worries or responsibilities, who hadn't broken hearts or promises. Robbie helped me realize that wasn't going to happen, but I could choose differently and stop whining. I quit the landscape job in order to come here—to Florence, where Rachelle was living with our boys. Before I left Sioux Falls, I gave Robbie the ring as a token of a promise I made to myself that day—that I would do better. High school, up to that point, was the best part of my life. Only I could change that." He looked across the counter between them. Amanda was crying, soft and silent as she wiped at her cheeks. Her emotion thickened the lump in Steve's throat, but he didn't let it stop him. Not all tears were bad ones. "It wasn't easy, but I became a presence in my boys' lives. I got a job in the parts department of a local car dealership and I've worked my way up to manager. Rachelle offered to reduce the child support I owed her, and I was able to pay it off in a few years. I haven't missed a birthday party or ball game unless I couldn't get the time off work. I bought my condo a few years ago—first time I've ever been a homeowner—and I did all of that, in part at least, because of your son."

"My son the murderer." Her eyes went wide as though she hadn't meant to say it out loud, but Steve didn't flinch.

"Your *son*," Steve said.

Tears rose to her eyes again and she blinked, looking to the side and wiping quickly at the corners.

He looked down at the ring again, hoping to give her a little more privacy. "It's been funny, getting this ring back." He turned it so that it caught the fluorescent light in the ceiling. "My son asked me about it and I talked about high school—I haven't ever talked about high school with him." He looked up at her. "I've lived my life in the present since I came back, afraid of looking behind me and afraid of looking to the right or left for fear I might fall off this path I am so determined to stay on. But now I'm wearing this ring, and people ask about it and I talk about a part of my life that was wonderful, but I thought I had to shut out. I told Coach that I'm trying to live in the now, and I am, but thinking back to the past again helps me look at the future different, too—bringing everything together."

He looked up at Amanda and something passed between them, something he couldn't explain other than it being . . . a feeling. "Thank you for returning the ring—it completed a circle for me."

"Thank you, Mr. Mathis, for coming and for telling me that story about Robbie and returning the chip. I will . . . treasure it."

"I did have a question for *you*, though," Steve said.

She was wary again, though not as steeped in it as she'd been when she'd pulled open the front door.

"What's the secret ingredient of your chicken fried steak?"

Tears welled into her eyes and she put a hand to her mouth.

After a moment, she lowered it. "Robbie told you about my chicken fried steak?"

Steve nodded. "Raved about it. Said you made it better than anyone—even *restaurants*." He raised his eyebrows when he said "restaurants," mimicking Robbie's teenaged awe.

She laughed, but it came out mixed with a sob. She took a deep breath and shook her head.

"Does that mean you're not going to tell me?"

She laughed again, a real laugh. "Mustard powder," she said, lifting her shoulders. "I put a little bit of mustard powder in the breading. That's all."

"Genius. Was Robbie's favorite color blue, or am I making that up?"

She wiped at her eyes again. "Bright blue, like on a Nestlé Crunch bar, not navy or baby blue."

"Right," Steve said, nodding. "I remember that. And he didn't root for the Cavs."

"Sorry, he was a Celtics fan."

Steve winced as though the knowledge was physically painful. She laughed, then went silent, her smile falling. "I don't talk about Robbie to anyone, Steve. Ever."

"I understand," Steve said. "I didn't talk about the past for a really long time, and then I did. And it was okay. It was even . . . good."

"Not the same, though, is it?"

He held her eyes, then shook his head but didn't look away. *Not the same, not hardly, but* . . . "Still might be good to talk about him, though."

She folded her arms and looked at the hardwood floor. "Robbie's Sunday School teacher did an interview for one of the tabloids. The parents of the girl he took to prom sold the pictures. My sister-in-law started a blog where she reported the details of his trial, peppered with stories from his childhood." Amanda looked up at him, but he could see a wanting there. She wanted to trust him, she wanted to feel safe. How on earth could he assure her?

Steve took off the ring and put it on the counter between

them. They both looked at it. "I have no agenda. I hold no judgment. The boy I knew helped me. As my ex-wife would say, he 'blessed my life.' " He paused, debating what else to say until he realized there was no reason to hold back. Not when she was so close to telling him to leave forever. He looked at her face and waited until she met his eyes. "I've read everything I could find about Robert Mallorie these last few weeks. He's not the young man I knew. Nothing can change what he did, I know that, nor the lives his actions affected, including yours, but I'm totally cool with thinking of Robbie. That's the only version I knew."

She closed her eyes in an almost pained kind of blink.

28

Amanda

Twenty-seven minutes

Amanda opened her eyes to see this man, a stranger, who had found her even though she was hiding. She still wasn't sure why he'd done it, but he was comfortable with who Robbie had been. He had a past and heartache and found a way to live again, and live well—the exact thing Robbie had told her to do in his letter. Amanda had thought a lot about Robbie's comment about counting time—her life *had* reset the day he took that gun to the Cotton Mall, and then the count had reset again the day the State of South Dakota killed him. Every day for two weeks she'd woken up with the memory of how long it had been since her son had been dead. She was tired of trying to make sense of what had gone wrong, worn-out from looking for some magic bean that would put all the hurt to rest. There was no magic bean, no trick to make it all better, not even Robbie's letter had been the salve she longed for, though it had helped immensely to hear his hopes for her future. But what if she could stop trying to make sense of everything? What if she stopped putting Robbie and Robert Mallorie together as one person? Maybe the dark would go away and the flickering light that had been getting a little bit bigger within her would grow bigger. Maybe that, more than anything, would help her live the way Robbie had wanted her to.

"Are you hungry, Amanda?" Steve asked, causing her to look

up at him again. He had put the ring back on his pinkie finger and laced his fingers together on top of the counter. "You haven't been in Cincinnati long, so you probably don't know about Randal's Diner."

Amanda smiled. "Their corn chowder was amazing."

His shoulders fell, but her mood lightened.

"My daughter and her husband took me there my first night in town." The same day Amanda had met Steve, in fact. The man she was only going to see that one time but who had found her somehow and didn't make her as nervous as other people did. "But I haven't been there since."

"Did you have the Portobello ravioli?"

She shook her head.

"Would you like to? We could have dinner and you can tell me about Robbie."

Robbie had given this man motivation to make his own life better. Steve's children had him in their life, which meant that if Robbie had never been born, or if that sledding accident had been worse than it was, Steve's life would be worse too. The ripples of Robbie's actions that day at the mall would never end, she knew that, and people would continue to suffer. But there was a different kind of ripple effect happening, too—one of goodness and hope. A rush of wind seemed to move out from the center of her chest, a letting go of something tight and confining. She could love her son and be glad for the years of joy he'd brought her. She *could*.

Steve was still holding her eyes. Amanda took hold of all the courage she could find hiding in the nooks and crannies of her head and chest. She allowed her shoulders to relax and her smile to lose any remaining stiffness. She could see in his eyes that he noticed the change. His eyes softened; his smile stretched a bit wider.

"I would like to try the ravioli and talk about Robbie, Steve. I would like that very, very much."

29

Steve

One year, eight months, fourteen days

Steve finished getting ready for work and headed to the kitchen, where he could smell coffee—Amanda always brewed the pot while he took a shower. The kitchen was empty, so he filled his "Just Married" mug, added a little cream, and then headed toward the French doors that led out onto the patio of their bungalow-style house in the Walnut Hills area of Cincinnati. They were ten minutes from Melissa's family and half an hour from Max and Rachelle in Florence. There were two extra bedrooms for when his other boys came to visit and plenty of honey-do tasks to keep Steve busy. Amanda had a flower garden, an enclosed backyard, and had recently been invited to join a neighborhood book group by the lady next door, who knew exactly who Amanda was.

From the inside of the French doors, Steve watched Amanda sip her coffee while looking at the pygmy Japanese maple tree they'd planted above Robbie's ashes last spring. Beauty had risen from ashes, literally, since then. Life for death. Hope for heartache. A living tribute to the boy he'd been.

Steve turned back to the house, letting her have her moment. He went back into the kitchen, made scrambled eggs for both of them, and was dividing their breakfast onto two plates when he heard the squeak of hinges and looked up in time to smile at the woman he'd fallen in love with against all odds. Because of a feeling. And courage.

"Hey there," he said, bringing the plates over to the Shaker table they'd found while antique-hunting a few months ago. He put the plate in front of her and then leaned in for a kiss. She placed her hand against his cheek so that he didn't pull back too soon.

"Hey yourself," she said as he went around to his side of the table. "This looks wonderful."

"Well, eggs are easy," he said with a shrug.

He glanced casually at the montage of photos on the wall behind her—Max's most recent family picture, taken when Kassie was seven months' pregnant with their now-newest grandchild, Ellen. Rachelle and Mitch from their ten-year wedding anniversary almost a year ago now, Melissa and her family right after Mason was born. There were several pictures from their earlier years, too—Steve with his boys when Garrett was just a baby, and Robbie's cross-country photo from his junior year. Steve and Amanda had managed to combine two pasts and make a future.

Last month the law firm in Sioux Falls that had represented Robert Mallorie had forwarded Amanda a letter. The young man who wrote it had been paralyzed by a bullet; his dad had been killed. In the letter, he explained that he was engaged and making peace with his past by finally responding to a letter Amanda had written his mother a few months after the shooting. Amanda had cried and cried over that letter, then put it in the little jewelry box Robbie had made in high school—the same box where she stored Robbie's last letter and the Christmas card Steve had sent to Coach, which had brought her to him that first time. There was also a printed e-mail in the box from a man named Ken, whose daughter had also been one of Robbie's victims. His wife had not handled their daughter's death well and recently passed away without finding solace, but he wanted Amanda to know that he had forgiven Robbie and held no ill will against Amanda. He apologized for waiting so long to write to her—he'd hoped it would be something he and his wife could do together once his wife had found some heal-ing—but that day had not come. He wished Amanda a happy future. Steve was humbled to be a part of that wished-for hap-piness.

"Lucy's birthday party tonight?" Steve asked when he looked away from the photos to focus on Amanda again. She'd cut her hair short and colored it a darker red, more like it was in the photos with her kids when they were little. She tucked a lock be-hind one ear, the morning light catching the baby pink polish of her fingernails. They'd gone to Decaturville last week and Amanda had met up with the woman who had helped her find Coach Miller that day she came looking for Steve. They'd gone out for manicures, and Amanda had remarked how wonderful it was to have friends again.

"Dinner is at six, cake and ice cream at seven in case you don't get out of work in time. I can hardly believe she's four years old already."

Steve winked at her and reached across the table to give her hand a squeeze. "With a future as wide as the sky."

She laughed and squeezed his hand back. "Someday it will only be a window."

"Then let's hope it has a fabulous view."

AS WIDE AS
THE SKY

Jessica Pack

ABOUT THIS GUIDE

The suggested questions are included to enhance
your group's reading of Jessica Pack's
As Wide as the Sky.

Discussion Questions

1. Each chapter begins with a timer—minutes, hours, days, months, and years—meant to show a "reset" point in each life of the point-of-view character in that chapter. Were you able to pinpoint what the reset point was for any of the characters?

2. Do you have a "reset" point of your own life?

3. The Kübler-Ross stages of grief are denial, anger, bargaining, depression, and acceptance. Can you match these stages with any of the characters in this story?

4. Did any of the characters in this story particularly stand out to you?

5. Were there any of the secondary characters in this story you would have liked to learn more about?

6. How has your life been affected by forgiveness, either as the giver or the receiver?

7. Do you think you could remain as close to your child as Amanda stayed with Robbie if he or she committed such a heinous crime?

8. How much of Robert Mallorie's crime do you feel was due to his mental illness, and how much because of the choices he made?

9. Have you experienced trauma in your life? If yes, how do you feel it has changed you? How have you found healing?

10. *Optional Question:* What are your feelings regarding capital punishment?

Read on for an excerpt
from Jessica Pack's next novel,
Whatever It Takes

The paper sheet crinkled as Sienna lay back on the exam table per the doctor's instructions. She stared at the fluorescent lights in the ceiling and imagined that the long breaths she was taking would pull calm over the fear like a tarp over the back of Daddy's pickup.

It will be okay, she told herself. She wished someone else were saying it. Holding her hand. Kissing her forehead. But she'd needed to come alone.

"Sienna is a pretty name," Dr. Sheffield said in a coffee-shop-conversation tone.

"Thank you." *Inhale. Exhale.*

"Wasn't there a *Seinfeld* episode about a girl named Sienna?" Dr. Sheffield pulled back the right side of the paper gown Sienna had put on five minutes earlier—opening in front, per the nurse's instruction.

"Yeah."

"Lift your right arm over your head, please."

Sienna raised her arm, bending at the elbow so that it curled around her head resting on that paper sheet. The doctor began the breast exam while the nurse stood like a centurion in the corner of the room to insure propriety, Sienna assumed. Wouldn't it be *more* appropriate to have *fewer* people looking at her half-naked self?

"Wasn't the episode about George dating a crayon?" the doctor continued.

"Yeah." Sienna and Tyson had found the episode a few years ago after yet one more person had brought up the reference to her name.

"So, Sienna is a color?"

"Yeah."

"Reddish brown?"

"Yeah." Dad had always said it was the color of sunset in the fall, when sunlight had depth and shadows were solid. Tyson had compared it to the red dirt in Hawaii where they'd taken their honeymoon a million years ago.

Dr. Sheffield's movements became slower, focused on the upper part of Sienna's right breast and confirming that the lump wasn't some macabre figment of Sienna's imagination. Sienna began anxiously reciting the poem she'd memorized in the fourth grade.

> *Who has seen the wind?*
> *Neither I nor you;*
> *But when the leaves hang trembling*
> *The wind is passing through.*

The poem had always made her think of the line of poplar trees that separated the backyard from the ranch. When the wind blew, the leaves sounded like a river and shimmered like thin sheets of metal. Wind was invisible, but you knew it was there because of what it left behind.

"That's the lump?"

Sienna nodded.

"Tender?"

"A little."

"Hmm. Let me check the other side. Put your left arm over your head."

Sienna closed her eyes and pictured the shimmery leaves of the poplar trees again, then added other images that gave her center. Acres of ranch land pulled tight against the horizon.

Daddy riding bareback through the pastures. Tyson with his shirt off throwing bales of hay onto the trailer. She could *see* the memories but could not get lost in them the way she desperately wanted to.

The doctor finished examining the left breast and pulled the paper gown over that half of Sienna's chest. She went back to the right side and moved more slowly for a second exam.

"Your mother had breast cancer?"

Inhale. "Yeah."

"When?"

Sienna did the math in her head. *Exhale.* "Twenty-three years ago, I guess. I was two when she died." The paperwork Sienna had filled out in the waiting area had asked about medical history, but not whether her mother's breast cancer had led to Mom's death. Sienna thought that an important oversight.

"Any other direct relatives with breast cancer? Aunt? Cousin? Grandmother?"

"I don't think so."

The doctor held her eyes and Sienna answered the unasked question. "I don't know my mom's side of the family. They're in Canada. Mom was an only child." So was Dad. So was Sienna. Sienna had determined she would be the generation to fill all six seats around a standard kitchen table. Each of the in vitro fertilizations had implanted three embryos and she'd fantasized that she might have to buy a bigger table. Each embryo had failed in one way or another. Were they to try again, which wasn't likely, she and Tyson would have to start over.

"Do you know what stage your mom's cancer was when she was diagnosed?"

"No."

"I'm sorry for all these sensitive questions." She was still palpating, pressing from angles Sienna had not known existed. "Do you know how long after diagnosis your mother passed away?"

"About six months." Sienna had outlived Mom by two years now.

The centurion nurse holding her chart cleared her throat. "Her dad has had prostate cancer," she said.

Sienna thought that sentence should have an exclamation point at the end for emphasis. *Both of my parents have had cancer. My mother died from it.*

"When was that, Sienna?" Dr. Sheffield asked.

"Last fall. They caught it early and Dad agreed to aggressive treatment. He's doing pretty good."

Dr. Sheffield nodded. "Did you notice in your self-exam that the lump moves?"

"Yeah." Google said that was a bad sign.

"It's small."

"Yeah." Google said that was a good sign.

The doctor pulled the right side of the drape closed, sat down on her rolling stool, and put out her hand for the chart. Paper charts—so twenty-first-century Wyoming.

"You can sit up, Sienna."

Sienna sat up and pulled the paper gown tightly closed, trying not to feel violated. Not by the doctor—by the lump.

Dr. Sheffield looked up from the chart, her expression sympathetic. "Thursday is your birthday?"

Sienna shrugged. She'd been dreading her twenty-fifth birthday since before she'd found the lump because the day would end with a Mom letter—letters Mom had written on her death bed as a way to remain a part of the life of the daughter she would never see grown. Over the years the letters had become a reminder that every happy day couldn't be all it *should* be because Sienna's mother wasn't a part of the day. Would this one also be full of advice about motherhood and enjoying the journey and treating her marriage as the most important relationship she would ever have?

On Sienna's twenty-fourth birthday, a year ago, they had scheduled the third round of IVF and she'd still known what hope felt like. She'd added another half dozen items to her Amazon nursery wish list and imagined watching her freckle-faced daughter grow up the way her mother hadn't.

This is not how my life was supposed to go, she wailed in her mind.

Deep breath.

Hold it together.

She had the whole drive back home to fall apart.

Connect with Us

Visit us online at
KensingtonBooks.com
to read more from your favorite authors, see books
by series, view reading group guides, and more.

Join us on social media

for sneak peeks, chances to win books and prize packs,
and to share your thoughts with other readers.

facebook.com/kensingtonpublishing
twitter.com/kensingtonbooks

Tell us what you think!

To share your thoughts, submit a review,
or sign up for our eNewsletters, please visit:
KensingtonBooks.com/TellUs.